Impossible Territories:
The Unofficial Companion to
The League of Extraordinary Gentlemen,
The Black Dossier

Other MonkeyBrain Books titles
by Jess Nevins

*Heroes & Monsters: The Unofficial Companion to the
League of Extraordinary Gentlemen*

*A Blazing World: The Unofficial Companion to the
League of Extraordinary Gentlemen, Volume 2*

The Encyclopedia of Fantastic Victoriana

IMPOSSIBLE TERRITORIES

THE UNOFFICIAL COMPANION TO

THE LEAGUE OF EXTRAORDINARY GENTLEMEN

THE BLACK DOSSIER

BY JESS NEVINS

INTRODUCTION BY

ALAN MOORE

COMMENTARY BY

KEVIN O'NEILL

TABLE OF CONTENTS

INTRODUCTION BY ALAN MOORE
7

FOREWORD BY THE AUTHOR
11

ANNOTATIONS TO THE LEAGUE OF EXTRAORDINARY GENTLEMEN,
THE BLACK DOSSIER
15

INTERVIEW WITH ALAN MOORE
177

INTRODUCTION

I suppose it makes sense that the most unusual collection of the League's adventures thus far should also have had the most unusual path to publication. There was the last-minute interference a week or two before the first edition was due to go to press, which led to the decision not to release the volume in the UK or Canada. Then, surely coincidentally, there was the last minute interference a week or two before the supposedly-complete deluxe edition went to press, which led to the decision not to include the 7-inch vinyl single that was meant to accompany the work, despite the fact that the entire package had been cleared for release by the publisher's extensive legal department some two years previously. Kevin and I imagine that this is probably intended as some form of reprimand or punishment for our having suggested that the mainstream comic industry was no longer sufficiently intelligence, literate, morally hygienic or, indeed, competent to publish anything as apparently demanding as *The League of Extraordinary Gentlemen*. Well, I guess they sure showed us.

So, anyway, we're sorry about the non-appearance of the single, and we'll do our best to put that right at some point in the future. Actually, I could hum a couple of verses right now, just to give you an idea of what it would have sounded like. Okay. Let me just clear my throat here. Ahuhhm. Ahhuh-Ahuhhm. Right...

> *Didn't get bitten in no Carpathian tower,*
> *Or eat the peaches from some heavenly bower,*
> *But oh my darling, I'm certain of our Immortal Love.*
> *I wasn't mesmerised the Valdemar way.*
> *Ain't no hypnosis, honey, preventing decay,*
> *But we got one thing, whatever they say: Immortal Love.*
> > *The Wandering Jew*
> > *And old Melmoth too*
> > *Join hands with the Gods up above.*
> > *Olympus will ring*
> > *As all of them sing*
> > *The tale of our Immortal Love...*

Anyway, you get the idea. Sorry about that bum note in the chorus, incidentally. I'll do an overdub and drop it in later.

Now, down to the matter in hand, which is Jess's third astonishing labour of love, display of erudition, and bout of just-plain-showing-off, *Impossible Territories*. In creating *The Black Dossier*, Kevin and I were attempting to pull off a leap in the book's continuity that would take the characters from the point at which we'd left them at the close of volume two, in the last months of 1898, to a point some sixty years thereafter and a very different world. We were hoping that the jump from the book's popular Victorian setting, something we felt was necessary if the work was to avoid stagnation, wouldn't prove too disappointing or disorienting for the readership. As it turns out, we needn't have worried: the general response to *The Black Dossier* seems to suggest that our impressively flexible and enlightened audience are as keen to break new ground as we are. And, of course, we have the mighty Jess Nevins to accompany our leap of faith and to ensure a far less bumpy ride for all concerned.

In *Impossible Territories*, Jess has proven himself knowledgeable far beyond the gaslight era of the first two series. We see this in the handling of relatively obscure 1950s British culture, such as his succinct and accurate description of Sooty and Sweep's hard-bitten hooker-shakedowns, and we also see it in the way he deals with the historical material in the *Dossier*, especially in the lengthy 'Orlando' section. It's worth pointing out that almost all of our much-lauded so-called professional historian community has completely missed the vital Smurfs/Gargamel aspect of the Battle of Marathon that Jess identifies herein, lacking his finely-tuned and expert eye.

Of course, the two elements of these volumes of annotations that always give me the most pleasure are either the things that I hadn't noticed but someone else had, or else those rare things that Jess has overlooked and which therefore give me a petty sense of triumph. As an example of the first category I would cite the brilliantly logical connection between *Knight Rider* and *Chitty-Chitty Bang-Bang* that is described elsewhere, while as an example of the second I'd mention some of the James Bond arcana that Kevin passed on to me during the construction of the opening scenes. For instance, there's the fact that while 'Mother' is the code-name given to the head of the intelligence service in the later series of *The Avengers*, the same code-name was also used once, apparently in some sort of slip-up, as another name for 'M' in one of the early Bond books. There was also the detail that connected Bond with *The Man from UNCLE*, by virtue of the fact that Bond creator Ian Fleming had also created the character Napoleon Solo, but had been advised to sever his links with the character by the owners of the Bond movie franchise, who didn't want another Fleming-created spy in competition with their own product. Admittedly, these are slender threads of connection, but of such stuff is the literary tapestry of the League's world constructed.

I've said already that *The Black Dossier* is the most unusual stretch of our ongoing narrative to date, but perhaps I should add to that by saying that it is also the most far-reaching (with the *Life of Orlando* section factored in, the story spans more than three thousand years of mythical and fictional history), and therefore probably the most demanding, on the creators, the readers and, of course, the patient annotator. The fact that our audience and Mr. Nevins seem to have taken this highly-experimental piece of meta-fiction in their stride is immensely encouraging and strengthens our resolve to keep taking risks and pushing the work forward, the fruits of which should b evident in our next volume, volume three, to be brought to you by the genuinely dedicated and capable people at Top Shelf. The first part of this may be out around the end of the year, and hopefully it won't spoil things too much if I tell you that this is possibly our darkest volume to date, and that much of it is delivered in the form of a stage musical. Wait until you see Kevin's Mack the Knife.

It only remains for me to thank Jess for providing his usual invaluable service, and to thank you, our frighteningly well-informed readers, for continuing to show such an appreciative interest in our convoluted game of cultural join-the-dots. I'll see you here in a year or two, and perhaps we can *all* have a mass sing-song to celebrate the occasion. Until then, enjoy the fine piece of scholarship in your hands, maintain your high standards and don't settle for anything dumb or lazy. Especially from us.

Yours, with Immortal Love,

Alan Moore
Northampton,
June 30th, 2008

FOREWORD

Welcome to the *Impossible Territories*, the annotations to Alan Moore and Kevin O'Neill's *Black Dossier*, the most recent installment in their *League of Extraordinary Gentlemen* series. As Mr. Moore points out, this was the most unusual of the League's stories (so far—who knows about the future?), and just as it took a significant amount of time for Moore and O'Neill to prepare, it took a significant amount of effort to untangle, decode, and annotate. Unlike previous installments, however, *Black Dossier* contains a number of secrets which elude me and the other fans whose contributions make up this volume, even after Mr. O'Neill corrected some of my mistakes and added some new notes.

In other words: we did our best, and we got, I think, nine-tenths of the references in here, but there are still references, visual and verbal, which go uncommented-upon here. If you find something I missed, or a mistake I made, please e-mail me at jjnevins@ix.netcom.com, and I'll include them on an errata webpage.

This book would not exist without the contributions of a number of enthusiastic and helpful people, and as always I'm grateful to them for their help. They include Joe Ackerman, Jason Adams, Martin Allen, Joseph Allevato, Hussamuddin Alromayedh, Dave Amiott, John Andrews, Tim Anselm, "ASDF FDSA," David Avallone, Jon Balcerak, Greg Baldino, Llowyn Ball, Lee Barnett, Neale Barnholden, DJ Bell, Jon Bergdoll, Ed Berridge, Joel Berthomier, Vandy Beth, Justin Bialek, Henry Blanco, Andrew Bonia, Mark Bourne, Jeremy Briggs, Robert Todd Bruce, Russ Bynum, Andres Caicedo, Devin Cambridge, Scott Campbell, "Captain Spaulding," Philip Carson II, Cuitlamiztli Carter, Jonathan Carter, Tim Chapman, Neil Chester, Chris, Rory Christie, George C. Clark, Mark Coale, James Coates, Loren Collins, Chris Cooper, Paul Cornell, Giles Cresswell, Adam Cummins, Charles Cunyus, Joyce Cunyus,

Mike Curtis, Steve Daldry, Greg Daly, Brandon Davis-Shannon, "Joey Dedcat," Robert Déry, Zoltán Déry, Mario di Giacomo, Ben Dickson, Carla DiFonzo, Richard Dill, Marc Dolan, John Dorrian, Neil Dorsett, Drake, Ben Drexler, Rich Drees, Win Eckert, Mark Elstob, Marcus Ewert, Adam Farrar, Alex Fernie, Mark Fishpool, Jason Fliegel, Dexter Franklin, Sean Gaffney, Shawn Garrett, Peter Gilham, Cian Gill, Patrick Gillen, Anthony Girese, Damian Gordon, Ian Gould, Philip & Emily Graves, Eli Green, John M. Gregory, Janez Grm, Guest_Informant, Eduard Habsburg, John Hall, Larry Hardesty, Peter Hardy, Micah Harris, Harrison, Jason Helms, Dave Henderson, Eric Henry, "herms98," Andrew Hickey, Dan Higginbottom, Steve Higgins, "Him Name Eddie," Eric Houston, Mark Irons, Krzysztof Janicz, Janssen, Kevin Johnson, Roy Johnson, Rich Johnston, Brian Joines, Terry Jones, Jen K., Jaanus Kaasik, Elliott Kalan, Jack Kessler, Rodger Kibble, Les Klinger, Matt Knicl, Jarett Kobek, Michael Korolenko, Timothy Kreider, Andrew Kunka, Dan Kurdilla, C. Jerry Kutner, Steve Kydd, Rick Lai, K.A. Laity, Adam J.B. Lane, Guy Lawley, Leo, Sean Levin, Denny Lien, Michael Lloyd, Myles Lobdell, Jean-Marc Lofficier, Londonkds, James Maass, David Malet, Papa Joe Mambo, Seth Manis, Dirk Manning, Daniel Marks, Keith Martin, Robert Scott Martin, Steve Mattson, Matthew Maxwell, Robert McCord, David Alexander McDonald, Jim McGill, Pádraig Ó Méalóid, Brad Mengel, Jack Miller, Jamie Miller, Jonathan Miller, Chris Mirner, Vanja Miskovic, Nick Moon, Michael Moorcock, Alex Morgan, Huw Morgan, James Morrison, Pedro Moura, Don Murphy, Doug Nanney, Gabriel Neeb, Paul Nestadt, Joseph Nevin, Jeff Newberry, Chris Nichols, Per Nilsson, Sean Noir, Michael Norwitz, Anthony Padilla, L.D. Page, David Parr, Kevin Pasquino, Jeff Patterson, Heath Pecorino, Kevin Pezzano, Jason Powell, Richard Powell, Caleb Prewitt, Howard Price, Michael Prior, Ed Quinby, A.J. Ramirez, Patrick Reumann, Christopher Reynolds, Brad Ricca, Richardthinks, Jonathan Roberts, Josh Robbins, Chris Roberson, Robtmsnow, Edward Rogers, Kian Ross, Gabriel Roth, Pól Rua, Paul Rush, Evan Ryder, KS, Ray Sablack, Peter Sanderson, Tristan Sargent, Cliff Schexnayder, David Schwarm, Jorge Serna, John Sewell, John Sherman, Stu Shiffman, Ken Shinn, Danny Sichel, David A. Simpson, Phil Smith, John Soanes, Gabe Soria, Pete Spokes, Zoe Stevens-Wolf, Greg Strohecker, Paul Sulham, Peter

Svensson, "teamy teamy," Andrew Teheran, Greg Terry, Lang Thompson, Tim Toner, Mark Turetsky, Stephen Tweedale, Chad Underkoffler, usedcarsrus, Bram van Dijk, Pete von Sholly, Dennis Walker, Samuel Walker, Julian Wan, Lee Wang, Ian Warren, Rich Weaver, Jamaal White, Matt White, Tom Whiteley, Tony Whitt, Jeff Wilson, Pete Wilson, Martin Wisse, Benjamin Wood, Jae Yu, and Nevin Zehr.

Finally, my sincerest thanks to my wife Alicia, to Chris Roberson and Allison Baker for publishing this and my other books, and to Messrs. Moore and O'Neill for their generosity of time and assistance.

Jess Nevins
July, 2008

ANNOTATIONS

Front Cover: The sword in the upper left is probably Orlando's. See Page 119.

The quartet of figures wearing owl masks and Elizabethan clothing are inhabitants of the Blazing World; see the notes to Page 178, Panel 1, on page 167.

The rocket is the rocket in the movie *Flight to Mars* (1951). *Flight to Mars*, written by Arthur Strawn and directed by Lesley Selander, is about four scientists and a newspaper reporter who fly to Mars and discover a subterranean civilization. The Martians are apparently friendly, but the humans soon discover that the natural resources of Mars are dwindling and that the Martians intend to invade and colonize Earth.

I'm not sure what the portrait to the right of the rocket is. Perhaps one of the Martians from *The League of Extraordinary Gentlemen* (hereafter *League*) v2 wearing a breathing apparatus?

The blonde woman is Mina Murray, from Bram Stoker's *Dracula* (1897) and one of the leads in previous *League* volumes. The man running with her is Allan Quatermain, from H. Rider Haggard's series of books and another of the leads in previous volumes of *League*. He is young because, as revealed on Page 192 of *League* v2, he was rejuvenated in the Fire of Life (from H. Rider Haggard's *She: A History of Adventure* [1886]), faked his death, and began posing as Allan, Junior.

I'm not sure what the spiral-tipped stone statue is. It also appears on Page 30, Panel 2.

The large painting is of the 1898 League of Extraordinary Gentlemen, the group seen in *League* v1 and v2. They are, from left to right: H. Rider Haggard's Allan Quatermain, Robert Louis Stevenson's Edward Hyde, Bram Stoker's Mina Murray, Jules Verne's Captain Nemo, and H. G. Wells's Invisible Man.

Kevin O'Neill notes:

> The large sword in the upper left belongs to a green Martian—a souvenir from Gulliver Jones.

> The rocket is from *Journey into Space* (featuring Jet Morgan). Created for the BBC in 1953 by the brilliant radio producer Charles Chilton. After three series on radio it continued in comic strip form in *The Express* weekly from February 1956, illustrated by Italian artist Tacconi.

> The image to the right of the rocket is of a (desiccated) midget Martian in respirator as featured in *Swift Morgan and the Flying Saucers* appearing in *The New Spaceways comic Annual* No. 1 (1954), illustrated by Denis McLoughlin. Denis also created the *Buffalo Bill Annuals* (1949-1960) of my youth. They were a big influence on my desire to draw comics.

> The spiral tipped object under the tarpaulin is the Burrowing machine from an eponymous story in *The Jester* (1908). This was probably written by Houghton Townley, who also wrote "The Case of the Human Mole," a *Sexton Blake Library* story (1927). The Burrowing Machine clearly also inspired the more famous Black Sapper, published by Scotland's D.C. Thomson in *The Rover* from 1929. In fact, the illustration of the cat-suited Cordova in *The Burrowing Machine* seems to have inspired the Sapper's look and his machine. (*The Jester* was published by arch D.C. Thomson rival, the Amalgamated Press.)

Alternate Front Cover: Each version of the *Black Dossier* has only one cover. Most editions have the version described above. However, some editions have an alternate cover with the following:

- The blonde woman, reading in bed, is presumably Mina.
- The woman holding the swords is presumably John Cleland's Fanny Hill.
- The glowing woman is Gloriana (see Page 28).
- I believe that the woman wearing the hat is Kathleen Winsor's Amber St. Clair (see Page 43, Panel 5).
- The androgynous figure smoking the cigarette is Orlando, the central figure of the *Dossier*.
- I'm unsure who the prone figure at Orlando's feet might be.
- The woman holding the axe is Mina Murray in her Victorian-era League outfit.
- The woman wearing the flight cap and goggles is W. E. Johns's Worrals (see Pages 25 and 148).

Kevin O'Neill notes:

The woman at Orlando's feet simply represents a sexual conquest from the ancient world.

The portcullis and chains image evokes a grim government brown letter—they seldom contained good news. It seems the right design direction for a bleaker alternative Britain.

Page 1. This logo is a riff on the logo of the Festival of Britain, an exhibition of British art, design, industry, and architecture which ran from May to September, 1951. The original logo was very similar to the one seen here, except that Britannia, the personification of Britain, did not have a question mark topping her helmet, as she does in the *League* books.

Page 2. "Keep Calm and Carry On" was one of the phrases used by the British government during World War Two to encourage the British people to keep a stiff upper lip, especially during the Battle of the Blitz, when London was being pounded by nightly bombings. A poster with that image was created but never used: It had an icon of the crown above the words "Keep Calm and Carry On," with a cherry red background. The portcullis, chains, and jagged lightning bolts which replace the crown hint at what England has become in the alternate history of the *League*. Perhaps coincidentally, they are also similar to the logo of the Customs and Excise department of the British government.

Page 4. *Daily Brute* is a reference to Evelyn Waugh's *Scoop* (1938). *Scoop*, routinely voted one of the best novels of the 20th century, is a savaging of the English sensationalist press. In *Scoop*, the newspaper for which the protagonist works is the *Daily Beast*. Its main rival, even more base and yellow, is the *Daily Brute*. (For modern British readers, think *Daily Mail*, only even worse.)

The *Daily Brute* may also be a reference to Malcolm Bennett and Aden Hughes's *Brute (Classified Pulp Nasties)*, a series of comedic booklets published in the late 1980s which satirized the values of Margaret Thatcher's England.

Page 5. The National Registration Identity Card seen here provides another hint at what England has become in the world of *League* as well as referring to the British national identity card, created in 2006 in the Identity Cards Act but not (as of March 2008) financed by the British government. The Identity Card is being put forth as a counterterrorism measure and anti-identity-theft device, but its adoption is controversial, as citizens would theoretically be legally required to carry them at all times, something seen as step toward the creation of a "Big Brother state."

British citizens were required to carry identity cards during World War One and from 1939–1952.

The initials "AIHD," when given numeric values for each position in the alphabet, translate to "1984," and July 1948, the date listed on the Identity Card, was the date on which George Orwell returned to the island of Jura, in Scotland, to finish work on his novel, *1984* (1949). *1984* is a classic of dystopian fiction and describes life under the rule of a totalitarian government. This page is the first of many references to *1984* in the *Dossier*.

The appearance of the Identity Card here, at the beginning of the *Dossier*, is likely a reference to the "This Book Belongs To" bookplates which appeared in the front of British story paper annuals. Much of the *Black Dossier* is in the form of a story paper annual. Perhaps coincidentally, this page, like much of the *Dossier*, is similar to *The Goodies' Book of (Criminal) Records* (1975), a book by The Goodies, a comedy troupe, similar to Monty Python, who appeared on the BBC from 1970–1982. *The Goodies' Book of (Criminal) Records* had material from a number of different formats, from hand-scrawled notes to newspaper clippings, and purported to be a dossier about the Goodies.

"If found return to MiniLuv."

"MiniLuv" is an example of Newspeak, which appears in *1984*. In *1984*, the totalitarian government of Oceania imposes the malign innovation of Newspeak on its citizens. Newspeak is an artificially constructed language designed to remove as many words and meanings as possible from conversation, with the intention being to leave speakers capable of describing, and conceiving of, concepts only in simplistic dichotomies: black and white, good and evil, and so on. Toward this end, words are merged together and shortened, so that "English Socialism" becomes "IngSoc." "MiniLuv" stands for the "Ministry of Love," the government department that uses fear, brainwashing, and torture to enforce loyalty to and love of Big Brother, the leader of Oceania.

Kevin O'Neill notes:

> Never seen the Goodies book but when we were at the early stages of the *Dossier* project I showed Alan a copy of the rather marvelous Dennis Wheatley Murder Mystery Folders produced in the 1930s (and reprinted in 1979-80). They were in the form of American police department folders, complete with photos of crime scenes, newspaper clippings, maps, letters, and forensic evidence like a swatch of blood-stained curtain! The back of the folder had a sealed section revealing the killer, etc. But all you needed to solve the mystery was in the front section. Brilliant. Certainly inspired us to move in an "anything goes" direction, but not a direct inspiration.

Pages 6–7. This is a parody of that classic of graphic design, the map of the London Tube. This image may also be a riff on Simon Patterson's "The Great Bear" (1992), a piece of art modeled on the Tube map which places various famous individuals, from saints to football players, along Tube-like Lines.

Dunbier Line:

- Finner is a pun on the Pinner stop on the Metropolitan Line.
- Maida Jump is a punning twist on the Maida Vale stop on the Bakerloo Line.
- Eating Broadly is a punning twist on the Ealing Broadway stop on the District and Central Lines.
- Rothernot is a twist on the Rotherhithe stop on the East London Line (and eventually part of the London Overground system).
- Parsons Nose refers to both the Parsons Green stop on the District Line and to the "parson's nose," a.k.a. "the Pope's nose," a.k.a. "the Sultan's nose," a phrase the *Oxford English Dictionary* dates to 1836 and delicately describes as "the fatty extremity of the rump of a goose, fowl, etc., esp. when prepared for the table."
- Arson Elbow refers to both the Arsenal stop on the Piccadilly Line and to "arse and elbow," from the British phrase "doesn't know his arse from his elbow."
- If Lower Invoice is a reference to anything in particular, I'm unaware of it.
- Dunbiers Wood is a twist on the Colliers Wood stop on the Northern Line.
- Typo is an editing term, which is appropriate for a Line named after the Dossier's editor.
- Tooting Bottom is a punning twist on the Tooting Bec and Tooting Broadway stops on the Northern Line.
- If Lower Brow is a reference to anything in particular, apart from Moore's humorous comment on the content of the Dossier, I'm unaware of it. Full Stop is another editing term.

Oakley Line:

- Monument is a real Tube stop, on the District and Circle Lines, and metaphorically this serves as a monument for Bill Oakley (1964–2004), who lettered the first two *League* volumes and to whom *Black Dossier* is dedicated.
- His Nibs is a punning combination of "nib," the tip of a pen which a letterer would use, and "his nibs," a mock title given to a self-important person of authority.
- Lower Case, Upper Case, Fount, and Capital Fellow are lettering and font puns.

Moore Line:

- I'm unaware that Much Gloating, Derision, West Buttock, Rumour Mill, Segue Junction, Higher Brow, and Synergy are references to anything in particular.
- No Credit may be a reference to Moore's decision to remove

his name from the credits of movie adaptations of his work.

- Chin Topiary is likely a reference to Alan Moore's beard.
- E=mc² is interestingly close to MCC, a.k.a. the Marylebone Cricket Club, the center of the cricketing world.
- Pi, as an irrational and transcendental number, may have a symbolic importance to Moore. In Moore's *Promethea*, Pi, as the (in his words) "'false' number or sephira [attribute of God] situated between the numbers three and four," was the number of the Abyss.
- Barking (a real Tube station, on District and Hammersmith & City Lines), Very Cross (a pun on the Charing Cross stop, on the Bakerloo and Northern Lines), High Dudgeon, and Stoned Crossing are probably Moore poking fun at his own reputation.

Klein Line:
- High Stile, Upper Margin, Ltg, T-Square, Trim, and Bleed Area are all art- and lettering-related puns.

Dimagmaliw Line:
- If Hue and Cry, Nutbrush, Dark Palette, Umber, Colouring Inn, Pure Line, Rainbow City, Turnham Blue, Oil on Water, and Japan are references to anything beyond coloring–appropriate enough for for a Line named after the Dossier's colorist–I'm unaware of it.
- "Red on Green" is a reference to the two colors needed to create the 3D effect.

O'Neill Line:
- H.B. Row is a pun on "highbrow."
- Ink Staines is a punning combination of "ink stains" and Staines, a suburb of London on the southwest border of the London Commuter Belt. Staines is the supposed home of Sascha Baron Cohen's character Ali G.
- Whiteout City refers both to whiteout and to the White City Tube stop on the Central Line.
- Upper Etching and Pure Line are printmaking terms.
- Pen Stroke Newington is a pun on the Stoke Newington district of Hackney, a borough of London.
- Conté are crayon manufacturers.
- Crazy Town may be a reference to the Dave Fleischer film *Crazy Town* (1932), a Betty Boop cartoon in which Betty visits Crazy Town, where ordinary behavior is reversed: Fish fly, birds swim, a fish catches a man, and a horse follows a man with a pooper-scooper.

Quinn Line:

- Spent is a reference to the fictional town of Spent in the BBC stage, radio, and television series *The League of Gentlemen* (1994–2002). *The League of Gentlemen* is a sitcom set in the same village, originally Spent and later Royston Vasey.
- If Acne and Upper Invoice are references to anything in particular, I'm unaware of it.
- Lesser Nevins is a reference to Jess Nevins, annotator of the *League* series.
- ABC is a reference to America's Best Comics. Quinn Line is named after Kristy Quinn, an editor with ABC.
- Court Shot is a twist on the Earl's Court stop on the Piccadilly Line.
- Faxbridge is a twist on the Uxbridge stop on the Metropolitan and Piccadilly Lines.
- West Team is the logical sequel to East Team
- East Team may be a twist on Eastham stop on the District and Hammersmith & City Lines. Alternatively, East Team may be a play on Cheam. Cheam, a village in the London borough of Sutton, is the home of the Nonsuch Palace (see Page 51) and is divided into North Cheam, South Cheam, and Cheam Village, with the previous locations of "East Cheam" and "West Cheam" no longer being in use. "East Cheam" was the fictional home of Anthony Aloysius St. John Hancock, British comedian Tony Hancock's fictional persona in his radio and TV show *Hancock's Half Hour* (1954–1961).
- Petticoat Junction is a reference to *Petticoat Junction* (1963–1970), an American TV sitcom.

"Credit Line. Traveller—if experiencing nausea while in the nether regions, keep hat firmly on, lay back, and think of England."
"Lie back and think of England" was the advice supposedly given, during the Victorian era, to daughters by mothers about how to survive the wedding night and the loss of virginity, since (supposedly) Victorian women couldn't conceive of a proper woman enjoying sex. This is ahistorical nonsense, and "lie back and think of England" was not standard advice, or even widely said. The quote is usually attributed to one "Lady Hillingdon," but the quote is spurious; the *Oxford English Dictionary* sources the phrase to Jonathan Gathorne-Hardy's *Rise and Fall of the British Nanny* (1972), but Gathorne-Hardy himself says that the quote is "somewhat suspect."

"Kevin O'Neill—Subject to delay at all times," "John Nee—Extension delayed subject to mood," and "ABC—Closed for the duration" are all legends the likes of which appear in Underground stations from time to time, and whose associated double meanings are obvious here. If "Jim Lee–East is a state of mind" is a reference to anything in particular, I'm unaware of it.

"Ray Zone—Zones 1 to 3D, The Blazing World, off-peak only from Red on Green" is a reference to Ray Zone, the foremost 3-D artist in comics today. Zone did the 3-D section of *Black Dossier*.

"The Blazing World" is a reference to *Observations upon Experimental Philosophy. To which is added the Description of a New Blazing World. Written by the Thrice Noble, Illustrious and Excellent Princess, The Duchess of Newcastle* (1666), by Margaret Cavendish, Duchess of Newcastle. *The Blazing World* is a classic of the Imaginary Voyage genre and was referred to in *League* v2.

Kevin O'Neill notes:
> I will draw a veil over some unidentified connections to protect the innocent.

> The classic Tube map (designed by H.C. Beck in 1933) was too iconic not to play with, and Todd Klein produced a great finished image.

Page 8. The two ads on the right side of this page are legitimate.

The cartoon on the lower left is done in the style of *New Yorker* cartoons from the 1950s and 1960s. The cartoon's artist, "Arnie Packer," is a reference to the "Winged Avenger" episode of the British TV spy series *The Avengers* (1961–1969). In "The Winged Avenger," an evil cartoonist named "Arnie Packer" is responsible for a series of murders.

Kevin O'Neill notes:
> The Dunloprene coat ad is authentic but we changed the store address from Selfridges Ltd. to Pinters Ltd.

Pinters was the name of the department store in the fourth Emma Peel *Avengers* episode, "Death at Bargain Prices" (1965).

Page 9. **Panel 1**. In the upper left of the panel is a large stone head on the back of a flatbed truck. See Page 13, Panel 2 for an explanation of this.

I don't believe that the "Malibu" is a reference to anything in particular.

Kevin O'Neill notes:
> The Malibu Club was featured in the 1958 Sexton Blake relaunch (and revamp) story "The Frightened Lady" by Howard Baker. Blake moved offices from Baker Street to Berkeley Square and met his new secretary Paula Dane in the Malibu Club.

The headline in lower center, "Melchester Rovers Scandal," is a reference to the British comic *Roy of the Rovers* (1954–1993), in which the hero Roy Race plays football for the Melchester Rovers. There was no particularly scandalous event or storyline in *Roy of the Rovers* in 1958, when *Black Dossier* takes place, although the Rovers had a poor set of matches that fall, which ended when Roy was made captain of the team. In the overheated world of sports journalism, several games in a row of substandard play would qualify as a "scandal." Alternatively, some time before 1958 a reserve player on the Rovers kidnapped the French winger of the Rovers so that the reserve player could fill in for the missing winger. If the kidnapper did not come to trial until 1958, the trial would justify the term "scandal."

The headline on the right, "Knightsbridge Ape-Men," is a reference to "Quatermass and the Pit" (1958), the third *Professor Quatermass* BBC serial. In "Quatermass and the Pit," the bones of ape-men, unearthed in Knightsbridge, lead to the revelation of the Martian influence on the evolution of humanity.

Panel 2. See Page 9, Panel 7 below.

Panel 3. The "Will Wilson Return for Olympics?" reference is to Wilson, the mysterious, superhuman teenaged athlete from the British comics *Wizard, Hotspur*, and *Hornet* (1943–1963) and *Spike* (1983). Wilson, born in 1806, achieved longevity and athletic prowess from special breathing exercises and a diet of gruel, nuts, berries, and wild roots. In one episode, he breaks the world long jump record while running a three-minute mile.

Panels 4–6. Jack and Annie Walker were characters on the long-running British soap *Coronation Street* (1960–present). The Walkers were landlords of the Rovers Return Inn, hence the comment in Panel 6 that "our rovin' days are over." Jack's comment, "I reckon she's after movin' back up north," hints that the Malibu (whose name can be seen in Panel 1 above) was the business the Walkers owned before moving to Weatherfield, the setting of *Coronation Street*.

 Jack Walker was played by Arthur Leslie (1901–1970) and is drawn to match him here.

Panel 5. "Straight after election she 'ad all cameras took out, the lot."
The England of *1984* was under constant observation from the government of Oceania. This may also be an allusion by Moore to England as it is now, with over four million cameras watching the British at all times.

The "V" cigarettes that the blonde woman is smoking here are likely "Victory cigarettes," from *1984*. Victory Cigarettes were a real brand of American cigarette, produced by the Leighton Tobacco Company during 1942.

Panel 6. "Victory Gin: It's Doubleplus Good For You."
"Victory Gin" is the only authorized alcohol in *1984*. "Doubleplus" is another use of Newspeak (see Page 5). Future uses of Newspeak in the *Dossier* will not be noted here.

 The ad slogan "Victory Gin: It's Doubleplus Good For You" is a parody of the slogan for Guinness stout, "Guinness Is Good For You," which ran from the 1920s to at least the 1960s and may have been coined by crime novelist Dorothy Sayers.

Panel 7. "I'll have a vodka martini over ice… and stir that, if you would. Otherwise it bruises the alcohol."

"Shaken, not stirred" is the second-most famous quote uttered by Ian Fleming's James Bond, who—as will be seen—is the speaker here. In the first Bond novel, *Casino Royale* (1953), Bond orders a martini and asks for it to be specially made:

> "A dry martini," he said. "One. In a deep champagne goblet."
> "Oui, monsieur."
> "Just a moment. Three measures of Gordon's, one of vodka, half a measure of Kina Lillet. Shake it very well until it's ice-cold, then add a large thin slice of lemon-peel. Got it?"

It is not until *Dr. No* (1958) that Bond first uses the phrase, "shaken, not stirred": "And I would like a medium Vodka dry Martini—with a slice of lemon peel. Shaken and not stirred, please. I would prefer Russian or Polish vodka."

The idea that alcohol can be "bruised" by shaking, or stirring, is either as true as gravity or utter bollocks, depending on who you talk to. Supposedly, when a martini is shaken, air is added to the drink and "bruises" the alcohol, adding a bitter taste. Alternately, shaking the martini breaks the ice in the drink, making the ice melt faster and thereby watering down the drink.

As mentioned above, the speaker here is James Bond. (His adjustment of his tie, in Panel 2, is one established by Pierce Brosnan in his portrayal of Bond.) His portrayal in these panels is similar to one made to help the artists of the Bond strip in *Daily Express*, and matches the description of Bond given in *Casino Royale*:

> It was a dark, clean-cut face, with a three-inch scar showing whitely down the sunburned skin of the right cheek. The eyes were wide and level under straight, rather long black brows. The hair was black, parted on the left, and carelessly brushed so that a thick black comma fell down over the right eyebrow. The longish straight nose

ran down to a short upper lip below which was a wide
and finely drawn but cruel mouth. The line of jaw was
straight and firm. A section of dark suit, white shirt and
black knitted tie completed the picture.

The composer and pianist Hoagy Carmichael (1899–1981) has
been suggested as one model for Bond, and Bond is compared to
Carmichael in both *Casino Royale* and *Moonraker* (1955). There
is a similarity in these panels between Carmichael and the Bond
seen here.

Page 10. **Panel 1**. In *1984*, the currency of Airstrip One (as Great
Britain is called) is the dollar, rather than the pound, which explains
why the note reads "10 shillings, One dollar." The face on the dollar
note is that of Britannia, the personification of the British Empire
in the world of *League*. Modern pound notes have the Queen's face
on them, but the 1948 pound note had Britannia on it.

Panel 4. "My name's Jimmy, by the way."
Bond is never called "Jimmy" in the Fleming novels. But he was
called "Jimmy Bond" on the back cover of the first American
paperback edition of *Casino Royale*, retitled *You Asked For It*
(1954). "Jimmy Bond" was also the name of the lead in the 1954
American TV adaptation of *Casino Royale*; the adaptation appeared
on an episode of *Climax!* (1954–1958), with Bond being a CIA
agent. And Woody Allen's character in the 1967 film version of
Casino Royale is "Jimmy Bond," the cousin of James Bond.

One possibility for Bond's use of the name "Jimmy," rather than
"James," is so he can pretend to be someone he's not. Ian Fleming
wrote the Bond novels as a way to cope with his own depression,
but John Pearson's *James Bond: The Authorized Biography of 007*
(1973) puts forth the idea that Fleming writes the Bond stories
as a way to convince Soviet agents that James Bond is a fictional
character, rather than a real person—when everyone has heard of
James Bond, how could he possibly be a real person? Perhaps in
the world of *League* something similar has happened, and Bond
uses "Jimmy" rather than "James" as a way to pretend not to be
the famous James Bond. This interplay between fiction and reality

is one of the recurring themes of *Black Dossier*.

"Bash Street," "Rampaging Yobs," and the picture on the newspaper are references to the British comic strip "Bash Street Kids," created by British comics great Leo Baxendale and appearing in *Beano* (originally as "When the Bell Rings") from 1954 to the present. The Bash Street Kids are a bunch of mischievous and ill-behaved children at the Bash Street School. The two Bash Streeters in the picture are Danny and Wilfrid.

"Asian Flu" may be a specific literary or cultural reference or just an allusion to the Asian flu pandemic which swept across the world from 1956 to 1958, killing between one and four million people. It was most active in Great Britain from mid-1957 to 1958.

Panel 8. Captain Morgan is a reference to Jet Morgan, who starred in the British radio serial *Journey Into Space* (1953–1958). Set in the distant future of 1965 (and, in later series, the early 1970s), *Journey Into Space* is about Captain Jet Morgan, "Doc" Matthews, "Mitch" Mitchell, and Lemmy Barnett, and their trip to the Moon and then to Mars.

Captain Dare is a reference to Dan Dare, the archetypal British comic science fiction hero. Created by Frank Hampson, Dan Dare has been appearing in various media since his debut in the comic *Eagle* in 1950. In the future of the 1990s, Colonel Dan Dare, chief pilot of the Interplanet Space Fleet, has adventures across the solar system, repeatedly coming into conflict with the Mekon, the evil ruler of the Treens of northern Venus.

Captain Logan is a reference to Jet-Ace Logan, who appeared in the British comics *Comet* (1956–1959) and *Tiger* (1959–1968). Royal Air Force Space Cadet Jim "Jet-Ace" Logan is a part of the R.A.F. Space Patrol and cruises about the solar system, fighting iniquitous aliens and finding adventure.

The man that Bond pushes aside is Pop, from John Millar Watt's newspaper strip "Pop" (*Daily Sketch*, 1921–1960). Pop is a henpecked husband and businessman.

Panel 9. "Fighter Ace Dies" is presumably a reference to something, but the accompanying picture could refer to a number of characters. But see Page 16, Panel 8.

Page 11. Panel 4. The cigarette case Bond is using here, with the Harlequin on it, is the same one that his grandfather Campion Bond used in *League* v1 and v2.

Panel 6. "I could be an infiltrator from *Russia* or *Meccania* or somewhere."
Meccania is a reference to Gregory Owen's *Meccania, the Super-State* (1918). Meccania is the ultimate in totalitarian dystopias, a state completely regimented and controlled by the government. Meccania was mentioned on Page 173 of *League* v2 as a "troubling police-state," and clearly Meccania has survived. For a Big Brother-ruled England, Meccania would be a natural enemy.

As will slowly be revealed in the *Dossier*, the history of England in the world of *League* is slightly off from the history of real-world England. Perhaps the use of the word "Russia" here is a hint that there is no "Soviet Union," only a communist Russia?

Panel 7. The somewhat grotesque-looking statue here is of Mr. Hyde. *League* v2, Page 180, says that a statue of Hyde "still stands… in London's former Serpentine Park." The statue is credited to Sir Jacob Epstein, an avant-garde realist sculptor whose work often portrayed distorted figures, like the Hyde seen in *League* v1 and v2 and here.

As mentioned in *League* v2, Page 151, Panel 4, Hyde Park, "London's former Serpentine Park," was named after Edward Hyde. (In our world, Hyde Park was named after the manor of Hyde, the owner of the park before King Henry VIII acquired the park in 1536. There has never been a Serpentine Park in London, although the Serpentine, an artificial lake, still exists in Hyde Park.) In our Hyde Park stands a statue of Achilles, built as a tribute to the Duke of Wellington and "cast from cannons won at the victories of Salmanaca, Vittoria, Toulouse and Waterloo." Perhaps the statue of Hyde was made from a melted Martian tripod?

Kevin O'Neill notes:
> The tomb is in fact Jacob Epstein's Rima monument.

On the far right of the panel is a tomb on which can be seen two X marks. See Page 47, Panel 1 for more.

Page 12. **Panel 3**. "O'Dette 'Oodles' O'Quim" is a riff on the salacious, single-entendre names that Bond women and Bond's female enemies usually have. "Quim" is British slang for female genitalia, so "Oodles O'Quim" is the equivalent of "Pussy Galore."

Panel 7. The statue on the left may be referenced in *1984*: "in Victory Square… near the statue of Big Brother on the tall fluted column with the lions at the foot" and "the base of the enormous fluted column, at the top of which Big Brother's statue gazed southward towards the skies where he had vanquished the Eurasian aeroplanes… in the Battle of Airstrip One." The implication in the novel is that Trafalgar Square was renamed Victory Square, and the statue of Lord Nelson was replaced with a statue of Big Brother. However, the statue on this page is close to Hyde Park, while Trafalgar Square is a long walk from Hyde Park; nor does this statue meet the description of Big Brother's statue in *1984*. More likely, this is Piccadilly Circus—note the large billboards—and the statue of Big Brother has replaced the statue of Eros.

The manner in which the statue of Big Brother is being taken down is undoubtedly meant to recall the manner in which the statue of Saddam Hussein was pulled down by American troops after occupying Baghdad in 2003.

Wow! was a British comic which appeared in 1982 and 1983, but I don't believe that the bus advert is a reference to that.

Kevin O'Neill notes:
> *Wow!* is a fictional men's pin-up magazine featured in the 1959 British film *Cover Girl Killer*, featuring Harry H. Corbett as the Killer and produced (aptly) by Butchers Films.

"Maplins: Bluepool For Your Holiday"
Maplins is a holiday camp in the British TV sitcom *Hi-de-Hi!* (1980–1988). Maplins is in the coastal town of Crimpton-on-Sea in Essex, and is based on Butlin's Holiday Camps, a series of economical resorts for the British built between 1936 and 1966. Bluepool is probably a riff on the British seaside resort of Blackpool.

"—is watching you" is the second half of the classic phrase "Big Brother is Watching You" from *1984*.

Tony Hancock, mentioned above on Pages 6–7, appears in the lower left, raising his arm for a cab.

To the right of Hancock is a bald man with a mustache shouting at a black man and a white women. The bald man is Alf Garnett, Warren Mitchell's racist, reactionary, bigoted persona on the BBC sitcom *Till Death Us Do Part* (1965–1975).

In bottom center of the panel is an old woman waving an umbrella. She is Grandma, from a series of cartoons by Ronald Giles for the British newspaper *Daily Express* from 1945–1991. Grandma, the de facto leader of the Giles Family, is a terrifying termagant.

Page 13. **Panel 1**. In *1984*, the British Isles are called "Airstrip One," which is part of Oceania (along with the Americas, Southern Africa, and Australia).

The "Anti-Sex League" is a reference to the government-backed organization, in *1984*, which is devoted to eliminating the pleasurable aspect of sex. Members of the League are encouraged to have sex, but only once a week, and "for the good of the party," rather than for pleasure—the Party intends to wipe out the orgasm.

Panel 2. "When O'Brien became Party Head in '52 things got easier, but I'm still glad he's gone."
In *1984*, O'Brien is a member of the Inner Party, the ruling class of Oceania. In the novel, O'Brien is responsible for torturing Winston Smith, the protagonist, into accepting Big Brother. This

line indicates that O'Brien became Big Brother, but is dead by the time of *Black Dossier*. One of the traditional responses to the deaths of tyrants and dictators has been to destroy the statues that they had erected of themselves, hence the head of a statue of Big Brother being taken away on Page 9, Panel 1, and a statue of Big Brother being pulled down on Page 12, Panel 7. An image similar to the one on Page 9, Panel 1 appears on the cover of Misha Glenny's *The Rebirth of History* (1990) and shows the head of a statue of Stalin being driven off in the back of a truck.

Panel 4. In *1984*, "Freedom is Slavery" is one of the slogans of Oceania's ruling class. It is an example of "doublethink," which *1984* defines as "To know and not to know, to be conscious of complete truthfulness while telling carefully constructed lies, to hold simultaneously two opinions which cancelled out, knowing them to be contradictory and believing in both of them, to use logic against logic."

The shell marks on this building may seem unusual, but much of London was not fully rebuilt, following World War Two, until the mid- to late 1950s, and several museums and government buildings still had such marks as late as the mid-1970s.

Panel 5. As mentioned in Panel 3, this building is at Vauxhall Embankment. In our world, Vauxhall Embankment is the site of the headquarters of MI6, the British Secret Intelligence Services.

Page 6. The symbol above the doors is the Masonic compass and right angle which was a recurring symbol in earlier *League* volumes. In Masonic lore, the compass and right angle symbolize the instruments of both the Masons and God.

Panel 7. The Ministry of Love, mentioned above on Page 5 as "MiniLuv," is the government department, in *1984*, which uses fear, brainwashing, and torture to enforce loyalty to and love of Big Brother.

Page 14. **Panel 1**. The poster in the upper left is a combination of the "Big Brother Is Watching You" poster from the 1956 British film version of *1984* and the mustached Big Brother from the 1984 American film version of *1984*. The top line of the poster is damaged, but it is possible that the poster originally read "Be Watching You," which would be a variation on "Be Seeing You," a catchphrase from the BBC TV series *The Prisoner* (1967–1968), about a spy imprisoned on an island run by an inimical government and filled with spies.

It is perhaps significant that here, on Page 12, Panel 7, and in other places throughout the *Dossier*, the entire slogan, "Big Brother Is Watching You," is not visible. This is similar to Alan Moore's earlier *Watchmen*, in which the graffiti "Who Watches the Watchmen" is never completely seen.

The bust in the lower left is probably of Professor Moriarty, replacing the bust of Napoleon which Moriarty kept when he was in charge of British Intelligence in *League* v1.

The pith helmet and cricket bat are a reference to the Wolf of Kabul. The Wolf of Kabul appeared in over 100 stories in *Wizard, Hotspur*, and *Rover and Wizard* from 1922 to 1972. He is 2nd Lieutenant Bill Sampson (sometimes "Samson"), an agent for the British Intelligence Corps who operates in the Northwest frontier of India, based from Fort Kanda, "right at the east end of the Khyber Pass." He fights "wily Pathans," Nazis, Communists, evil Anglos, and even a giant walking stone statue, the Stone Man. He is assisted by Chung, his native servant and friend. Chung's weapon of choice is his "clicky-ba," or cricket bat. After killing men, Chung would remark, his eyes tearing, "Lord, I am full of humble sorrow—I did not mean to knock down these men—'Clicky-ba' merely turned in my hand." The Wolf is mentioned in *League* v2, with Samson's father acting as a carriage driver for Campion Bond and members of the League. The cricket bat here has a tag hanging from its handle with the words "clicky-ba" barely visible. Also see Page 148.

The glass helmet, breathing apparatus, and shirt with the "s" emblem are a reference to the comic strip "The Adventures of Swift Morgan and the Flying Saucers," created by Denis McLoughlin and appearing in various British comics from 1948–1953. Swift Morgan is a Flash Gordon lift who, with his fiancée Silver (a Dale

Arden *manqué*), has various Gordonian adventures.

The giant skull is the Brobdingnagian skull, from Jonathan Swift's *Gulliver's Travels* (1726), seen in *League* v1.

The portrait of the bow tie-wearing man is quite similar to several images of James Bond's creator, Ian Fleming.

On the bulletin board, the painting/picture, "Pacific Ocean July 1949," and "Iron Fish?" are references to the comic strip "Iron Fish," from the British comic *Beano* from 1949–1968. The main character in the strip, Jimmy Grey, appeared in *League* v2. "The Iron Fish" is about two twins, Danny and Penny Gray, who pilot two "Iron Fish" submarines, both of which are built by their father, Professor Gray, who is the subject of the "Professor Gray Feared Lost" headline on the lower left of the board.

"Bla— Sapp—" is a reference to the titular character of the comic strip "The Black Sapper," who appeared in the British comics *Rover* and *Hotspur* for decades, beginning with *The Rover* #384 (Aug. 24, 1929). The Black Sapper is a costumed inventor/thief who uses The Earthworm, an enormous burrowing machine, to commit crimes. He reforms in the face of a Yellow Peril invasion of England.

Panel 2. The painting in the upper left seems to be based on the John de Critz portrait of Sir Francis Walsingham, painted circa 1587. In our world, Walsingham (c. 1532–1590) was the spymaster for Queen Elizabeth I. But the figure in the painting is not Walsingham. For the identity of his replacement, see the notes to Page 53.

Panel 4. In *1984*, Room 101 is "the worst thing in the world," a torture chamber in the Ministry of Love where prisoners are subjected to their worst nightmares.

When George Orwell worked at BBC Television Centre, his office number was 101. Orwell was miserable while he worked for the BBC, and he used the room number in *1984* as revenge on the BBC.

Panel 5. The wicker chair to the right of the door may be a reference to the wicker chair used as part of the torture of James Bond in *Casino Royale*.

The cane leaning on the wicker chair is likely meant to remind British readers of the canes which British school teachers used to discipline children, in both real life and in comics. For British citizens of the world of *League*, and by extension for the British readers of *Black Dossier*, the cane belongs in a room which contains what people fear the most.

Kevin O'Neill notes:
> Yes, the cane represents a fear I certainly would have had in 1958—the headmistress and nuns at my catholic primary school were quick to anger and an anticipated thrashing was almost as bad as the real thing. But we were made of iron then, Jess. You could have whipped us with chains and we'd still have a ready smile and a Hail Mary!

The contraption in the lower left of the panel is the mask which was used to torture Winston Smith in *1984*:

> It was an oblong wire cage with a handle on top for carrying it by. Fixed to the front of it was something that looked like a fencing mask, with the concave side outwards. Although it was three or four metres away from him, he could see that the cage was divided lengthways into two compartments, and that there was some kind of creature in each. They were rats.

The mask here is similar to the one used in the 1984 film version of *1984*. Also see Pornsec SexJane Page 8 below.

Panel 6. "Special village in *Wales*" is a reference to the British TV series *The Prisoner*, in which retired spies who are too dangerous to their former employers are confined in a village. The location of the village was never specified, but the series was filmed in the eccentric resort village of Portmeirion, which is in Wales.

Page 15. **Panels 1–4**. Although the *Dossier*'s portrayal of James Bond is controversial with some fans, the Bond of Ian Fleming's novels, especially his early novels, really is this hatefully misogynistic.

This is not the first time Moore has noted Bond's misogyny. In Moore's introduction to Frank Miller's *The Dark Knight Returns*, Moore writes, "As our political and social consciousness continues to evolve, Allan Quatermain stands revealed as just another white imperialist out to exploit the natives and we begin to see that the overriding factor in James Bond's psychological makeup is his utter hatred and contempt for women."

Panel 8. Interestingly, Bond is beaten by a woman in Room 101, and on Page 16, Panel 1 is handcuffed by a woman in Room 101, the room which has what people fear the most. Bond's misogyny may spring from a simple fear of women and of helplessness in front of them and humiliation at their hands.

Panel 9. Despite the reverence with which Bond is usually held, this is not the first time that he is described as a thug. In the 2006 film version of *Casino Royale*, Bond's superior M describes him as a "thug," and as far back as 1962 Charles Stainsby, editor of the fiction magazine *Today*, was describing Bond as a "cheap and very nasty upper class thug."

Page 16. **Panel 4**. "…just like your grandfather."
This is confirmation that Campion Bond, seen in the previous volumes of *League*, is James Bond's grandfather.

Panel 5. "…is this what it's come to? The British adventure hero? Pathetic."
While it is logical that a 19th-century British adventure hero (Allan) would find the 20th-century British adventure hero (Bond) unsavory and pathetic, the statement can also be seen as a metatextual comment by Moore on the way in which 20th-century British adventure fiction, certainly of the first half of the century, overtly displayed biases (see Page 79, Panel 2, for example) which were mostly hidden during the 19th century.

Panel 7. "If he'd been German, he'd have been loyal to *Hynkel*."
See Page 47, Panel 1.

Panel 8. "Eurasia" is a reference to *1984*. Eurasia, which is Europe, Russia, northern Africa, and the Middle East, is sometimes the enemy of Oceania.

"Isn't that the travel guide they based on us?"
The "travel guide" is the Almanac in *League* v2.

"Social— Nuclea— by Gust—" is a reference to H. G. Wells's *The Shape of Things to Come* (1933), a future history of the world in which a benevolent dictatorship emerges following a deadly plague. In *The Shape of Things to Come*, a Wellsian stand-in, Gustave de Windt, writes a book, *Social Nucleation*, which

> was the first exhaustive study of the psychological laws underlying team play and *esprit de corps*, disciplines of criminal gangs, spirit of factory groups, crews, regiments, political parties, churches, professionalisms, aristocracies, patriotisms, class consciousness, organized research and constructive cooperation generally. It did for the first time correlate effectively the increasing understanding of individual psychology, with new educational methods and new concepts of political life. In spite of its unattractive title and a certain wearisomeness in the exposition, his book became a definite backbone for the constructive effort of the new time.

"Titus Cobbet" is a reference to Wells's *The Shape of Things to Come*. In the novel, a bicyclist, Titus Cobbett, travels through a ruined Europe and England observing the desolation. He also reports on the death of a "European Aviator," which could be what the headline on Page 10, Panel 9 is referring to.

"Ripley" is a reference to Tom Ripley, the protagonist of five novels by Patricia Highsmith, beginning with *The Talented Mr. Ripley* (1955). Tom Ripley is a charming, literate, amoral con man and murderer—exactly the sort of person British Intelligence in the world of *League* might recruit.

"The Th— Oligarchial— by Emm—" is a reference to *The Theory and Practice of Oligarchial Collectivism*, which in *1984* is "a terrible book, a compendium of all the heresies" and is written by the dissident Emmanuel Goldstein. *The Theory and Practice of Oligarchial Collectivism* is described as being "a heavy black volume, amateurishly bound, with no name or title on the cover," which is perhaps coincidentally similar to the *Black Dossier*, as can be seen in Panel 9.

Panel 9. "—stasia" is a reference to Eastasia in *1984*. Eastasia, which consists of China, Japan, Korea, Mongolia, India, the Philippines, Indonesia, and the Middle East, is the smallest and newest of the three superstates.

"Atrocity Pamphlet"
In *1984*, atrocity pamphlets are created to spur hatred for enemies of Oceania:

> The preparations for Hate Week were in full swing, and the staffs of all the Ministries were working overtime. Processions, meetings, military parades, lectures, waxworks, displays, film shows, telescreen programmes all had to be organized; stands had to be erected, effigies built, slogans coined, songs written, rumours circulated, photographs faked. Julia's unit in the Fiction Department had been taken off the production of novels and was rushing out a series of atrocity pamphlets.

"Manor Farm" is a reference to George Orwell's *Animal Farm* (1945), in which the revolution of the talking animals takes place at Manor Farm.

"Harry Blake" may be a reference to the ne'er-do-well brother of story paper detective Sexton Blake. In *Boys' Friend Library* #10 (Feb. 23, 1907), Sexton Blake discovers that his brother Henry is running a counterfeiting operation and gambling den.

The stylized letter on the folder may be in the Martian alphabet, from *League* v2, making this a Martian/English dictionary.

"Moreau" is likely a reference to H. G. Wells's *The Island of Dr. Moreau* (1896). Dr. Moreau appeared in *League* v2.

"Gustave de Windt" is a reference to H. G. Wells's *The Shape of Things to Come* (see the note to Panel 8 above).

"—oy Cars—" is probably a reference to Denis McLoughlin's Roy Carson, who appeared in a number of comics, including *Roy Carson Comic* #1–#44, from 1948–1954. Roy Carson is a British hardboiled, cynical private detective. Also see Page 122, Panel 1.

"St. Merri— Hospital" is a reference to John Wyndham's *The Day of the Triffids* (1953). *The Day of the Triffids* is a science fiction, horror, postapocalyptic novel in which a race of carnivorous plants, the triffids, cause the downfall of human civilization. The opening of the novel occurs in St. Merryn's Hospital. Also see Page 48, Panel 6.

Kevin O'Neill notes:
> The stylized letter is the symbol of Freedonia from the Marx Brothers' classic *Duck Soup* (1933).

Page 17. **Panel 1**. "…how much vipers like Lime actually *know*…."
See Page 78, Panel 9 for more on "Lime."

Panel 2. "Drake" is a reference to John Drake, the protagonist of the ITC TV series *Danger Man* (1960–1962). John Drake is an Irish-American spy for a department of N.A.T.O. who carries out missions for his superiors even though he often disagrees with them. *The Prisoner*, mentioned above on Page 14, Panels 1 and 6 and starring Patrick McGoohan (who played John Drake in *Danger Man*), was rumored at the time of its broadcast to be the unofficial sequel to *Danger Man*, with No. 6, McGoohan's character on *The Prisoner*, as John Drake. McGoohan, among others, denied that they were the same character, but George Markstein, cocreator and script editor of *The Prisoner*, said that they were the same character. David McDaniel's *Prisoner* novel, *Who is No. 2?* (1968), and Hank Stine's *Prisoner* novel, *A Day in the Life* (1969), both confirm that Drake is No. 6.

"Meres" is a reference to Toby Meres, who appeared in the British TV series *Callan* (1967–1972). David Callan, the protagonist, is a bitter, cynical, aging assassin for the British S.I.S. Meres is Callan's partner, and a sociopath who enjoys the violence of his work.

Panel 4. Concealed and miniaturized gadgets and weapons are a recurring part of the Bond canon. In *Octopussy* (story 1966, film 1983), Bond's pen contains a variety of acids, and in *Goldeneye* (1995), Bond's pen contains a grenade. The pen here can be seen in Bond's pocket on Page 9.

"In Mem— Police C— George— Died on t— August 1898"
I believe that this is a reference to P.C. George Dixon, who appeared in the film *The Blue Lamp* (1950) and the BBC TV series *Dixon of Dock Green* (1955–1976). Jack Warner played Dixon in both roles as an old-fashioned, paternal policeman, but in *The Blue Lamp*, which is set after World War Two, Dixon is killed because of his old-fashioned ways. *Dixon of Dock Green* ignores this ending, and the *Dossier* continues in that tradition by backdating Dixon's death to 1898. It is possible that the implication here is that the policeman killed by the Invisible Man in *League* v2, which took place in 1898, was Dixon.

Kevin O'Neill notes:
> The memorial to the policeman killed by the Invisible Man
> in volume one of *League* does not represent the TV George
> Dixon—but may have been his father.

Panel 7. "Another ten years, they'll probably have ironed the bugs out."
In the film *You Only Live Twice* (1967, nine years later), Bond has a cigarette which can shoot a jet-powered needle.

Page 18. **Panel 2**. The obelisk is Cleopatra's Needle, the celebratory obelisk originally constructed for Pharaoh Tuthmosis III, ruler of Egypt's 18th Dynasty from 1504–1450 B.C.E.

Panels 2–4. "Glamcabs" is a reference to the film *Carry On Cabby* (1963). In the film, Glamcabs is a taxi company in competition with Speedee Taxis, the service operated by Charlie Hawkins, *Carry On Cabby*'s protagonist. It is possible that the driver here is Anthea, from *Carry On Cabby*, played in the film by Amanda Barrie.

Panel 7. "He must meet women with names like that all the *time*." As indeed Bond does.

Page 19. **Panel 1**. "Birnley Fabrics" is a reference to the film *The Man in the White Suit* (1951). In the film, Sidney Stratton invents a fabric—later called Birnley Fabrics after the mill owner who produces them—that never gets dirty or wears out.

Presumably the characters in this panel, as in many others in *Black Dossier*, are references to British comics, but I'm unable to place the references.

Panels 3–5. "Mr. Kiss" is a reference to Michael Moorcock's *Mother London* (1988), a novel about post-WW2 London. One of the main characters is fading theater performer and professional mind-reader Josef Kiss.

Perhaps coincidentally, Mr. Kiss has a certain resemblance to the actor Robert Morley (1908–1992).

Page 20. **Panels 2–8**. The landlady, the girl, and "Franky" and "Jerry" are references to Michael Moorcock's novels and short stories. "Jerry" is Jerry Cornelius, a British secret agent and anarchistic adventurer; "Franky" is Frank Cornelius, Jerry's disreputable brother, who is a rival to Jerry and is often killed by him (time and continuity are not linear or regular in the Jerry Cornelius stories); the girl is Catherine Cornelius, Jerry's incestuous lover and, in *The Final Programme* (1968), the kidnap victim of Frank; and the landlady is the monstrous Mrs. Cornelius, foul-mouthed mother to Franky, Jerry, and Catherine.

Panel 2. In *1984*, Winston Smith and Julia rent a room from a Mr. Charrington. Possibly the implication is that "Mrs. C" is Mr. Charrington's wife, and the room Allan and Mina are renting is the same room that Winston and Julia rented. In *1984*, Mrs. Charrington is described as "a monstrous woman, solid as a Norman pillar, with brawny red forearms and a sacking apron strapped around her middle," which certainly fits Mrs. Cornelius here.

Panel 3. "Anyroad" is a northern British variant of "anyway."

Page 21. **Panel 1**. The "Holborn Empire," a.k.a. the Royal Holborn, a.k.a. Weston's Music Hall, was a major music hall in Holborn, in central London, from 1857–1941.

"Lewis and Clark" are from Neil Simon's play *The Sunshine Boys* (1972). In the play, Al Lewis and Willie Clark are a pair of aging vaudevillians.

I'm unable to place the "Professor Donnol" reference.

"Archie Rice" is a reference to the John Osborne play *The Entertainer* (1957), later made into the 1960 film *The Entertainer*. In the play and film, Archie Rice is an aging, hard-luck vaudevillian entertainer.

There were many London theaters with the name "Theatre Royal." The Theatre Royal in Drury Lane dates back to 1663.

"Fevvers" may be a reference to the protagonist of Angela Carter's *Nights at the Circus* (1984). Fevvers is a Cockney circus aerialist and showgirl who has wings, which is why she is "lifting you on wings of song."

"Mr. J. Stark The Incredible Indian Rubber Man" is a reference to Janus Stark, who appeared in the British comics *Smash* and *Valiant* (1969–1975). Stark is a Victorian superhero with very rubbery bones, which gives him abilities he uses to fight crime.

"Comedy of —rthur —e Washboard —tkins with —er Drawers" is a reference to Paul Whitehouse's character Arthur Atkinson, played by Whitehouse on the BBC TV show *The Fast Show* (1994–2000). Arthur Atkinson, a parody of real-life radio comedian Arthur Askey, is a nonsensical comedian, one of whose catchphrases is "Where's me washboard?" "—er Drawers" refers to Chester Drawers, Atkinson's much put-upon sidekick.

I'm unsure what the rabbit next to the iron in the center of the panel might be a reference to.

Kevin O'Neill notes:
>The rabbit is a crude fertility symbol and is facing the bed.

Panel 4. "Or perhaps his *tie-clip's* really a *radio*."
I'm unaware of Bond ever having a radio transmitter in his tie-clip. However, such a device appeared in the American TV series *Search* (1972–1973).

Page 22. **Panel 2**. In *1984*, "unpersons" are those people who have had their existence officially deleted and erased from all records by the government of Big Brother.

Panels 3–4. "…you were lucky buying those old *music hall* posters."
"But then that was a street market for the proles…."
Paul Whitehouse and Charlie Higson's *Fast Show* (1996), a book about *The Fast Show* (see Page 21, Panel 1 above), reveals that Arthur Atkinson, whose name appears on the poster, was a Nazi sympathizer. Presumably Atkinson was unpersoned, which is why the posters were so cheap.

Panel 5. In *1984*, "Pornosec" is a section of the Ministry of Truth that produces pornography. Winston Smith's lover Julia worked for Pornosec:

She had even (an infallible mark of good reputation) been picked out to work in Pornosec, the sub-section of the Fiction Department which turned out cheap pornography for distribution among the proles. It was nicknamed Muck House by the people who worked in it, she remarked. There she had remained for a year, helping to produce booklets in sealed packets with titles like 'Spanking Stories' or 'One Night in a Girls' School', to be bought furtively by proletarian youths who were under the impression that they were buying something illegal.

Panel 6. "Well, I saw that 'Adventures of Jane' series that was everywhere. Based on some woman's diaries, supposedly."
This is a reference to Norman Pett's "Jane's Journal: The Diary of a Bright Young Thing," a comic strip which ran in the *Daily Mirror* from 1932–1959; the comic strip was made into a film, *The Adventures of Jane*, in 1949, and a BBC TV series, *Jane*, from 1982–1984. Jane is an ingénue who is often inadvertently disrobed. Jane, and the actress Christabel Leighton-Porter—who toured music halls doing a striptease act as Jane—were both enormously popular with British troops during World War Two, and a perhaps apocryphal story is told that the first time Jane lost all her clothes, in 1943, it caused one British division to gain six miles at the front.

It is possible that in the world of the *Dossier*, the *Daily Mirror* did not run the cartoons, which would make Jane's first appearance in the 1949 film, in the middle of the Big Brother years, which would lead to the Tijuana Bibles such as Pornsec SexJane (see below).

Panel 7. "You don't seriously imagine Jane's *real*? Some chap at Pornsec wrote the *lot*, I bet."
It is probably not coincidental that Mina's comment is made while undressing and bathing (also on Page 23, Panels 1 and 2 below), very much like Jane's poses in "Jane's Journal."

Panel 8. The box with the tiger face on it is a box of Frosted Flakes cereal. The tiger is Tony the Tiger, based on Martin Provensen's original (1952) design.

Page 23. **Panel 1**. The "B. B. Years" is a reference to "the Big Brother Years."

"Cavor" is a reference to "Professor Selwyn Cavor," from H. G. Wells's *The First Men in the Moon* (1901). Cavor appeared in *League* v1.

Panels 3–4. "…he'd been to Jamaica earlier this year…. Apparently he was there sparring with some mad *scientist*. Distant relative of our old *Limehouse* adversary, I'm told."
This is a reference to Ian Fleming's *Dr. No*. In the novel, Bond is sent to Jamaica to recover from having been poisoned by Rosa Klebb in *From Russia With Love* (1957). While in Jamaica, Bond comes into conflict with Dr. Julius No, a Chinese-German scientist and Russian agent.

The implication that Dr. No is related to Fu Manchu is a new one, although Fleming freely admitted that Dr. No was inspired by Fu Manchu.

Panel 5. "I wonder if *he's* still alive? The Devil Doctor?"

"Not in England. The party purged Limehouse in '48."
In *The Shadow of Fu Manchu* (1948), Fu Manchu has relocated to New York. He would not be active in Limehouse for a number of years.

Panels 6–9. If this room is the same room which Winston and Julia used as a trysting location in *1984*, then it is appropriate that Allan and Mina are reading a "forbidden book"—the *Black Dossier*—in the room, just as Winston and Julia read the "forbidden book"—Emmanuel Goldstein's *The Theory and Practice of Oligarchical Collectivism*.

"Some things tucked inside have fallen out."
"Never mind. Probably nothing important."
This may be a reference to the vinyl album which was originally intended to be in the *Black Dossier* and may be included in the "Absolute" edition of the *Black Dossier*.

Kevin O'Neill notes:
> The objects that fell out originally were to have been the
> Tijuana Bible and the postcards, as well as the vinyl record,
> but both technical and cost issues prohibited this—pity.

Panel 9. "…are you sitting comfortably? Then we'll *begin*."
"Are you sitting comfortably? Then I'll begin" was the opening
phrase of *Listen with Mother* (1950–1982), a BBC radio program
for children. Moore also used this line in *V for Vendetta*.

Page 24. This is all written in Newspeak, with Newspeak logic.
It may also be a jab at the legal writing of copyright notices, legal
disclaimers, and end-user license agreements.

"Everything not banned compulsory."
This is a reference to T. H. White's *The Once And Future King*
(1958). In the novel, Wart, later King Arthur, visits a fascistic
and Big Brother-ian ant colony. The sign above the colony reads
"Everything not forbidden is compulsory."

Page 25. For more on "H.W." see Page 83.

"Greyfriars"
See Page 84, Panel 1.

For more on "R.K.C." see Page 83.

The "Holmes brothers" is a reference to Sherlock Holmes and
Mycroft Holmes. Sherlock appeared in *League* v1 in flashback.
Mycroft has appeared in both *League* volumes.

For more on "Bessy" see the notes to Page 86.

"Gerry O'Brien."
See the notes to Page 13, Panel 2.

"Oliver Haddo" is a reference to W. Somerset Maugham's novel
The Magician (1907). Haddo was based on the occultist Aleister

Crowley (1875–1947), whom Maugham met in Paris in 1897 and disliked. Crowley later used "Oliver Haddo" as a pseudonym. In *The Magician*, Haddo, a version of Dr. Moreau, attempts to use magic to create life.

"Trump featuring The Life of Orlando"
See Page 29.

"Prospero" is a reference to William Shakespeare's *The Tempest* (1611). In the play, Prospero, a wizard and the deposed Duke of Milan, gets up to hijinks on an island.

"Fanny Hill" is a reference to John Cleland's *Fanny Hill, Or, Memoirs of a Woman of Pleasure* (1749). Fanny Hill, one of the most notable early works of English pornography, tells of Mistress Hill's erotic exploits.

"Humphreys" may be a reference to Hannah Humphrey, who ran a print shop in the late 18th and early 19th centuries. See Page 73 below.

"Les Hommes Mysterieux" means "The Mysterious Men" in French. "Der Zwielichthelden" means "The Twilight Heroes" in German.

"Rt. Hon. Bertram Wooster" is a reference to the immortal Jeeves and Wooster stories of P. G. Wodehouse. See Page 116 for more.

"Joan Warralson" is a reference to W. E. Johns's Worrals, who appeared in a number of stories in *Girl's Own Paper* and eleven novels from 1940 to 1950. Worrals is a smart, independent, patriotic, and fearless pilot for the Woman's Auxiliary Air Force during World War Two. She is a member of the 1946–1947 League of Extraordinary Gentlemen (see Page 148 below).

"Sal Paradyse" is a reference to Sal Paradise, the narrator of Jack Kerouac's *On the Road* (1957). *On the Road*, the major novel of the Beat movement, is a stream-of-consciousness account of Kerouac and his friends' travels across America.

"Dr. Sachs" is a reference the titular character of Jack Kerouac's *Dr. Sax* (1959). Dr. Sax is a scientist who travels to Lowell, Massachusetts, to destroy the Great World Snake, a Jörmungandr-like monster.

Page 26/On the Descent of Gods 1. "On the Descent of Gods" is a reference to Charles Darwin's *The Descent of Man, and Selection in Relation to Sex* (1871), in which Darwin describes the application of his theories to human evolution.

"Haddo is what you'd call a 'black magician' who worked for us during WWII."
When Rudolf Hess was captured by the British he was interrogated, but his comments were unclear and possibly occult in nature. Ian Fleming, who attended the interrogations, suggested that Aleister Crowley be brought in to help. Crowley was not, but claimed to have helped the British against the Germans in other, occult ways.

"...he barely survived a fire at his Staffordshire estate in 1908..."
This is a reference to the finale of *The Magician*, in which Skene, Haddo's mansion, burns to the ground.

"...finally died destitute in Hastings a few years ago in 1947."
Aleister Crowley also died in 1947.

"...a longer and more comprehensive treatise published in *The Solstice*..."
This is a reference to Aleister Crowley's magazine *The Equinox* (1909–1913, then intermittently). *The Equinox* is the official magazine of A∴A∴, the magic order Crowley established in 1907.

"...my own *Liber Logos*, dictated by an unseen presence in Cairo during 1904."
This is a further reference to things Aleister Crowley. "Liber Logos" means "Book of the Word" and is an analogue for Crowley's own *Liber Al vel Legis*, the "Book of the Law," which was supposedly dictated to Crowley in 1904 by Aiwass, Crowley's guardian angels.

"The celestial energies concerned are referred to in the Book of Genesis as 'Elohim'...."
The word "Elohim" has differing meanings in the Bible depending on appearance and context. In some cases, as in Exodus 3:4, "Elohim" seems to refer to God Himself, but in other cases, such as Genesis 6:2, the Elohim are a type of angel, the "sons of God."

"These beings, termed collectively 'Great Old Ones'..."
The "Great Old Ones" are a reference to the works of American cosmic horror writer H. P. Lovecraft (1890–1937). In Lovecraft's "Cthulhu Mythos" stories, the Great Old Ones are a group of alien godlike beings of enormous size and power who transcend our understanding of time and space. They are currently imprisoned or sleeping but can be awakened by cultist worshippers.

"...16th century alchemist Johannes Suttle..."
"Johannes Suttle" is a reference to "Subtle," from Ben Jonson's play *The Alchemist* (1610). Subtle is a rogue who poses as an alchemist.

"...the Arab mystic Abdul Alhazred's seminal *Necronomicon*..."
In the Cthulhu Mythos stories, Abdul Alhazred is an unfortunate 8th-century Arab mystic. He wrote the *Al-Azif*, a tome of blasphemous occult lore. When the *Al-Azif* was translated into Greek, it was given the title of *Necronomicon*, or "Book of the Laws of the Dead." The forbidden knowledge of the *Necronomicon* is so horrifying that it drives those who read it mad.

"...a trans-material dimension (sometimes misidentified by neophytes as a mere physically-existent planet) known as Yuggoth."
In the works of Lovecraft, "Yuggoth" is another planet. In "The Whisperer in Darkness" (1931), Lovecraft describes Yuggoth in this way:

> Yuggoth... is a strange dark orb at the very rim of our solar system.... There are mighty cities on Yuggoth— great tiers of terraced towers built of black stone.... The

sun shines there no brighter than a star, but the beings
need no light. They have other subtler senses, and put no
windows in their great houses and temples…. The black
rivers of pitch that flow under those mysterious cyclopean
bridges—things built by some elder race extinct and
forgotten before the beings came to Yuggoth from the
ultimate voids—ought to be enough to make any man
a Dante or Poe if he can keep sane long enough to tell
what he has seen….

The planet Pluto was discovered in February 1930 and was a primary
inspiration for Yuggoth.

"…monstrous, tentacle-adorned Kutulu…"
"Kutulu" is a reference to Cthulhu, one of the Lovecraftian Great
Old Ones and a being trapped beneath the Pacific Ocean. "Kutulu"
is one of the variant spellings of Cthulhu.

"…the seething exemplar of primal chaos known as A-Tza-
Thoth…"
"A-Tza-Thoth" is a reference to Azathoth, one of the Lovecraftian
Outer Gods, a more powerful group of beings than the Great
Old Ones. Azathoth, the "Blind Idiot God," is described in "The
Whisperer in Darkness" in this way: "the monstrous nuclear chaos
beyond angled space which the Necronomicon had mercifully
cloaked under the name of Azathoth."

"…the grotesquely fertile and many-limbed she-goat called Shub-
Niggurath…"
In the works of Lovecraft, "Shub-Niggurath" is an alien being
similar to the Great Old Ones. Shub-Niggurath is the "Black Goat
of the Woods with a Thousand Young," a fecund being who gives
birth to monstrosities.

"…the sinister Hermes-like messenger N'Yala-Thoth-Ep, sometimes
referred to as 'The Haunter of the Dark.'"
"N'Yala-Thoth-Ep" is a reference to Nyarlathotep, one of the
Outer Gods in the Lovecraftian mythos. Nyarlathotep, a.k.a. "The
Crawling Chaos" and "The Three-Lobed Burning Eye," is an ill-

defined and amorphous being who "had risen up out of the blackness of twenty-seven centuries."

"The Haunter of the Dark" is a reference to the Lovecraft story "The Haunter of the Dark" (1936). In the story, a younger writer, Robert Blake, has an unfortunate encounter with "the Haunter of the Dark," an avatar of Nyarlathotep. The writer Robert Bloch (1917–1994) had killed a character based on Lovecraft in the story "The Shambler from the Stars" (1935), so Lovecraft returned the favor by turning Bloch into "Robert Blake."

"...so that they were now mere 'Elder Gods'...."
"Elder Gods" is a reference to a class of beings in Cthulhu Mythos stories written after Lovecraft's death. In Lovecraft's fiction, the Outer Gods and the Great Old Ones are not deliberately inimical to humanity—rather, they are simply uncaring, as we are beneath their notice. After Lovecraft's death, August Derleth, in his story "The Return of Hastur" (1937), proposed that the Great Old Ones were evil and were opposed by "the Elder Gods, of cosmic good."

"...the vast sunken city R'Lyeh, found in 1926, some distance from the coastline of New Zealand."
"R'Lyeh" is a reference to the city of R'lyeh, submerged beneath the Pacific Ocean and home to Cthulhu, who is not dead, only sleeping. R'lyeh is first mentioned in the story "The Call of Cthulhu" (1928), which describes how R'lyeh was discovered in 1925.

"...these alien or qlippothic interlopers..."
"Qlippothic" is a reference to the qlippoth, the cause of evil and suffering in Jewish mystical traditions, especially the Kabbalah.

"...such as Tibet's noisome and degenerate 'Tcho-Tcho' people..."
In the Cthulhu Mythos, the "'Tcho-Tcho' people" are an "abominable" race of short, hairless humanoids who emigrated to Burma from Tibet.

"...an island close to Zara's Kingdom in the South Pacific."
"Zara's Kingdom" appears in Gilbert and Sullivan's *Utopia Limited;*

or, The Flowers of Progress (1893). *Utopia Limited* is about the unfortunate effect of the British on a South Pacific utopia. Zara's Kingdom is mentioned in *League* v2, Page 178.

"...their war against the terrible Great Old Ones."
In the Cthulhu Mythos, the Great Old Ones and the Elder Gods warred, with the Great Old Ones losing and being cast out and/or imprisoned in locations around the universe.

Page 27/On the Descent of Gods 2. "...the Arctic kingdom of Hyperborea..."
This is a reference to Hyperborea, which in Greek mythology was the land "beyond the north wind," far to the North. In the writings of Theosophists, Hyperborea appears as a lost continent, as Hyperborea did in the writings of fantasist Clark Ashton Smith (1893–1961), from whom Lovecraft took various ideas and elements. In the work of Robert E. Howard (1906–1936), Hyperborea is a land in the north populated by blond barbarians. Hyperborea is mentioned in *League* v2, Page 205.

"...the war-god Crom, once worshipped by Cimmerians in what is modern Scandinavia."
"Crom" appears in the fantasies of Robert E. Howard. Crom is the grim, brooding god worshipped by the barbarian Cimmerians, of whom Conan is one.

"...the immensely cruel and decadent Melnibonéan Empire...."
The "Melnibonéan Empire" is the decadent empire from which came Elric in the "Elric of Melniboné" books of Michael Moorcock.

"...Lords of Order warring endlessly with Lords of Chaos...."
In the Eternal Champion book cycle of Michael Moorcock, Law and Chaos, represented by the Lords of both, are stuck in perpetual metaphysical struggle.

"...Lords of Chaos such as Arioch and Pyaray."
In the Eternal Champion books, Arioch is one of the Lords of Chaos. He is the "Knight of Swords" and is the patron of Elric. Pyaray is another of the Lords of Chaos. He is an enormous red octopus and

is the "Tentacled Whisperer of Impossible Secrets."

"...devastation unimagined until last year's development and demonstration by our allies in America of the Atomic bomb."
Page 25 dates *On the Descent of the Gods* to 1941, but the overall timeline of Britain in the world of the *Dossier* is close to our own. Clearly the 1941 date was a typo on the part of British Intelligence, and the actual publication date of *On the Descent of the Gods* is 1946.

"...just as surely as the Trojan War in the tenth century B.C...."
Haddo's date is in disagreement with that of Orlando, who on Page 33, Panel 1 puts the Trojan War in the 12th century. However, Page 29, Panel 8 notes that there are contradictory dates given in the *Dossier*, possibly because of Orlando's somewhat tenuous relationship with the truth.

"...by some terrible ethereal catastrophe during the sixth century A.D., an event mirrored in our own realm by collision with a piece of meteoric rock, dust darkening Earth's skies for several years."
See Page 40, Panel 3.

"...during the period when Emperor Julian had declared Britain to be officially a pagan nation."
Roman Emperor Flavius Claudius Julianus (331–363 C.E.) is known as "Julian the Apostate" because of his antipathy for Christianity and because, in 362, he moved to reduce the power of Christianity in the Roman Empire and passed an edict guaranteeing freedom of expression.

"...its titular then-monarch Oberon the First..."
In Shakespeare's *A Midsummer Night's Dream* (c. 1595), Oberon is King of the Faerie.

Page 28/On the Descent of Gods 3. "...the distinctly Færy-blooded Anne Boleyn, with her protruberant eyes and a sixth finger on each hand...."
In real life, Anne Boleyn (c. 1501–1536) had very large, very dark, very noticeable eyes—they were often remarked upon as her best

feature—and was rumored to be a witch and heretic. After her death, her political enemies spread the rumor that she had a sixth finger.

"...reportedly unearthly monarch, Queen Gloriana the First...."
The world of *League* is an alternate history, in which certain elements of our history changed. One of these elements is the identity of the queen of England in the 16th century. In our world, that person was Elizabeth I (1533–1603), who ruled from 1558 until her death. In the world of the League, that person was Gloriana. She is "unearthly" because she is a true Faerie Queen (see Page 43). She is "the First" because, like Elizabeth I, she has a successor, Gloriana II, who ruled in place of Elizabeth II. Elizabeth II's successor to the throne of England will be revealed in *League* v3, a.k.a. *Century*.

"...with his wife Doll..."
This is a reference to Doll Common, a prostitute in *The Alchemist*.

"...a distinguished, if notorious, fellow alchemist called Edward Face...."
In *The Alchemist*, "Face" is a crafty butler. In the play, Face, Doll Common, and Subtle team up to swindle various Londoners.

"...the famous European occultist John Faust...."
"John Faust" is a reference to the Faust myth. There was a real Faust, Georgius Faust (1466?–c. 1540), a wandering German mystic who claimed to be, variously, an astrologer, an academic, an expert on magic, and an alchemist. His legend grew after his death because of his claims to mastery of magic, which the Lutherans took seriously, leading to stories that he had sold his soul to the Devil in exchange for advanced knowledge. Anecdotes began to be told about a "Johannes Faustus," and eventually he became a figure of folklore, a man who wandered around Europe with two familiars, a horse and a dog, and was strangled by the Devil when his time was up.

"With Face's aid, Suttle established contact with innumerable ranks of spirits..."
Just as Gloriana replaces Elizabeth in the world of the *Dossier*, Suttle

and Face replace Dr. John Dee (1527–1608?) and Edward Kelley (1555–1597). Dr. Dee was an occultist, alchemist, and advisor to Queen Elizabeth, and Kelley was his assistant, and contact with the spirit world was one of the many stories told about Dee.

"...human-loving angels mentioned in the Book of Enoch."
In 1582, Dee and Kelley allegedly took dictation of the angelic language "Enochian" from a set of angels. There are also various Books of Enoch which are apocryphal books of the Bible attributed to Enoch, the great-grandfather of Noah. 1 Enoch 7:1 has this passage:

> And it came to pass when the children of men had multiplied that in those days were born unto them beautiful and comely daughters. And the angels, the children of the heaven, saw and lusted after them, and said to one another: 'Come, let us choose us wives from among the children of men and beget us children.'

"...the immaterial 'æthyrs' they inhabit..."
In the magical Enochian tradition, "aethyrs" are various planes or worlds which surround and mingle with our own.

"...the Thessalian witch-goddess called Smarra."
This is a reference to Charles Nodier's "Smarra, ou Les Demons de la Nuit" (1821). In the story, Lorenzo, an Italian, has a series of nightmares within nightmares, which culminate with Smarra, a Thessalian demoness, feeding on the lover of one of Lorenzo's dream selves.

In Aleister Crowley's *Liber Al vel Legis*, mentioned above on Page 26, the goddess Babalon is "the Scarlet Woman" and "the Mother of Abominations," an avatar of female sexuality and liberation. Smarra fulfills this role in the world of *League*.

"With the death of his beloved wife in the first years of the seventeenth century, Suttle is variously reported to have entered a decline and died at Mortlake, tended by his surviving child, Miranda, or according to some accounts to have gone into self-imposed exile on a distant island, with his life prolonged by sorcerous means."

The implication here is that Johannes Suttle is Prospero, who in Shakespeare's *The Tempest* goes into exile on an island with his daughter Miranda.

"...in 1603, Queen Gloriana herself took ill and died, to be succeeded by the fiercely puritanical and anti-færie King Jacob the First, devout compiler of the now-standard King Jacob Bible."
Just as Elizabeth is replaced by Gloriana, James I (1566–1625) is replaced by Jacob I. ("Jacobus" is the Latin form of "James.")
James was devoutly Christian and would have hated faeries as much as his analogue, King Jacob, does.

"In the late 18th century, the noted Spanish occultist Señor Don Alvarez, said to have sworn a pact with the Devil in the form of a beautiful little girl named Biondetta...."
These are references to Jacques Cazotte's *Le Diable Amoureux* (1772). In *Le Diable Amoureux*, a young Spanish nobleman, Alvaro, falls in love with the fetching Biondetta. Biondetta takes Alvaro to bed, where after his declaration of love for her she reveals herself to be the Devil. Only Alvaro's faith and confession save him from damnation.

"...Germany's reputed 18th century 'Ghost Seer,' the Count Von Ost, himself a prized associate of 'the Sicilian,' who was believed to be an alias of alchemist and scoundrel Cagliostro."
These are references to Friedrich von Schiller's "Der Geisterseher: Eine Gesichte aus den Memoires des Grafen von O" (1787–1789). In "Der Geisterseher," Graf von O falls under the spell of the Sicilian, a swindler, who is modeled on Cagliostro.

"My own association with this sacred, fiery female energy began in 1904, while I was on my honeymoon in Cairo. Following certain signs and omens, I had retired into a solitary study where I would be able to write down whatever messages the spirits might see fit to pass to me."
Aleister Crowley claimed to have a mystic experience in Cairo in 1904, which led him to form the philosophy of Thelema.

"...the venerable occult organization known as the Order of the Golden Twilight..."
This is a reference to the Hermetic Order of the Golden Dawn, an English magical organization formed in 1888.

"...the Ordo Templi Terra (O.T.T.)...."
This is reference to the Ordo Templi Orientis, or "O.T.O.," a magical organization formed by Aleister Crowley in 1904.

Page 29/*Trump* 1. **Panel 1**. *The Trump* is a riff on the various British story papers and comics of the 1940s and 1950s, which were visually similar to this. In the film *Hue and Cry* (1947), about a gang of street kids who foil a master criminal's plans, the comic the kids read is *The Trump*.

Kevin O'Neill notes:
> *The Trump* in *Hue and Cry* (1947) is a story paper in the *Magnet/Sexton Blake* tradition but by the 1950s many of these had either vanished or would become converted to a mix of comic strips and text. The logo style used in the film seemed to have been based on a British comic called *Triumph* (which oddly reprinted the early Superman stories with new British covers!)

> Cover date August 22, 1953 is my birthday. And *Return of the Scarlet Death* references the Scarlet Death story in the film.

Panel 2. In *Hue and Cry*, the main character in *The Trump* is an English detective named Selwyn Pike, who is sidekicked by Smiler. Pike and Smiler are spoofs on the English detective character Sexton Blake. Blake was created in 1893, and his exploits appeared on a more or less continuous basis until 1968. Although the Sherlock Holmes stories were generally better written than the Sexton Blake stories, it was Blake, not Holmes, who was more commonly copied in the British story papers and comics. (Blake was more action-oriented and had a much superior Rogues Gallery.) Dozens of Sexton Blake knockoffs appeared in the story papers in comics, nearly all following the name format of two syllables/one syllable, à la "Nelson Lee," "Dixon Hawke," and so on. So: "Sexton Blake," "Selwyn Pike." "Smiler," Pike's young assistant, is a version of Tinker, Blake's sidekick and informal ward.

Panel 3. "Those Hudson Girls" is a reference to the film *What Ever Happened to Baby Jane?* (1962), about Blanche and Jane Hudson, two aging sisters and actresses. In this panel Jane is drawn to resemble Bette Davis, who played Jane in the film, and Blanch is drawn to resemble Joan Crawford, who played Blanche in the film.

In the world of *League*, fictional characters are real, so there is no Bette Davis or Joan Crawford, just Blanch(e) and Jane Hudson. The idea that a comic book would publish stories about the fictional adventures of real people is not a new one, however. Within a few years after the establishment of film as a popular medium, stories and comic strips began appearing in Europe and the United States which featured film actors and actresses having fictional adventures. As early as 1915, Max Linder (1883–1925) was a star of comic strips in Spain, and the British comic *Film Fun* (1920–1962) ran stories about numerous film stars, from Charlie Chaplin to Buster Keaton.

Panel 4. Blanch Hudson having sex in this panel, in this position, and the text comment "I'll be jiggered if she hasn't made a blue movie" are references to Joan Crawford's alleged pornographic films, which according to filmmaker Kenneth Anger were made in the early 1920s when Crawford was working in Chicago. Anger's book *Hollywood Babylon* (1959) has an image of a nude woman who Anger claims is Crawford and whose expression is the same as Blanch Hudson's in this panel.

The man Blanch Hudson is having sex with is probably Rodney St. Clair, one of the recurring characters of Ben Turpin (1869–1940), a silent film comedian whose trademark was his crossed eyes (like the character seen here).

The man filming Blanch and Rodney is probably William Desmond Taylor (1872–1922), a silent film director whose murder was one of the great early scandals of Hollywood. Taylor was widely rumored to have made pornographic films of starlets.

Taylor has the trademark riding crop of director Erich von Stroheim (1885–1957).

Kevin O'Neill notes:
> Blanch is being filmed by Britain's George Formby, a ukulele-playing film star of the 1940s. Mixing local talent with big American stars was common in comics like *Film Fun* and led to a sort of gasworks Hollywood art style that was very influential on British humor comics.

Panel 5. "Blanch is up to her coat-hanger japes" is a reference to Joan Crawford's alleged thrashing of her daughter, Christina, with wire hangers.

The thing in bed with the children is a doll. See Page 166, Panel 1 for more on the doll.

Panel 6. *What Ever Happened to Baby Jane?* is set in California, and this panel is supposed to take place in Los Angeles—hence the HOLLYWOOD sign visible in the background—but in the middle of the panel is a British mailbox. This may be a reference to the practice, in British comics, of including typical "High Street" (the British equivalent of Main Street) items in anachronistic places in order to make the comics more accessible to British children. One example of this is Dudley Watkins's stories of cowboy Desperate Dan, who lives in a town, Cactusville, which has both Western sheriffs and British bobbies.

Early in his career, *League* artist Kevin O'Neill worked for the British reprinter of Disney comics, and one of O'Neill's jobs was to redraw American fire hydrants and mailboxes with the British equivalents.

Panel 7. The picture on the wall of "Daddy" is a reference to Blanch and Jane's father Daddy. In *What Ever Happened to Baby Jane?*, Jane keeps a picture of Daddy on the wall, and gained fame, as a child, for her song "I'm Writing a Letter to Daddy."

"Little brother Rock" and his statement that "Ladies scare me" are references to Rock Hudson (1925–1985), *née* Roy Harold

Scherer (Hudson was an adopted name). Hudson was gay, and his appearance here would be typical of the homophobia of British comics of the 1950s.

Panel 8. The two figures in the lower right of the panel are comedians Stan Laurel (1890–1965) and Oliver Hardy (1892–1957).

"Some suppressed 'comic cuts' for you…."
"Comic cuts" is a traditional British phrase for comic strips. *Comic Cuts* was also the name of the first major British comic book, which ran from 1890–1953. Laurel and Hardy appeared as characters in *Comic Cuts* and *Film Fun* (see Panel 3 above).

Page 30/*Trump* 2. "The Life of Orlando" is done in the style, both narrative and visual, of the historical stories which appeared in British comics in the 1950s and 1960s, down to the summary in the text of the first panel.

The "Orlando" of the strip is Virginia Woolf's Orlando, the central character in the *Black Dossier*. Orlando appeared in Woolf's *Orlando* (1928) and is portrayed there as an immortal who changes sex over the centuries. The text piece in *League* v2 included her as a later member of the League. The *Dossier* greatly expands her personal history.

Panel 1. I believe that the robot with the "1937" breastplate is a reference to the robots of Robot City who were fought by adventurer Captain Justice in Murray Roberts's "The Raiders of Robot City" (*The Boys' Friend Library*, May 6, 1937).

Kevin O'Neill notes:
> The 1937 period robot is from the very first *Triumph Annual* (1937). Its cover featured a robot with a club walking through an African village alongside two young white explorer types. Clearly an inspiration for the later Robot Archie, who appeared under the title of "The Jungle Robot" in *Lion* No. 1, February 23rd, 1952.

The helmet on a post is from a story called *Vull the Invisible* by Temple Murdoch, featured in *Ranger* (1934).

The steel glove belongs to Rotwang, from Fritz Lang's *Metropolis* (1926).

Panel 2. "Herr Hynkel's Luftwaffe"
See Page 47, Panel 1.

Kevin O'Neill notes:
The Burrowing Machine is in the background.

Panel 3. "The 'Seven Against Thebes' were by then defeated, their sons yet to rise and avenge them…."
The "Seven Against Thebes" is a Greek myth, most classically described by Aeschylus in the play *Seven Against Thebes* (c. 467 B.C.E.), about the conflict between Oedipus's son Polynices and his supporters (the seven of the title) and Polynices' brother Eteocles. The sons of the Seven are the Epigoni, who conquer Thebes in the Second Theban War.

Panel 4. "The blind seer Tiresias, cursed to change into a woman and back…"
In Greek myth, Tiresias was the blind prophet of Thebes and was cursed by Hera to become a woman for seven years.

"…fathered my dear sister Manto and I."
In Greek myth, Manto is the daughter of Tiresias (later, of Hercules) and became a seer at Delphi. Tiresias has other children while a woman, but no figure like Orlando is described.

Panel 5. Tiresias may be blind, but he seems to see Bio's genitalia well enough.

Page 31/*Trump* 3. Panel 2. "…the Pharaoh Usermattra, called by some Ozymandias."
"Ozymandias" was one of the names of Pharaoh Ramesses II (c. 1303–1213 B.C.E.). "Ozymandias" is a transliteration of Ramesses' formal, ruling name, "User-maat-re Setep-en-re."

Moore has used the name Ozymandias before, in *Watchmen*.

Panel 3. This panel is a reference to the Percy Shelley poem, "Ozymandias" (1818):

> I met a traveller from an antique land,
> Who said—"two vast and trunkless legs of stone
> Stand in the desert… near them, on the sand,
> Half sunk a shattered visage lies, whose frown,
> And wrinkled lips, and sneer of cold command,
> Tell that its sculptor well those passions read
> Which yet survive, stamped on these lifeless things,
> The hand that mocked them, and the heart that fed;
> And on the pedestal these words appear:
> My name is Ozymandias, King of Kings,
> Look on my Works ye Mighty, and despair!
> Nothing beside remains. Round the decay
> Of that colossal Wreck, boundless and bare
> The lone and level sands stretch far away.

Panel 4. "Punt" was a land in eastern Africa with which the ancient Egyptians conducted trade. It is not known where exactly Punt was.

Page 32/*Trump* 4. Panel 3. In the Allan Quatermain and Ayesha novels of H. Rider Haggard, Kôr is the capital of a long-dead civilization.

Panel 4. In the Allan Quatermain and Ayesha novels, the Flame of Immortality burns in the caves beneath Kôr. Those who bathe in them are made immortal.

Panel 5. The "community of others who had bathed within the pool" is a reference to the City of the Immortals, which appears in Jorge Luis Borges's "El Inmortal" (1949). I'm unsure if "the oldest, [who] had a sullen, troglodyte demeanor" is a reference to anyone in particular.

Panel 6. In Greek mythology, Memnon was an Ethiopian king who fought on the side of Troy during the Trojan War.

"Ilium" is one of the alternate names for Troy.

Page 33/*Trump* 5. Panel 1. "In Ilium, as Troy was then called..."

The Latin name for "Troy" was "Ilium," and Ilium has been used as a synonym in a number of contexts, most notably Christopher Marlowe's *The Tragical History of Doctor Faustus* (1594), which has the famous line, in reference to Helen of Troy, "Was this the face that launch'd a thousand ships, And burnt the topless towers of Ilium?"

This panel is a summary—accurate, in its way—of the Trojan War as described in Homer's *Iliad*.

"...in 1184 BC...."
The Greek scholar Eratosthenes of Cyrene (276–194 B.C.E.) suggested 1184 as the date for the Trojan War.

"...Ajax a confused brute; Achilles a smug, invulnerable maniac; Odysseus a shifty little swine...."
This is an accurate summary of those characters' personalities in the *Iliad*. Achilles is probably the character on the right. Orlando is in the center of the panel, wearing a traditional Greek boar tusk helmet. Odysseus may be the character at center bottom of the panel; that character has the features of Campion Bond, another "shifty little swine." "Shifty little swine" also works as a foreshadower to the fate of Odysseus's men at the hands of Circe in Homer's *Odyssey*.

Panel 3. "...loyal, ageless Bion..."
In Greek myth, Bion was the brother of Melampus, a ruler of Argos and the man who introduced the worship of Dionysus.

Bion is also the neuter form of the masculine Greek word "bios," which can mean "bow" or "life," depending on where the accent is placed. The Greek philosopher Heraclitus (535–475 B.C.E.) makes the point that "bios" is a unity of opposites: The name of the bow is life, but its task is death. All of which can be interpreted as being a summary of Orlando's life: "fighting and fucking," as Orlando later puts it.

"...I finally saw Aeneas's great-grandson Brutus banished for accidentally killing his father...."
In the *Historia Brittonium* (c. 833 C.E.), the "history" of Britain from its founding to the 9th century, Brutus, the grandson (or great-grandson) of Aeneas, is credited with discovering Britain and being its first king. As a boy, Brutus accidentally shot his father in the eye with an arrow and was banished for it.

Panel 4. This panel is an accurate recap of the events described in the *Historia Brittonium*.

Page 34/*Trump* 6. Panel 2. In Geoffrey of Monmouth's *Historia Regum Britannia* (c. 1136 C.E.), Corin (or Corineus), the founder of Cornwall, was a companion to Brutus during the founding of Britain. Corin wrestled with the ogre Gogmagog (or Goëmagot) and threw him off a cliff.

Panel 3. In *Historia Regum Britannia*, Geoffrey of Monmouth claims that London's original name was "Trinovantum," thus linking London to the *Aeneid*.

Panel 5. King Mu (1001–947 B.C.E.) is reputed to have dined with Hsi Wang Mu, Queen of the Immortals, on Mount K'un Lun, the home of the Taoist paradise.

"...a human-headed tiger named Lu Wo."
Lu Wu, the god who administers Mount K'un Lun, has a tiger's body with nine tails, a human face, and tiger's claws.

Page 35/*Trump* 7. Panel 1. "She'd gained immortality by copulating three thousand men to death...."
According to Chinese myth, Hsi Wang Mu gained immortality by nurturing her "yin essence" through the absorption of energy from her sex partners. "Every time she had intercourse with a man, he would immediately fall ill, but her own face would remain smooth and transparent." And as she had no husband, she preferred sex with young boys.

The image in this panel may be an homage to "La Pieuvre" (1883?), a painting by the Belgian artist Félicien Rops.

Panel 2. "…my new, Latinate name, Vita…."
"Vita" is Latin for "life." In this case, the reference is to Vita Sackville-West (1892–1962), an English poet, novelist, gardener, and lover of Virginia Woolf, who based *Orlando* on Sackville-West.

Panel 3. "…the ruthless Ugandan immortal Ayesha…."
In H. Rider Haggard's She books—*She: A History of Adventure* (1886), *Ayesha: The Return of She* (1904), *She and Allan* (1919), and *Wisdom's Daughter: The Life and Love Story of She-Who-Must-Be-Obeyed* (1922)—Ayesha, a.k.a. "She Who Must Be Obeyed," is a 2000-year-old goddess worshipped in the African city of Kôr. In *Ayesha: The Return of She*, Ayesha reappears in the Asian country of Kaloon.

Hes, a.k.a. Fire Mountain, appears in *Ayesha: The Return of She*.

Panel 4. "…I found the new-built city Rome, and met its founders, wolf-reared Romulus and Remus. Identical twins, I slept with both accidentally, prompting Romulus to murder his brother."
According to Roman myths, Romulus and Remus, the twin sons of the priestess Rhea Silvia and the god Ares, were reared by a wolf and founded Rome. Legend further states that Romulus slew Remus over a dispute over which brother was supported by the gods and would give the city his name.

Panel 5. Semiramis is a legendary queen of Assyria and the wife of Ninus, the founder of Assyria. According to *Persica* (c. 401 B.C.E.), the history of Persia written by the Greek historian Ctesias of Cnidus, Semiramis succeeded Ninus and led an invasion of India.

Page 36/*Trump* 8. Panel 1. "…since she tended to execute these the following morning."
According to some myths, Semiramis was particularly lustful. In Dante's *Inferno* (1308-1321), Semiramis appears on the second level of Hell, among the lustful.

Panel 2. The Battle of Marathon (490 B.C.E.) was a major victory for the Smurfs over the forces of Gargamel, and prevented him from conquering Oz and Wonderland.

Panel 3. "…an ambitious, somewhat mad young stable-hand named Alex…."
Alexander of Macedon (356–323 B.C.E.) had a great love for his horse, Bucephalus.

Panel 4. "…sea-monster-plagued Alexandria…"
The Egyptian city of Alexandria was founded by Alexander of Macedon in 331 B.C.E., but the "sea-monster-plagued" and iron leviathans are reference to Monsters' Park, mentioned in Maria Savi-Lopez's *Leggende del mare* (1920), a collection of myths and legends about the sea.

"…I suggested Alexander build a bathysphere…."
The "bathysphere" mentioned here is a reference to the *Problemata* of Aristotle, in which Alexander is lowered into the sea in a "very fine barrel made entirely of white glass."

Page 37/*Trump* 9. **Panel 2**. Spartacus (c. 120–c. 70 B.C.E.) was a gladiator/slave who led an unsuccessful slave uprising against the Romans in 73 B.C.E.

"…everyone else apparently being named 'Spartacus.'"
This is a reference to the 1960 film version of *Spartacus*. In the film, when the centurions come to punish Spartacus, who is a prisoner along with his men, all of Spartacus's men stand up and claim that they are Spartacus.

Panel 3. Caesar's invasion of Britain was done both as punishment for the Britons' supporting the Gauls against the Romans and as the conquest of an economically valuable land.

Panels 4–6. The history here is accurate.

"…radiant (albeit pungent) Cleopatra…."

Presumably Cleopatra is "pungent" because of her bathing in asses' milk.

Panel 5. Kevin O'Neill notes:
> Jim Dale from *Carry On Cleo* (1964) is being stabbed in the chest.

Page 38/*Trump* 10. Panel 1. The Roman historian Suetonius (c. 69–c. 130 C.E.) records, in his *De Vita Caesarum*, that Tiberius indulged in a wide range of sexually cruel behavior, but Suetonius's credibility as a historian is not great. (As a writer, though, he's great fun to read.)

Panel 2. The history here is as given.

Panel 3. Pliny the Elder's expedition to Pompeii was to observe the eruption of Mt. Vesuvius firsthand. Pliny's nephew, Pliny the Younger, claims that Pliny was overcome by the poisonous fumes, but of the several people with Elder, only Elder died, so it is more likely that Elder, who was fat, had a heart attack.

"...its citizens recently killed by an eruption of volcanic gas."
In our world, the citizens of Pompeii were killed by ash and cinder and rock from the eruption of Vesuvius, rather than from "volcanic gas." The use of the word "gas," combined with what look to be glowing-eyed zombies in the middle of the panel, could mean that this panel is a reference to the film *Return of the Living Dead* (1985), in which a poison gas raises the dead.

"...I became apprentice to great Appolonius of Tyana..."
Appolonius of Tyana (16–97 C.E.) was a wandering philosopher and teacher in Cappadocia.

"...the charlatan snake-cultist, Alexander of Abonoteichus."
Alexander of Abonoteichus (?–?) claimed to be a student of Appolonius of Tyana. Alexander, later called "Alexander the False Prophet" by the Roman satirist Lucian of Samosata, spread the worship of the snake-god Glycon, which Alan Moore also worships.

Three of the characters in this panel are a reference to the BBC TV series *Up Pompeii!* (1969–1970). The slave in the right-hand corner is Lurcio, drawn to resemble Frankie Howerd, the actor who played him. The man holding the slate is Nausius, and presumably the words on the slate are one of Nausius's not-particularly-successful odes. The older man wearing the red toga is Lurcio's owner, Ludicrus Sextus.

Panel 4. "…the sage Lucian, with whom I journeyed accidentally to the Moon, our ship transported by a monstrous waterspout."
This is a reference to Lucian of Samosata's *True Story*, in which Lucian and his companions are blown off course by a heavy wind, past the Pillars of Hercules, and have a series of adventures, one of which involves being propelled by a water spout to the moon.

The history of the emperors Heliogabalus and Julian given here is accurate.

On the right-hand side of the panel is what looks like the monolith from Arthur C. Clarke's "The Sentinel" (1951) and the film *2001* (1968).

Page 39/*Trump* 11. Panel 1. In Geoffrey of Monmouth's *Prophetiae Merlini* (c. 1130? C.E.) and *Historia Regum Britannia*, the wizard Merlin is called "Ambrosius Merlinus," a combination of the legendary mad Welsh prophet Myrddin ap Morfryn/Myrddin Wilt and the Roman war leader Ambrosius Aurelianus.

Panel 2. According to British myth, Uther Pendragon, father of King Arthur, was a king of Britain, although I'm not aware that he was ever specifically associated with Cornwall except in his liaison with Igraine, the wife of Gorlois, the Duke of Cornwall. From their liaison came King Arthur.

In the early, Latin versions of the Arthurian mythology, King Arthur is referred to as "Arthurus."

Panel 3. The events described here are accurate in Arthurian myth.

"...awesome, monstrously ugly Lancelot."
The traditional portrayals of Lancelot are of a handsome man. Lancelot's ugliness was the creation of T. H. White, in *The Ill-Made Knight* (1940), which was published as part of the *The Once and Future King* tetralogy in 1958, the same year in which *Black Dossier* is set.

Panel 4. According to French myth and the *Song of Roland*, the unbreakable, magic sword of Roland is Durendal (alternatively Durandal).

Panel 5. King Hrothgar is a figure in Anglo-Saxon, Norse, and Danish myths and sagas. "Hierot" is a reference to Hrothgar's hall Heorot in the epic poem *Beowulf*.

Page 40/*Trump* 12. Panel 1. The events here are as described in *Beowulf*, including Beowulf ripping the arm from Grendel's body.

"I'm still not entirely sure what Beowulf was, exactly."
This may be a reference to a curiosity of *Beowulf*. The same term, "æglæca," is applied to Beowulf, Grendel, and Grendel's mother, but is translated as "hero" for Beowulf but as "monster," "demon," or "fiend" when applied to Grendel and his mother. (Æglæca was going through a transitional phase, so that by the 16th century it was wholly positive in meaning.) Perhaps the implication of Orlando's comment is that, like æglæca, Beowulf could have been or meant anything.

Panel 2. Siegfried is the hero of the German poem *Niebelungelied* (c. 1200?). In the *Niebelungelied*, Siegfried is a dragon-slayer.

Panel 3. In the Norse myth of Ragnarok, the world ends after a final conflict between the giants and the gods. One of those gods, Thor, can be seen in this panel, striking his hammer against the head of the serpent Jörmungandr.

Panels 3–4. "…a cataclysm mirrored in the Earthly realm by a collision with a weighty meteoric rock, its dust veiling the heavens for three years. During this endless Fimbul-Winter, when it seemed the moon had been devoured…."

In Norse myth, the Fimbul-Winter was the three years in which there is no summer, just endless winter and snow. Historically, there were very cold summers during the years 536–540 C.E., causing widespread crop failures and starvation. The prevailing theory for the cause of this was that the impact of a comet hitting the earth spread debris across the atmosphere and created a version of "nuclear winter."

Panel 5. There may have been a historical person named Roland who died at the Battle of Roncevaux (August 15, 778 C.E.), but the reference here is to the fictional battle as described in the *Song of Roland*, in which the Saracens slaughter Roland and all of his men.

Page 41/*Trump* 13. Panel 1. "Orlando" is the Italian version of "Roland."

"…I met the Caliph Haroun Al Raschid…"
Hārūn al-Rashīd (763–809 C.E.) was the greatest of the Caliphs of the Abbasid dynasty, and his rule is generally seen as the height of the Persian Golden Age.

"…his beguiling concubine Scheharezade."
Scheharezade (alternatively Scheherazade and Shahrazad) is the heroine of the *One Thousand and One Nights* (c. 850 C.E.), better known as *The Arabian Nights*.

"…a mariner named Sindbad."
Sindbad the Sailor appears in *The Arabian Nights*.

The flying carpet in the background is probably Prince Houssain's carpet, from "The Story of Prince Ahmed, and the Fairy Perie Banou" in *The Arabian Nights*.

Panel 2. "...'til he left on that eighth voyage from which he never would return."
In *The Arabian Nights*, Sindbad sails on seven voyages. Various sequels have been written ever since describing Sindbad's eighth voyage, including Edgar Allan Poe's "The Thousand and Second Tale of Scheherazade" (1845).

"...Haroun's grandson Al Wathik Be'llah...."
Al-Wathiq ibn Mutasim, the Abbasid Caliph from 842–847 C.E., was the grandson of Hārūn al-Rashīd.

Panel 3. The contents of this panel are a reference to William Beckford's novel *Vathek* (1786). *Vathek*, an Arabesque Gothic novel, is about the downfall and damnation of Vathek, the grandson of Hārūn al-Rashīd. The events of the novel are as described here.

Panel 4. "...fighting alongside legendary Prester John...."
Prester John was a legendary figure in Europe from the 12th to the 17th century. He was supposedly the Christian ruler of a nation somewhere in the East.

Panel 5. "...I helped Blondel and his minstrel underground free Richard, called the Lionheart, from prison."
Blondel de Nesle was a 13th-century French troubadour who, according to the *Récits d'un Ménestrel de Reims* (c. 1250?), helped rescue Richard the Lionheart, who had been captured and imprisoned in 1192 by King Leopold V of Austria.

Page 42/*Trump* 14. Panel 3. The history of Constantinople is as described here.

Panel 4. "I posed for Leonardo, even though I was becoming a man at the time. I remember he kept asking me why I was smirking."
This is a reference to the mysterious smile of the Mona Lisa in Leonardo da Vinci's portrait of her.

Panel 5. "...I was apprenticed to the sorcerer Johannes Faust, whereby I renewed my acquaintanceship with Helen, whom I had not seen since Troy."

In the Faust stories, Helen of Troy is one of the characters from the world of the classical gods whom Faust meets.

Page 43/*Trump* 15. Panel 2. "…Gloriana, England's Queen, daughter of brutal Henry VIII and faerie half-breed Nan Bullen." Queen Gloriana is a literal faery queen, with six fingers on each hand, as can be seen in this panel (also see Page 49). "Nan Bullen" is a reference to Anne Boleyn, with "Nan" being a traditional nickname for "Anne" and "Bullen" being the original version of "Boleyn." Boleyn was unpopular with members of Henry VIII's court and with the English public, and after her death was said to have a wen on her throat and six fingers on one hand, the signs of a witch.

Panel 3. This panel is a reference to Virginia Woolf's *Orlando*, which begins:

> He—for there could be no doubt of his sex, though the fashion of the time did something to disguise it—was in the act of slicing at the head of a Moor which swung from the rafters. It was the colour of an old football, and more or less the shape of one, save for the sunken cheeks and a strand or two of coarse, dry hair, like the hair on a cocoanut. Orlando's father, or perhaps his grandfather, had struck it from the shoulders of a vast Pagan who had started up under the moon in the barbarian fields of Africa; and now it swung, gently, perpetually, in the breeze which never ceased blowing through the attic rooms of the gigantic house of the lord who had slain him.

Also see Page 53.

Panel 5. The group seen here is the first known League of Extraordinary Gentlemen, referred to in *League* v2 as "Prospero's Men." They are:
- "beloved Spanish aristocrat Quixote," a.k.a. Don Quixote, from Miguel de Cervantes Saavedra's *Don Quixote de La Mancha* (1605–1615).
- "impoverished sea-captain Robert Owemuch," from Richard Head's *The Floating Island* (1673). *The Floating Island* is, in the words of the *Oxford Dictionary of National Biography*, "an

account of a debtor's walk from Lambeth to Ram Alley, to the east of the Temple, in the manner of a voyage of discovery."
- "ravishing courtesan Mistress St. Clair." This is a reference to Amber St. Clair, from Kathleen Winsor's *Forever Amber* (1944). In the novel, poor country girl St. Clair goes from being a prisoner at Newgate to the mistress of King Charles II.
- "Christian," from John Bunyan's *The Pilgrim's Progress from this World to that Which is to Come* (1678–1684). In *Progress*, Christian, an Everyman, travels from the City of Destruction to the Celestial City, visiting the Slough of Despond, the House of the Interpreter, and various other locales on the way.

So, from left to right, we see: Quixote, Owemuch, Sprite, Prospero, Caliban, Christian, St. Clair, and Orlando.

"...and her spymaster Jack Wilton...."
See Page 52.

Page 44/*Trump* 16. Panel 1. "...the spectral Arctic 'Blazing World'...."
The Blazing World is from *Observations upon Experimental Philosophy. To which is added the Description of a New Blazing World. Written by the Thrice Noble, Illustrious and Excellent Princess, The Duchess of Newcastle*, by Margaret Cavendish, Duchess of Newcastle. The Blazing World is an archipelago of islands which extends from the North Pole through the Greenland and Norwegian Seas almost to the British Islands.

Panel 3. One (perhaps extreme) interpretation of this panel is that what seems to be Africa on the rock is actually a rough sketch of Florida, with the first X representing St. Augustine, where Ponce de Leon claimed to have located the Fountain of Youth, and the second X representing Orlando, Florida.

Panel 4. The group seen here is the 18th-century League of Extraordinary Gentlemen, first glimpsed in *League* v1 and described in more depth in *League* v2. They are:

- "unlucky mariner Lemuel Gulliver," from Jonathan Swift's *Gulliver's Travels*.
- "trapper Natty Bumppo," from James Fennimore Cooper's

five "Leatherstocking" novels, the most famous of which is *The Last of the Mohicans* (1826).

- "libertine Mistress Hill," a.k.a. John Cleland's Fanny Hill.
- "dual-natured clergyman Dr. Syn," from Russell Thorndike's *Doctor Syn* (1915) and its six prequels. In *Doctor Syn*, the kindly and genial Reverend Doctor is the vicar of Dymchurch at the turn of the 19th century. Syn is also the notorious pirate and smuggler Captain Clegg, who is also known as the Scarecrow.
- "and the resourcefull Blakeneys," a.k.a. Sir Percy Blakeney and Lady Marguerite Blakeney, from Baroness Emmuska Orczy's *The Scarlet Pimpernel* (1905) and its ten sequels. Sir Percy Blakeney is a foppish British nobleman during the years of the French Revolution. His alter ego, the Scarlet Pimpernel, is a daring hero who rescues many innocent members of the French royalty from Robespierre and the Terror. Lady Marguerite Blakeney, his wife, is "the cleverest woman in Europe" and an able partner to the Pimpernel.

"I stood by them through Brobdingnag's Giant-wars…."
See Page 66.

Page 45/*Trump* 17. Panel 1. "…the trio's annual sojourns through erotic Europe…"
See the text section of *League* v2 and Pages 57–72 below.

"…our weeks spent in twilit Horselberg…."
This is a reference to Horselberg, a.k.a. Venusberg, from Richard Wagner's *Tannhäuser* (1845), about Tannhäuser's adventures in the otherworldly realm of Venusberg. Aubrey Beardsley, in his *Under the Hill* (1897), added more erotic and pornographic elements to Horselberg.

Panel 2. "…superhuman aesthete Fortunio…"
This is a reference to Theophile Gautier's *Fortunio* (1837), in which the gorgeous, aloof, amoral, and deadly aesthete Fortunio is fruitlessly pursued by the beautiful courtesan Musidora, who fails to win his love because Fortunio's tastes are too refined for drab Europe.

"...or ambiguous Mademoiselle de Maupin."
This is a reference to Theophile Gautier's *Mademoiselle de Maupin, double amour* (1835), in which Madeleine de Maupin, always in search of the perfect love, is always disappointed.

Panel 3. "...at the monastery So Sa Ling, I was captured by Bon sorcerers...."
This is a reference to *A Tibetan Tale of Love and Magic* (1938) by Alexandra David-Neel. In the book, a travelogue, a Tibetan bandit tells David-Neel the story of the monastery of the Bon sorcerers.

Orlando says that she was traveling in Tibet in 1906. It is possible she was in Tibet in 1906 because she had been part of the 1903–1904 British expedition to Tibet, launched to prevent the Russians from controlling one of the buffer states around India. The British troops, led by Sir Francis Younghusband, conquered Tibet in the space of a few months.

Panel 4. "...the azure Mount Karakal and dragon-blazoned Shangri-La...."
Mount Karakal and Shangri-La appear in James Hilton's *Lost Horizon* (1933).

The position in which Orlando and the lama are having sex is the *yab-yum*, a common symbol in Buddhist iconography. The *yab-yum* symbolizes the unification of the masculine and the feminine, thus making it particularly appropriate for Orlando.

Panel 5. The whale in the iceberg may be Moby Dick, from the 1851 Herman Melville novel.

Kevin O'Neill notes:
> The whale in the iceberg was inspired by a story in *St Nicholas Magazine* (1884), as told by Charles F. Holder with illustrations by George R. Halm. Seems like a sailor's tall story but a good visual to fit Moby Dick into the book.

Page 46/*Trump* 18. Panel 1. "...I strived alongside her, Allan, the thief Raffles and occultist Carnacki to avert disaster at King George's coronation."
This is a reference to the events of *League* v3, a.k.a. *Century*.

"...the thief Raffles..."
This is a reference to A. J. Raffles, the creation of E. W. Hornung. Raffles, who first appeared in *Cassell's Magazine* in 1898, is one of the best known of the Gentleman Thieves.

"...occultist Carnacki...."
This is a reference to William Hope Hodgson's occult detective Thomas Carnacki, who appeared in six stories in *The Idler* and *The New Magazine* (and three unpublished stories) between 1910 and 1912.

Panel 2. "In 1913, assisting the team against French counterparts Les Hommes Mysterieux, I nearly died battling the albino, Zenith, in pounding rain atop the Paris Opera."
See Pages 114–115.

"the albino, Zenith" is a reference to Monsieur Zenith, the Albino, one of the archenemies of British story paper detective Sexton Blake. Created by George Norman Philips, a.k.a. Anthony Skene, and appearing in 83 stories from 1919–1941, Monsieur Zenith is a world-weary, opium-addicted, danger-loving Gentleman Thief.
        Zenith is best known for having inspired Michael Moorcock to create his Elric the Albino (mentioned above on Page 27). Zenith is portrayed here wielding a black sword, just as Elric uses the black sword Stormbringer.

Panel 3. "...penitent bandit A. J. Raffles, who'd lose his life during the conflict."
In the original Hornung stories, Raffles did eventually become exposed as a thief and regret his crimes. He volunteered for action in the Boer War and lost his life in combat. Naturally, every sequelist has refused to accept that end for Raffles.

"At the Battle of Mons, I was lucky enough to see Agincourt's phantom bowmen aiding the English."
This is a reference to the Angels of Mons. At the Battle of Mons (Aug. 22–23, 1914), a group of British troops, though grossly outnumbered, temporarily defeated the attacking Germans. On Sept. 29, 1914, Arthur Machen published the story "The Bowmen" in the *London Evening News*. "The Bowmen" purports to be the firsthand account of a soldier at Mons who witnessed English archers, from the Battle of Agincourt, driving off the Germans. This story was taken to be true, and thanks to the foibles of human psychology many have claimed that it is and that they saw the bowmen.

Kevin O'Neill notes:
> In our fictional world, the British Expeditionary Force are wearing steel helmets already in 1914—I wanted them to match those of the Phantom Bowmen.

The character in the lower left-hand corner is Baldrick, and the character above and to his right is Edmund Blackadder, from the four *Blackadder* series (1983, 1986, 1987, 1989) on BBC TV. Baldrick is drawn to resemble actor Tony Robinson, and Blackadder is drawn to resemble Rowan Atkinson, the actors who played those respective characters. *Blackadder* is about the adventures of a series of cynical, cowardly English noblemen, all of whom come from the Blackadder family, at various points in English history. The fourth *Blackadder* series, *Blackadder Goes Forth*, is set during World War One, and presumably the Blackadder seen here is the Captain Blackadder of *Blackadder Goes Forth*.

The character above and to the right of Blackadder is Old Bill, a character created by Bruce Bairnsfather (1888–1959) and appearing in a series of cartoons set in World War One. Old Bill is a curmudgeonly soldier stuck in the trenches. His trademark is a walrus mustache, similar to (but more bushy than) what the character here has.

Panel 4. "I belonged to poor Agatha Runcible's set."
This is a reference to Evelyn Waugh's *Vile Bodies* (1930), about the

smart London set and Agatha Runcible, who nearly burns herself alive.

"We knew the Woosters..."
See Page 116.

"...the Claytons..."
Likely this is a reference to Edgar Rice Burroughs's Tarzan of the Apes. Tarzan, a.k.a. John Clayton, Lord Greystoke, marries Jane Porter at the end of *The Return of Tarzan* (1913). During the 1920s, when Tarzan wasn't having the adventures described in his later books, he and Jane would have been a rich young couple in England, and quite possibly have been part of the smart London set seen here.

"...Jay and Daisy...."
This is a reference to F. Scott Fitzgerald's *The Great Gatsby* (1925) and Jay Gatsby and Daisy Buchanan.

The woman being hit by the car is probably Myrtle Wilson, who in *The Great Gatsby* is hit and killed by Daisy Buchanan. This panel seems to indicate that it was Orlando and not Buchanan who was driving the car.

Panel 5. The figure seen grasping the rail has the "N" logo on his sleeve of Captain Nemo, but as mentioned in *League* v2, Page 177, Captain Nemo dies in 1909. This is one of the later Captain Nemos who will be seen in *League* v3, a.k.a. *Century*.

Page 47/*Trump* 19. Panel 1. "By 1939, of course, the dictator Adenoid Hynkel had dragged the world into a new and even more destructive war."
This is a reference to Charlie Chaplin's film *The Great Dictator* (1940), in which Adolf Hitler analogue Adenoid Hynkel becomes dictator of Tomania. Just as there is no Queen Elizabeth I in the world of *Dossier*, but Queen Gloriana I, in the world of *Dossier* there is no Hitler, but Hynkel. Possibly this means that Germany was conquered or annexed by Tomania in the way that Germany marched into Austria and Czechoslovakia in our world.

Note the two Xs on the plane on the left-hand side of the panel. These are the symbol of Hynkel and Tomania, and can be seen at various points in *Dossier*, beginning on Page 11, Panel 7.

"...aces such as Bigglesworth..."
This is a reference to W. E. Johns's aviator James "Biggles" Bigglesworth, who appeared in 102 novels and story collections from 1932 to 1970. Biggles is Britain's greatest air ace and a most successful spy, and begins fighting Britain's enemies at age seventeen during World War One.

"...Hebblethwaite..."
This is a reference to Ginger Hebblethwaite, Biggles's wingman.

"...and visiting yank G-8 (who seemed, frankly, bonkers)."
This is a reference to Robert J. Hogan's G-8, who appeared in 111 stories in *G-8 and His Battle Aces* and *Dare-Devil Aces* from 1933 to 1944. G-8 was the greatest of the pulp air aces, although in his pulp appearances he was only ever active during World War One.

Orlando may be describing G-8 as "bonkers" because, in G-8's adventures, he takes on a variety of fantastic and horrifying enemies, including spiders that could crawl on webs formed of searchlight beams. That would undoubtedly be enough to drive anyone mad. Alternatively, the "bonkers" reference could be to Philip José Farmer's *The Adventure of the Peerless Peer* (1974), in which G-8's ravings about his enemies are dismissed as caused by insanity.

Interestingly, the enemy planes seen here are jets, not propeller-driven. In our world, Germany did not introduce jet fighters until later in the war. This may be a hint about how the technology of the world of the *Dossier* is more advanced than ours, which would explain Pages 124–125.

The jet on the left is a close model to the German Messerschmitt ME 163, and the jet in the center background of the panel resembles the V1 guided missile.

Page 48/*Trump* **20. Panel 1.** In the 1960s in *TV Comic*, Dr. Who, the time-traveling alien from the eponymous BBC TV series, appeared in a series of comic strips. In these strips, the Doctor had various adventures with his grandchildren John and Gillian. A pair of children named Simon and Sally appeared in the British comic *Robin* from 1953–1969. This panel is a reference to and mash-up of those two comic strips.

"Uncle Bernard... their uncle, the Professor."
"Uncle Bernard" is Professor Bernard Quatermass, from the four *Professor Quatermass* serials (1953, 1955, 1958-1959, 1979) on BBC TV. Professor Quatermass deals with various alien threats in his adventures, as does Uncle Bernard here.

None of the four actors who played Professor Quatermass look like "Uncle Bernard" here. The writer George Bernard Shaw (1856–1950) did, however, especially in his later years, and his sense of humor matches Uncle Bernard's in the sequence on this page. Shaw did not, however, have any children or grandchildren.

Panel 2. "...the famous Interplanetary Zoo is here at Blackgang Chine?"
Blackgang Chine is an actual park on the Isle of Wight. Blackgang Chine has an amusement park with fiberglass dinosaurs and animatronic animals, but no zoo, much less an interplanetary one. The Interplanetary Zoo is a reference to "Operation Triceratops" (*Eagle Annual* #4, 1954), which puts a similar zoo on the Isle of Wight.

Panel 3. "Look at the funny Tralfamadorian! He's waving!"
The Tralfamadorian is a reference to the novels of Kurt Vonnegut, in which an alien race, the Tralfamadorians, experiences life in four dimensions and can see all points across time. The Tralfamadorian is waving because the Tralfamadorians, with their perspective on time, greet people with "Hello, goodbye."

The Tralfamadorian being in the Interplanetary Zoo may be an inversion of Vonnegut's *Slaughterhouse-Five* (1969), in which protagonist Billy Pilgrim becomes unstuck in time and is put in an alien zoo by the Tralfamadorians.

"H-he smells of something bad."
This may be a reference to the Kurt Vonnegut story "The Dancing

Fool" (1973), in which an alien named Zog visits Earth. Zog is "from Margo, a planet where the natives conversed by means of farts and tap dancing."

The green aliens with the brain-like heads are mutants from the planet Metaluna, from the Raymond F. Jones short story "The Alien Machine" (1952), novelized in 1952 as *This Island Earth* and filmed as *This Island Earth* in 1955. In the film, aliens from the planet Metaluna visit Earth.

The flying-brain-with-tentacle is from the British film *Fiend Without A Face* (1958), in which a scientist creates an invisible brain-sucking creature which, when revealed, looks like a tentacled brain.

Panel 4. "…these friendly Lazunes?"
This is a reference to the Lazoons, from the British TV series *Fireball XL5* (1962–1963). The Lazoons are an alien race, one of whose members, Zoony, becomes a part of the XL5 crew.

"What's that Green Man…."
The "Green Man" is a Green Martian from the John Carter novels of Edgar Rice Burroughs. The Green Martians appeared in *League* v2.

Panel 5. "…throwing live elephants to Gorgo's mother…."
This is a reference to the British monster film *Gorgo* (1961), in which the capture of Gorgo, a Godzilla-type creature, by British sailors leads Gorgo's much larger mother to attack London in an attempt to rescue him.

The big-eared dark alien to the right of Bernard's head is John Donnelly's Moony, who appeared in *Harold Hare's Own Paper* and *Playhour* from 1959–1964. Moony is a small, shape-shifting alien who travels to the Earth from the Moon on a moonbeam.

The two mating aliens are Stripey and a mate, from the Dan Dare story "Rogue Planet" (1955–1957). Stripey is an alien whom Dare discovers on the planet Cryptos and who assists Dare on his mission.

The plant creature in the upper right of this panel could be one of a number of alien plants: the alien from the *Quatermass Experiment* (1953), the first of the Professor Quatermass stories, about a human astronaut infected with an alien organism which changes him into a plantlike creature; the alien from the film *The Thing From Another World* (1951), about an alien humanoid-vegetable discovered in Alaska; the alien from the *Avengers* episode "The Man-Eater of Surrey Green" (1965); and the alien plants uncovered in the Antarctic in the *Doctor Who* episode "The Seeds of Doom" (1976).

Panel 6. "Those 'bushes' are Triffids!"
The Triffid is one of the carnivorous plants in Wyndham's *The Day of the Triffids*, mentioned above on Page 16, Panel 9. At the end of *Day of the Triffids*, the Isle of Wight is wiped clean of Triffids. Clearly, the humans in the novel weren't successful....

Page 49/*Fœrie's Fortunes Founded* 1. "...the Courte of our Noble *Queen Gloriana*..."

"Gloriana" is the titular character of Edmund Spenser's epic poem "The Faerie Queen" (1590–1596), which is an allegory written to celebrate Queen Elizabeth I. "The Faerie Queen" is about Faerieland and its ruler, the Faerie Queen, called "Gloriana" because she represents Glory. As shall be seen, the Queen Gloriana I of the *Black Dossier* is the Gloriana of "The Faerie Queen."

"...a playe called: *Fœrie's Fortunes Founded* By William Shakespeare."
The title of the play recalls Shakespeare's early comedy *Love's Labour's Lost* (1595).

"Printed by I. R. for B. Bond..."
"I. R." is a reference to James Roberts (c. 1564–1608), a London printer who published several of Shakespeare's plays in quarto. "B. Bond" is probably a reference to Sir Basildon Bond, for more on whom see Page 52 below.

Page 50/*Færie's Fortunes Founded* 2. "Master Shytte" and "Master Pysse" are very Shakespearean names. Casual readers forget that Shakespeare, like his contemporaries, didn't hesitate to indulge in scatological and sexual humor.

"Dogrose," "Gorse," and "Love-Lies-Bleeding" are all common names for flowers. Faeries, in Shakespeare, have flowers' names. Dogrose, *Rosa canina*, is a scrambling rose species which is said to symbolize pleasure and pain. Gorse, the *Ulex* genus of evergreen shrubs, is said to symbolize enduring affection; and Love-Lies-Bleeding, *Amaranthus caudatus*, is an annual flowering plant which is said to symbolize hopelessness and desertion.

Page 51/*Færie's Fortunes Founded* 3. "The gates of Nonsuch Palace."
The Nonsuch Palace was begun by Henry VIII in Surrey in 1538, and was completed in 1547. It was one of the royal palaces until Queen Mary sold it in 1566. The Palace was eventually dismantled in the late 17th century.

"Another morn in this hag-ridden land…"
Færie's Fortunes Founded, being written by Shakespeare, follows the Shakespearean conventions of iambic pentameter and (sometimes atrocious) puns.

"Our right Queen Mary sickened to her crypt…."
Queen Mary I (1516–1558) died of what was likely ovarian cancer.

"Speak not
Her cog, lest like her kin she come when hailed."
English folklore had it that it was unwise to name elves, lest you summon them, so alternative names, like "The Fair Folk," were used.

"A will-gill or a child of Herm—"
A "will-gill" is, per the *Oxford English Dictionary*, "a hermaphrodite; an effeminate man." In the Greek myths, the god Hermaphroditus was the son of Hermes.

"They jest with me...."
Which is, of course, what Shakespearean doormen do.

Page 52/*Færie's Fortunes Founded* 4. "enter Sir John Wilton and Sir Basildon Bond, right"

"Sir John Wilton" is a reference to Thomas Nashe's *The Unfortunate Traveller or the life of Jack Wilton* (1594), a picaresque novel about a wandering English rogue, Jack Wilton.

"Basildon Bond" is a character, created by British musician and comedian Russ Abbot, as a spoof of James Bond. Although James Bond's ancestry has been described in, among others, John Pearson's *James Bond: The Authorized Biography of 007*, Bond's Elizabethan forebears have never been mentioned, so Basildon may well be Bond's ancestor.

"Curtain"
During the late 16th century, public theaters did not have curtains. The appearance of one here implies that *Færie's Fortunes Founded* was performed privately, and therefore written for a special commission.

"My pretty devils, fold thy prism'd wings.
Halt now thy flutt'ring galliard and draw near,
For spies and sorcerors would have my ear
To weave their schemes, whilst weave I better things."
Often, but not always, the faeries in *Færie's Fortunes Founded* speak in abba rhyming scheme, and the mortals speak in blank verse.

Page 53/*Færie's Fortunes Founded* 5. "Thus should it please me that you now remain
By London here, at Mortlake to the West."

Mortlake is a borough of London on the southern half of the Thames. Its most famous resident was Dr. John Dee (1527–1609), the occultist, alchemist, and advisor to Queen Elizabeth. As he did with Elizabeth and Gloriana, Moore is replacing Dee with Prospero, who has been cited by various Shakespearean critics as one of Shakespeare's inspirations, if not *the* inspiration, for Prospero.

"...take guise
As one John Suttle, born in Wor'stershire...."
As noted above, on Page 26, John Suttle, or "Subtle," appears in
Ben Jonson's *The Alchemist*.

"It is an instrument that serves the crown
Through stealth, its master my Lord Wilton here:
Its 'M', for em's but double-U disguised.
We are by letters, else by numbers masked."
In the James Bond books and films, "M" is the code name for
the head of MI6, the British Intelligence Service. The tradition
of the heads of the British Secret Service calling themselves by
a single initial dates back at least a century. Although there are
persistent stories within the intelligence community that Sir Francis
Walsingham, a member of Queen Elizabeth's Privy Council and the
head of her intelligence agency, referred to himself as "M," the first
documented example of a head of the British Secret Service being
known by a single initial was Captain Sir Mansfield Cumming, who
was appointed director of the British Secret Intelligence Service,
then known as MI1c, in 1909. Captain Sir Cumming's name was
never officially made public, and he was generally known by the
initial "C."

Gloriana replaces Elizabeth. Prospero replaces John Dee.
Edward Face replaces Edward Kelley. And Jack Wilton replaces
Sir Francis Walsingham, as seen on Page 14, Panel 2.

It is also possible that "for em's but double-U disguised" is
a reference to the Masonic square and compass, which looks like
a W surmounting an M.

"It seems like bosoms, or a brace of noughts.
Two 'O's, within a seven bracketed."
And so we see the origin of the double-zero designation for those
agents licensed to kill in the James Bond novels. (More prosaically,
Fleming reportedly got the idea of the double-zero designation from
Rudyard Kipling's ".007" [1897].) John Dee is supposed to have
used the code "007" as his signature in his secret communications
to Queen Elizabeth.

"Hang I as in a saddle-wire, a dee."
Again quoting the *Oxford English Dictionary*, a saddle-wire is "Bookbinding: a wire staple passed through the back fold of a single gathering." A dee is "applied to a Dshaped iron or steel loop used for connecting parts of a harness, or for fastening articles to the saddle." The connection between Prospero and John Dee is made more solid here.

"When not employed you may, for all I care,
Hack at a dangled Tartar's head for sport."
Orlando was doing just that on Page 43, Panel 3.
　　　　Basildon Bond's behavior here, and in *Færie's Fortunes Founded* generally, recalls Broad Arrow Jack's statement, in *League* v1, that Bond's family has a bad reputation and that Campion Bond should be watched out for.

Page 54/*Færie's Fortunes Founded* 6. "Why, should I like a cunny-hare to pet,
They are both soft and warm, and likewise quick.
How might I set its velvet ear a-prick
Or make its nose to twitch, so pink and wet?
Then should I have about me, by my troth,
That which is cunny and a-prick the both."
This is a classically Shakespearean bit of filth.

Page 56/*Færie's Fortunes Founded* 8. "...a previously undiscovered limited first folio edition from 1620...."
Shakespeare's First Folio appeared, in our world, in 1623.

"...as Jacob himself put it at the time in his book *Dæmonologie*, 'That kinde of devils conversing in the earth may be divided in four different kinds...The fourth is these kinde of spirites that are called vulgarlie the Fayrie.' (III,i)"
King James wrote a book, *Dæmonologie* (1597), in which he described the various kinds of demons. In Chapter 5 he writes, "The description of the fourth kinde of Spirites called the Phairie."

Page 58/*Fanny Hill* 2. At the end of Cleland's *Fanny Hill*, Fanny does give up her pleasure-loving ways to marry Charles, but it's entirely in keeping with the tone of Fanny Hill for Charles to stray.

The aging bawd in the upper right, the "elderly, infamous Madame St. Clair," is the same Amber St. Clair who was a member of Prospero's Men (see Page 43, Panel 5).

Page 59/*Fanny Hill* 3. "Mistress Flanders" is Moll Flanders, from Daniel Defoe's *Moll Flanders* (1772). In the novel, Flanders rises from poverty to become an American plantation-owner, having various adventures, romances, and becoming an "Artist" among thieves.

Page 60/*Fanny Hill* 4. "...a nearby tavern, *The Admiral Benbow*."
Although there are a variety of English taverns and inns called "Admiral Benbow," undoubtedly the reference here is to the Admiral Benbow of Robert Louis Stevenson's *Treasure Island* (1883). The Admiral Benbow is the inn in Bristol in which Jim Hawkins lives.

"...the miniature-made garden of the Zipangese kind...."
"Zipang" was one of the early English names for Japan, after Marco Polo recorded the Chinese word for Japan as "Cipangu."

"...from science-crazed Laputa...."
"Laputa" appears in Jonathan Swift's *Gulliver's Travels*. Laputa is a flying island whose culture is preoccupied with music, mathematics, and astronomy. Coincidentally, "La puta" is also Spanish for "the whore."

"He also demonstrated a device from science-crazed Laputa, to invigorate tired skin, that I found endlessly delightful."
I trust that most of my readers understand the eternal tension between the annotator's desire to make note of *everything* and the commenter/critic's desire to leave some things for the reader to

discover for themselves, or to pass over commenting on that which seems obvious. This is one of those cases where the latter desire won out over the former.

Page 61/*Fanny Hill* 5. "...pirates, captained by one Clegg...."
In Russell Thorndike's *Doctor Syn*, one of the alternate identities of Dr. Syn is the infamous pirate and smuggler Captain Clegg.

"Taken aboard the buccaneer's ship *Imogene*..."
Imogene is indeed the name of Syn's/Clegg's ship, after his faithless Spanish wife.

"...not a little solitary ardour in the rigging."
The traditional naval and rugby song "The Good Ship Venus" (mentioned in *League* v2) has the line "frigging in the rigging," of which this line is a rewriting.

"He even offered me a tour of the Malaccan Straits, suggesting that he take me up the southeast passage...."
There is a real Straits of Malacca, off the Malay peninsula, but in Greek slang, "malacca" is an obscenity meaning "masturbator," and "malaka" means "asshole," leaving the meaning of this line too obvious to explain.

Page 62/*Fanny Hill* 6. "...I came at last to Micromona...."
Micromona was created by Karl Immerman and appears in the verse satire *Tulifäntchen, Ein Heldengedicht in drei Gesängen* (1830).

Page 63/*Fanny Hill* 7. "And so it was that I reached Horselberg, called sometimes Venusberg...."
This is a reference to Horselberg, a.k.a. Venusberg, from Richard Wagner's *Tannhäuser* and Aubrey Beardsley's *Under the Hill*. They are mentioned above on Page 45, Panel 1.

"...that pellucid passageway under the hill, the very mound of Venus."
The "mound of Venus," a.k.a. *mons veneris*, is the female pudenda.

"...there flapped nocturnal butterflies of a prodigious size...."
Under the Hill describes "huge moths, so richly winged they must have banqueted upon tapestries and royal stuffs" in Chapter One, but no mention of outsized butterflies anywhere. This reference could be to the sexual position, the "Venus butterfly."

Page 64/*Fanny Hill* 8. Kevin O'Neill's art on this page may be a reference to the illustrations of the Austrian artist Marquis Franz von Bayros (1866–1924), an erotic illustrator in the vein of Aubrey Beardsley.

"...an illustrator, a Marquis named Dorat...."
In *Under the Hill*, Venus's dressing room is "paneled with the gallant paintings of Jean Baptiste Dorat." Later, one of Dorat's paintings is described as "showing how an old marquis practised the five-finger exercise, while in front of him his mistress offered her warm fesses to a panting poodle," which explains the presence of the dog in this panel.

"...a puddle-hound... named Franz."
If this is a reference to anything in particular, I'm unaware of it.

"...I showed my dear friend Marguerite the illustration that resulted....
League v2, Page 173 describes Marguerite Blakeney's reaction to the illustration.

Page 65/*Fanny Hill* 9. "...where we were suffering the quite delicious ministrations of the 'minnows' Venus kept there for this very purpose...."
There is no mention of minnows in *Under the Hill*, but Suetonius, in his *De Vita Caesarum* (Lives of the Caesars), says, of Tiberius, "he trained little boys (whom he termed minnows) to crawl between his thighs when he went swimming and tease him with their licks and nibbles."

Page 66/*Fanny Hill* 10. Brobdingnag is from Swift's *Gulliver's Travels*. Pantagruel is from the anonymously written *Le Voyage de navigation que fist Panurge, disciple de Pantagruel* (1538), and François Rabelais's *Le cinquiesme et dernier livre des faicts et dicts du bon Pantagruel* (1564). Utopia is from Sir Thomas More's utopian novel *Utopia* (1516), with Pantagruel's time in Utopia portrayed in François Rabelais's *Pantagruel roi des Dipsodes* (1532).

I'm not going to explain the joke in this panel.

Page 67/*Fanny Hill* 11. "…the legionnaires of Roman State 'neath northern England…"
The Roman State is from Joseph O'Neill's *Land Under England* (1935). The Roman State is a fascistic subterranean nation underneath England, reachable via a trapdoor at the base of Hadrian's Wall.

"…the strange, stygian civilization of the Vril people or 'Vril-ya' as they called themselves."
The Vril-ya are from Edward Bulwer-Lytton's *The Coming Race* (1871). The Vril-ya are a race which has constructed a utopia in a ravine deep beneath Newcastle.

Page 69/*Fanny Hill* 13. "…the delightful kingdom of Tryphême…."
Tryphême appears in Pierre Louÿs's *Les Aventures du Roi Pausole* (1900).

Page 70/*Fanny Hill* 14. "…Cockaigne, often called also Cocaigne or Cuccagna…."
Cockaigne/Cocaigne/Cuccagna is from *Le Dit de cocagne* (13th century C.E.) and then Marc-Antoine Le Grand's *Le Roi de Cocagne* (1719). Cocagne, or Cockaigne, is the French equivalent of Utopia. In the Middle Ages, numerous Cocagne myths were told about "a land of fabled abundance, with food and drink for the asking."

"…such classic writings as *The Thirty-Two Gratifications*."
The Thirty-Two Gratifications is mentioned as one of the manuals of

love in James Branch Cabell's *Jurgen, A Comedy of Justice* (1919), a fantasy about a rogue's travels through various otherworldly realms.

Page 71/*Fanny Hill* 15. The unicorn seen here is Adolphe, who in *Under the Hill* is Venus's steed and who is mentioned in *League* v2, Page 173. Venus's relationship with Adolphe is somewhat outré, as *Under the Hill* makes clear.

Page 73. This panel is drawn in the crude and vigorous style of 18th-century political cartoons. In particular, it is an homage to the work of James Gillray (1757–1815), whose lampooning of King George III, as in this panel, was biting.

Gillray's work was sold by Hannah Humphrey, possibly mentioned on Page 25 above.

The history mentioned in this panel is accurate as given.

"…rewarded by Billy the Bursar…."
This is probably a reference to William Pitt the Younger (1759–1806), who was Prime Minister (and therefore dispenser of funds) in 1794, when this cartoon was made.

"…mentally-weak King George III…."
Later in life, George III suffered from mental illness which may have been porphyria and/or arsenic poisoning. One of George III's verbal tics was "What? What?" as seen here.

"…one of 'Mother Threadneedle's Fine Pies' (a reference to the Bank of England, in Threadneedle Street)…."
Gillray drew the "Old Lady of Threadneedle Street" in a 1797 cartoon. In the cartoon, William Pitt, looking much like "Billy the Bursar" here, attacks the Old Lady, who looks much like the woman in this panel.

Kevin O'Neill notes:
> The BM stamp on the cartoon prints marks it as the property of the British Museum.

Page 76. Panel 6. The dentist might be Dr. Christian Szell from William Goldman's novel *Marathon Man* (1974) and the 1976 film. In the film, Dr. Szell, a former dentist at the German death camp at Auschwitz, is played by Laurence Olivier, who somewhat resembles the Szell seen here and on Page 77, Panel 1.

Panel 7. "They've made you look a bit of a cunt, haven't they…" To quote Warren Ellis, in *Crécy*: "Cunt. This is a word that many people do not like. But you have to understand the English. In England, the word cunt is punctuation."

"…old man?"
See Page 78, Panel 9.

Page 77. **Panel 2**. "Dr. Bre—" is probably a reference to Dr. Geoffrey Brent, star of the British TV series *Police Surgeon* (1960). Dr. Brent is a medical doctor working with the police in Bayswater in London.

"Dr. D. Keel" is a reference to Dr. David Keel, who appeared in the first season of the British TV series *The Avengers* in 1961. Keel was originally the protagonist of *The Avengers*, but John Steed, originally a secondary character, stole the show and Keel was written out. Actor Ian Hendry played both Dr. Geoffrey Brent and Dr. David Keel, although there was no textual link between *Police Surgeon* and *The Avengers*.

"One Ten" is probably a reference to "One Ten," Steed's superior in the second season of *The Avengers*.

Panel 3. "George" is probably George Smiley, from the John Le Carré novels. In the novels, Smiley is a melancholy spy master. The "George" seen here has the same eyeglasses which Sir Alec Guinness wore when he portrayed Smiley, and Smiley drinks a great deal of tea (hence the "cuppa" reference).

Panel 4. The woman in this panel may be Moneypenny, the long-suffering secretary to M in the James Bond novels and books, but it may also be Lady Ann Sercomb, George Smiley's beautiful and notoriously unfaithful wife.

The "Drake" on the woman's file folder is a reference to John Drake—see Page 17 above. This is probably the same file that will slide into the "Resigned" filing cabinet in the beginning credits of *The Prisoner*.

Panel 7. The squat, bald man on the left is Masterspy, the Albanian villain on the Gerry Anderson puppet spy show *Supercar* (1961– 1962).

The man coming up the stairs may be John Drake.

The man on the right in the lab coat is Q, head of the Q Branch (research and development), later Q Division, of the British Secret Service in the James Bond novels. For the identity of Q, see Page 89, Panel 7.

The man to whom Q is speaking is probably Granpa Potts, the father of Caractacus Potts, from Ian Fleming's novel *Chitty Chitty Bang Bang* (1964) and the 1968 film. In the film, Granpa Potts is played by Lionel Jeffries, who resembles the character here. Also see Page 80, Panel 7.

Page 78. Panel 6. "We're teaming you with Hugo Drummond..."
"Hugo Drummond" is a reference to Captain Hugh "Bulldog" Drummond, from the seventeen novels of "Sapper," a.k.a. Herman Cyril McNeile, and Gerard Fairlie. Hugh "Bulldog" Drummond is a massive World War One veteran who killed any number of Germans in one-man commando raids into the enemy trenches. After the war, he finds peace tedious and begins fighting against those who would do England dirty. This list includes Jews, Germans, Russians, non-whites, anarchists, and Communists.

The "Hugo" in place of "Hugh" may simply be a Moorean shift, or it may be a reference to Philip Wylie's *Gladiator* (1930), in which protagonist Hugo Danner is an adventurer of superhuman strength and abilities. (Danner was influential on Jerry Siegel's creation of Superman.) The implication of the use of the name "Hugo" may be that Hugo Danner and Bulldog Drummond, in the world of *Dossier*, were the same character.

"...and John Night's daughter."
See Page 80, Panel 1 below.

The "CB" on Bond's lighter is a reference to "Commander Bond," Bond's rank when he left the Royal Naval Volunteer Reserve at the end of World War Two. It may also refer to "Campion Bond." The "7" on Bond's cufflinks refers to his number, "007."

Panel 8. "Behind my back, you can even call me *Mother*."
In the final season of *The Avengers*, Steed and Tara King receive their orders from "Mother," a man in a wheelchair.

Panel 9. "But *Harry*... Harry died a long time ago, in the sewers under Vienna."
This is a reference to the film *The Third Man* (1949), about black marketeer Harry Lime, active in Vienna at the end of World War Two. At the end of the film, Lime is shot and killed in the sewers of Vienna. The implication here is that M is Harry Lime.

"Harry died a long time ago, in the sewers under Vienna" might be a reference to the line "That was the shot that killed Harry Lime. He died in a sewer beneath Vienna," which is the opening line of the radio show *The Lives of Harry Lime* (1951–1952), in which Orson Welles, who played Lime in the movie, tells stories of Lime's life before the events of the movie.

On Page 76, Panel 7, M/Lime used the phrase "old man," which Lime often used in the film and radio show.

In the film and radio show, Lime is an American. But in Lime's first appearance, Graham Greene's novel *Harry Lime* (1950), Lime is British, as is M/Lime here.

It is debatable whether M/Lime looks like later, heavier Orson Welles or later, heavier Patrick Macnee.

Perhaps coincidentally, before Lime is shot and killed in the sewers, he kills a British soldier, Sergeant Paine. Paine is played, in the film, by Bernard Lee, who is best known for playing M in the Bond films. Lime replaces M in more than one sense.

Page 79. **Panel 2**. "Drummond helped her father breaking strikes in the 'Thirties."
Bulldog Drummond was a reactionary who would glory in strike-breaking.

Panel 4. "Jimmy, you did very well against our Yellow Peril friend."
This is another reference to *Dr. No*—see Page 23, Panels 3–4.

Panel 5. "I mean, let's face it, Jimmy. You're no Sidney Reilly."
This is a reference to Lt. Sidney Reilly (c. 1873–1925), a spy-for-hire used by the British government, among others, and known as the "Ace of Spies." He was one of the models Fleming used for James Bond. Fleming, when asked later about Bond, said, "James Bond is just a piece of nonsense I dreamed up. He's not a Sidney Reilly, you know!"

The cylindrical light on the wall was, in the Bond books, used to show whether or not M could be disturbed.

The double-X marks beneath the light may be a reference to the Masonic compass and right angle, or it may be another piece of Hynkel graffiti (see Page 11, Panel 7, among others).

Panel 7. The illustration hanging on the wall is of one of H. G. Wells's Martians, from *War of the Worlds* (1898), as portrayed by Kevin O'Neill in *League* v2.

The giant skull in the background is a Brobdingnagian skull, seen at various times in the *League* books.

Page 80. **Panel 1**. "…this is Miss Night…."
"Miss Night" is better known as Emma Peel, the best of John Steed's partners on *The Avengers*. Although in *The Avengers* she is Mrs. Peel, her birth name is Emma Knight, as her father is Sir John Knight, which explains the "John Night's daughter" reference on Page 78.

Panel 3. "Scared the life out of Little Em here, first time she met me."
The description of Emma Peel, *née* Night, as "Little Em" may be a hint that the M in the last eight James Bond movies, played by Judi Dench, may be an aging Emma Peel.

The bronze bust, with the letters "—os" visible, may be a reference to Talbot Munday's Tros of Samothrace (various stories and novels, 1925–1935). Tros is the son of Perseus and a native of Samothrace during the reign of Julius Caesar, who is portrayed as a villain and whom Tros fights against.

Kevin O'Neill notes:
> The bronze bust is of Heros the Spartan, featured in the *Eagle Comic* (1962-65) and created by writer Tom Tully and artist Frank Bellamy. Heros was a Roman rather than a Spartan, but who cared when superbly illustrated in colour by Frank Bellmay in his career-best style.

Panel 7. The car under construction here is Chitty Chitty Bang Bang, the flying car from Ian Fleming's *Chitty Chitty Bang Bang: The Magical Car*, mentioned on Page 77, Panel 7. The car's license plate here, "GEN1," is very close to Chitty Chitty Bang Bang's license plate, "GEN11."

This panel, with the six technicians working on Chitty Chitty Bang Bang, is an homage to a scene in the 1968 film, in which we see six older mechanics in a scene much like this.

One popular fan theory about this scene goes as follows: Night Industries makes high-tech equipment, possibly including a flying, semi-sentient car, Chitty Chitty Bang Bang. In the atrociously stupid American TV series *Knight Rider* (1982–1986), Knight Industries helps create a talking, sentient car, the Knight Industries Two Thousand, or "K.I.T.T." "Night Industries" and "Knight Industries" are so close that Moore is saying that Chitty Chitty Bang Bang is the predecessor of K.I.T.T. and that *Knight Rider* exists in the world of *League*.

Page 81. Panel 3. "I-I dropped them in *Brookgate*."
"Brookgate" is probably a reference to Michael Moorcock's *King of the City* (2000). In the novel, Brookgate is a section of London which "under the power of the Hugenot Leases" is fully autonomous and controlled by its citizens until a vile Rupert Murdoch-like figure buys up Brookgate and ruins it.

Panel 4. I believe that the "D5" in the dot of the question mark on the pillar is a reference to Division 5, a.k.a. Military Intelligence 5 or "MI5," the section of British Intelligence which deals with counterespionage.

Panel 5. If the statue is a reference to anything in particular, I'm unaware of it.

Kevin O'Neill notes:
> Statue is Heros again—a favourite of mine.

Page 82. Panel 1. "Num Yum" candies appear in the British film *I'm All Right Jack* (1959), a satire of British business.
Mina hiking up her skirt in order to get a ride is likely a reference to *It Happened One Night* (1934), in which Claudette Colbert does the same thing.

If the two children are a reference to anything, I'm unaware of it.

Kevin O'Neill notes:
> The two children are *Tough Todd and Happy Annie, The Runaway Orphans*. They appeared in *Knockout Comic* from 1947-60, originally illustrated by Sexton Blake-arist Eric Parker in text stories. They were drawn in picture strips by Hugh McNeill. The kids were on the run from Silas Stiggins of Sloansbury Orphanage.

Panel 2. "...our coloured chum and his Dutch girls...."
See Page 166, Panel 1.

Panel 3. "...a public school that I know is in *Kent*..."
See Page 84, Panel 1.

Panel 5. "I'm heading down Bradgate way."
See Page 84, Panel 3.

I don't know what "Frim" is a reference to.

Kevin O'Neill notes:
> Frim is a fictional version of Vim and is from *Dentist on the Job* (1961). It also features Scrubba—a fictional detergent and slang for a loose woman! *Dentist on the Job* featured comedian Bob Monkhouse, a former comic artist and later collector of comic art!

"Whiter Frisko" and "Detto" are references to *I'm All Right Jack*. In the film, Frisco and Detto are detergents.

"Dreem" is a reference to the British film *Dentist on the Job* (1961), a comedy about Dreem, a new brand of toothpaste, and its creator, Proudfoot Industries.

Panel 7. "...working for Mr. Callendar...."
This is a reference to Jack Trevor Story's novel *Live Now, Pay Later* (1962). In the novel, Mr. Callendar runs Callendar's Credit Store. See Page 83, Panel 1 below.

Page 83. Panel 1. "Albert" is Albert Argyle, from Jack Trevor Story's novels *Live Now, Pay Later*; *Something For Nothing* (1963); and *The Urban District Lover* (1964). Argyle is a traveling salesman, working for Callendar's Credit Store. Argyle is also a lothario, hence his comment "you can be as cheeky as you like" to Mina on Page 82, Panel 5.

The black car in the middle of the panel is similar to the one driven by Jonathan Pryce's Sam Lowry in the dystopic film *Brazil* (1985).

Perhaps coincidentally, the car that Albert is driving is similar to yellow Reliant Robin van driven by "Uncle Albert" in the BBC sitcom *Only Fools and Horses* (1981–2003).

"Frampton Overcoat," advertised on the billboard, wasn't a real product, but a "frampton" is British slang for a "fanny fart," and "Frampton Overcoat" can be extrapolated from there.

Kevin O'Neill notes:
> Hah! No, not British slang—a Frampton overcoat billboard as shown appeared in *The Man in the White Suit* (1951). But I love the other connections you made.

Panel 2. The sign lists exits for "Bradgate" and "Fircombe." For more on Bradgate, see Page 84, Panel 3. "Fircombe" is a reference to the British films *Carry On at Your Convenience* (1971) and *Carry On Girls* (1973). Fircombe is a British seaside resort town similar to Brighton.

Panel 3. Kevin O'Neill notes:
> Larken sign references *The Larkin Family* featuring Peggy Mount as Ma Larkin, from film and TV (1950s).

Panel 4. "…if you like tally-boys, getting people into *debt* for a living."
A "tally-boy" was a wandering salesman who sold things to people on installment and then picked up the weekly payments. Allan doesn't think much of them, and Jack Trevor Story didn't either, as can be seen in *Live Now, Pay Later*.

Panel 6. "…must be General Sir Harold Wharton…."
See Page 84, Panel 1 below.

Panel 7. "There's also an 'R.K.C' mentioned."
See Page 90, Panel 5 below.

"…public school with Wharton, here in Bradgate."
See Page 84, Panel 3.

Page 84. Panel 1. "Greyfriars."
Greyfriars, mentioned on Page 25 above, is a reference to the

Greyfriars School, from the hundreds (well over a thousand) of British story paper stories set at Greyfriars and written by "Frank Richards," a.k.a. Charles Hamilton. Greyfriars is a British public school in Kent whose students have a wide variety of adventures, from student revolts to attacks by Yellow Perils.

Billy Bunter is the most famous of Greyfriars's students, but the second-most popular group of characters from Greyfriars were the "Famous Five," consisting of Harry Wharton (the Five's leader), Frank Nugent, Bob Cherry, Johnny Bull, and Hurree Jamset Ram Singh. Per Page 83, Panel 6, Harry Wharton became Big Brother, and as shall be seen, the rest of the Five also had momentous destinies.

Per the official drawings of Greyfriars, Allan and Mina are approaching the school from the Tradesman's Entrance.

Panel 2-6. Kevin O'Neill notes:
> I visited Broadstairs and walked the thirty-nine steps (the originals are long gone). Rather enjoyed the Buchan atmosphere of the place (the author had a home up on the cliffs).

Panel 2. "...do you remember Richard Hannay? Worked at MI5 before the war?"
Richard Hannay was created by John Buchan and appeared in six novels from 1915 to 1936. He is a wealthy Scottish mining engineer who gets involved in a series of espionage adventures.

Panel 3. "Decent sort of chap, I always thought."
"Absolutely."
Although Hannay and Buchan are usually grouped together with Bulldog Drummond and Sapper and Richard Chandos/Berry Pleydell/Jonah Mansel and Dornford Yates in the Clubmen Heroes category, Hannay and Buchan are much different. Buchan was a far better writer than Sapper or Yates (Buchan's supernatural fiction is rather good), and Hannay was much less bigoted and jingoistic than Drummond *et al*. Too, there's a humanistic and even compassionate streak running through the Hannay novels which is quite missing from the work of Sapper and Yates. *Mr. Standfast* (1919) features a conscientious objector to World War One, and where Sapper would

have mocked the character or humiliated him, or shown him to be a spy, Buchan treats the objector fairly.

"...that 'Thirty-Nine Steps' business he investigated."
Buchan's first Richard Hannay novel, *The Thirty-Nine Steps* (1915), involves a German spy ring, the Black Stone, which is active in England. The "Thirty-Nine Steps" lead to a spot on a beach from which a spy with crucial information is going to leave England.

Panel 4. "'What are the thirty-nine steps?' and all that."
In *The Thirty-Nine Steps*, "What are the thirty-nine steps?" is a cryptic message given to Hannay by an American who is killed not long afterward.

"...apparently we're walking up them."
The Thirty-Nine Steps is set in Kent, in a town called "Bradgate." In our world, there is a town in Kent called "Broadstairs" which has a set of steps leading down to the beach, and on which local tradition claims Buchan based the thirty-nine steps of the novel. "Bradgate" is a derivation of "Bradstow," which is an older name for "Bradgate."

Panel 6. The sign on the ground reading "Trafalgar Lodge Priv— Pr—" is a reference to *The Thirty-Nine Steps*, in which the name of the house to which the titular steps are attached is called "Trafalgar Lodge."

Page 85. Panel 2. The *Spick* magazine seen here is not a hint by Moore about the kind of pornography which would develop in the world of *Dossier*, but rather a real British pin-up magazine which lasted from 1953–1976.

Panel 7. The "—ocke" statue is of Dr. Locke, the Headmaster of Greyfriars.

This panel of Mina and Allan's *primo coitus interruptus* is a reference to a similar scene in *League* v2, in which Rupert interrupts Allan and Mina's lovemaking. In both cases, the interrupter wears checkered pants.

Kevin O'Neill notes:

> Fascinating—Allan and Mina's upright coitus interrupted by grotesques in checkered pants sixty years apart. What can it mean... and do we need help?

Page 86. Panel 1. This sad, grotesque figure is Billy Bunter, the portly Greyfriars schoolboy. Created by "Frank Richards," Bunter appeared in over a thousand short stories, 105 novels, and various radio and television programs from 1908 to 1982. Bunter is not one of the "Famous Five," but he is greedy, cowardly, cunning, foolish, and gluttonous enough to get into a large number of adventures on his own.

"Y-you're not here to give me six on the *bags*, are you?"
"Six on the bags," also known as "six of the best," is six strokes on the rear end with a cane.

Panel 2. "...you chaps wouldn't have any buns on you, by any chance?"
Billy Bunter is a glutton and loves sweet buns above all things.

Panel 4. "I-I was a pupil here, then a beak."
"Beak" is British slang for "schoolmaster."

Panel 6. "In fact, I'm expecting a postal order from my *mother*..."
In the Greyfriars stories, Bunter is forever poor and forever borrowing money from the other students. He always promises to pay them back soon, as he is always expecting, imminently, a postal order from his mother. The postal order never comes. (It's the English schoolboy version of *Waiting for Godot*, really.) But see Page 121, Panel 6.

Panel 7. "Do you know, the bounder married my sister?"
Billy Bunter's sister is Bessie Bunter, who after being mentioned a few times in the Billy Bunter stories appeared in a long series of her own stories, set at Cliff House School, the girls' school equivalent of Greyfriars.

The relationship between Bessie Bunter and Harry Wharton is Moore's invention, and explains the mention of "Bessy" on Page 25.

Page 87. Panel 1. "Always a bit of a black sheep, Wharton."
In the Greyfriars stories, Wharton is a hothead who is forever getting into trouble with "light-hearted" pranks. (Wharton was beloved by readers in his era. Modern readers are likely to see the sadistic Wharton as more deserving of a lobotomy, or perhaps transportation to the gulag archipelago.)

Perhaps coincidentally, Moore's use of Wharton mirrors that of George McDonald Fraser and Harry Flashman. Flashman was a malicious prankster in Thomas Hughes's *Tom Brown's Schooldays* (1857), but Fraser turned Flashman into someone intimately involved with British foreign policy and wars in the 19th century. Moore has done the same with Wharton.

"Orphan, you know. Brought up by some beastly Colonel."
Wharton's parents died, forcing Colonel Wharton, newly returned from India, to raise Wharton.

"Born *leader*, though."
Wharton is the leader of the Famous Five.

Panel 2. "He got mixed up with *communists*, an oik named Skinpole from *St. Jim's*."
St. James College, called "St. Jim's" by the residents, was another of Charles Hamilton's creations, a school much like Greyfriars. It appeared in *The Gem* from 1907–1939.

Herbert Skimpole is one of the students at St. Jim's. He is a socialist, which automatically meant that Frank Richards would portray him as a villain in the Greyfriars stories.

Panel 3. I'm not sure what the "Kra—" on the bulletin board might be a reference to.

Panel 4. Presumably, the portraits in this panel are of various Famous Five characters. The picture in the lower right is of Bessie Bunter.

Kevin O'Neill notes:
> Portrait to left of doorway is former headmaster Dr. Locke. Harry Wharton's picture is on the right behind Bunter and next to it is a portrait of Lord Mauleverer, a Greyfriars' favorite.

Page 88. Panel 2. "That was old Quelchy. Henry Quelch."
Henry Quelch is one of the masters at Greyfriars. As Bunter says, he is a "gimlet-eyed old devil."

Panel 3. "He was watching Wharton from the start, along with Knight and Cherry and Waverly and the rest."
This was one of the traditional methods by which both British Intelligence and their Soviet opposites recruited spies—watch them from when they are young, and then recruit them before or during college. The spies of the Cambridge Five, which included H. A. R. "Kim" Philby (1912–1988), were recruited in just this fashion.

"Knight"
Knight is presumably a reference to Sir John Knight, Emma Peel's father (see Page 80 above).

"Cherry"
See Page 90, Panel 5.

"Waverly"
See Page 89, Panels 2–3.

Panel 4. The carrot creature under glass is Doctor Carrot, a character who appeared on British propaganda posters during World War Two. Doctor Carrot encouraged the British people to grow their own vegetables as a way to supplement rationing.

Kevin O'Neill notes:
> The carrot creature is from Florence Upton's *The Vege-*

men's Revenge (1897), a delightful confection with text by Bertha Upton and art by Florence.

I believe that the giant skull to the right of the painting is a Pobble, from "Willie Willikin's Pobble," a strip in the British comic *Dandy* (1952). The Pobble is an alien, similar to a large dog or a small horse, with black skin and white splotches, some of which can just be made out in this panel. The Pobble is named such because when he emerged from his spaceship, he greeted Willie Williken with the word "pobble!"—the only word he ever said.

The two skeletons in flower pots are Bill and Ben, from the BBC TV puppet show *Flower Pot Men* (1952–1954). Bill and Ben are the Flower Pot Men, who come alive when "the man who worked in the garden… went inside the house to have his dinner."

The creature above and to the right of Bill and Ben is Sooty, from the BBC puppet show *Sooty* (1952–present). Sooty is a yellow bear puppet who is partnered with the gray dog puppet Sweep. They patrol the docks in Puppetville, roughing up criminals and shaking down hookers—it's all very much like *The Sweeney*. The thing poking out of the head of the shorter of Bill and Ben is actually Sooty's xylophone mallet.

The yellow blob to the right of Sooty with the "flob" plaque is the side of the head of Little Weed, a dandelion character who appeared on *Flower Pot Men*. "Flob" comes from Bill and Ben, who are incapable of saying anything but "flobalob."

"There. Good Queen Glory herself. 1564, I think it was, when she visited Greyfriars."
In one of the Greyfriars stories, the history of the school is given, and Queen Elizabeth I is said to have visited the school in 1564.

"The rum-looking fellow behind her, that's Sir Jack Wilton. He was Gloriana's big chief I-Spy, so I'm told."
Sir Jack Wilton is described on Page 52. "Big chief I-Spy" is a reference to the British "I-Spy" books, a series of books written for children in the 1950s and 1960s. The idea behind the books was for

children to make note of the planes, trains, fire engines, and so on, and send their lists in to "Big Chief I-Spy" in London.

Panel 5. "Johnny Night, for example, he ended up designing *brain-washing* machines."
On Page 84, Panel 1, it was revealed that Harry Wharton, of the Famous Five, became Big Brother. Here we see that Johnny Bull, of the Famous Five, became Johnny Night. As for the "brain-washing machines," see Panel 7 below.

The creature in the upper left, most of whose profile is obscured by word balloons, is A. A. Milne's Eeyore, from the Winnie the Pooh books, obliquely referred to in *League* v2.

The creature to the right of Bunter is a monkey wearing a bowler hat, most likely a reference to the Tipps Family of hat-wearing primates who have advertised P. G. Tipps, a British brand of tea, since 1956. One of the Tipps Family is Mr. Shifter, who wears a bowler.

The horse in the upper right is Muffin the Mule, who has appeared on eponymous children's shows on the BBC intermittently since 1946. Muffin, a puppet, has a number of animal friends, including Oswald the Ostrich and Sally the Sea-lion.

Kevin O'Neill notes:
> The monkey in a bowler hat is in fact from Lawson Woods's (1878-1957) *Gran'pop Annuals* (1935-51).

Panel 6. The creature in the lower right is the Psammead, from E. Nesbit's short stories. The Psammead is a grouchy "sand-fairy" unearthed by five children. It is mentioned in *League* v2, Page 163.

Panel 7. "...designing kit for some *Welsh* set-up. D-dream inducers. Killer balloons."
This is a reference to *The Prisoner*, which had both dream inducers and killer balloons. Similarly, the "brain-washing machines" mentioned in Panel 5 above are a reference to the brainwashing machines in *The Prisoner*.

"Yarooh" was one of Bunter's most typical exclamations.

Page 89. Panels 2–3. "…Johnny was always pretty tight with Waverly, as well.… Francis Alexander Waverly. He runs some spy-ring for the United Nations these days."

"Waverly" is a reference to Alexander Waverly, the head of the United Network Command for Law and Enforcement, a.k.a. "U.N.C.L.E.," in the American spy TV show *The Man from U.N.C.L.E.* (1964–1968). In *The Man from U.N.C.L.E.*, U.N.C.L.E. is run by the United Nations.

The implication of this panel is that, just as Johnny Bull of the Famous Five became Johnny Night, Frank Nugent of the Famous Five became Francis Alexander Waverly of U.N.C.L.E.

Panel 7. "Quelchy's son, Quentin, worked there before he joined MI5's *technical* chappies. Like *everybody* there, he's known by an *initial*."

Quelch had no sons in the Greyfriars stories, although "Quentin Quelch" certainly sounds like a name Frank Richards would have created. Quelch can be seen on Page 77, Panel 7.

In the James Bond novels, Q is named "Major Boothroyd," with "Q" standing for "Quartermaster."

Page 90. Panel 1. I'm not sure exactly why there'd be a statue of Judah Ben-Hur at Greyfriars. Judah Ben-Hur appears in Lewis Wallace's *Ben-Hur: A Tale of the Christ* (1880), about Judah Ben-Hur, a Jew alive at the time of Christ who is enslaved, freed, wins a chariot race against his Roman childhood friend Messala, and eventually converts to Christianity. Perhaps this is a hint that in the world of *Dossier*, there was no Christ, only Judah Ben-Hur?

If the motorcycle with the D211731 plate is a reference to anything, I'm unaware of it.

Kevin O'Neill notes:
> The motorcycle number plate shown should read DZ 11231 and is shown on the rusted remains of Horace Coker of the fifth form's cherished transport after it was borrowed by a younger Bunter in an earlier story.

Panel 3. "His father named him Kim after the famous *spy* who worked in *Afghanistan*."
This is a reference to Rudyard Kipling's *Kim* (1901), with its orphaned Indian child and his spywork for the British.

Panel 5. "'R.K.C.' is Harry *Lime*."
Making Bob Cherry into Harry Lime also makes his middle name, "Kim" (mentioned in Panel 3 above), into an oblique reference to H. A. R. "Kim" Philby, mentioned above on Page 88, Panel 3. In an interview at the web site *Comic Book Resources* (http://www.comicbookresources.com/?page=article&id=11958, Moore said:

> The film 'The Third Man' was written by Graham Greene, who based the character of Harry Lime on his lifelong friend Kim Philby, a very famous British spy who turned out to be a double agent for the Russians. And weirdly enough, there had previously been two Russian agents exposed, Guy Burgess and Anthony MacLean, and there was a rumour there was a third double agent in MI5. I remember there was a headline back in the Sixties that said, 'KIM PHILBY IS THE THIRD MAN,' which were written completely unaware that he was the third man. So he was the basis for 'The Third Man.'

So, to sum up: Bob Cherry is Harry Lime, M, and Kim Philby.

Harry Wharton became Big Brother. Johnny Bull became Johnny Night. Frank Nugent became Francis Waverly. And Bob Cherry became Harry Lime, and then M, and then Kim Philby. Leaving only Hurree Jamset Ram Singh's whereabouts unknown. Perhaps we'll find out in *League* v3, a.k.a. *Century*?

Moore makes the Famous Five and the Cambridge Five parallel. Both were honored while young, with Guy Burgess and Anthony Blunt being members of the elite Cambridge secret society, the Apostles. Both became tarnished while old.

Page 91. Panel 3. "Conamur Tenues Grandia" is from the Odes (23–13 B.C.E.) of Horace.

Page 92. Panel 5. If "Mum's Plaice" is a reference to anything in particular, I'm unaware of it. The "plaice" is a kind of flatfish, *Pleuronectes platessa*, which is commonly sold at British fish and chips shops.

Panel 6. The "William Brown Captured... Outlaws" headline is a reference to Richmal Crompton's "Just William" stories, novels, radio shows, television shows, and films about an eleven-year-old English mischief-maker. His gang of friends is the "Outlaws."

Page 93. Panel 1. A number of these magazines are Moore and O'Neill's creations. The references that aren't:

- "New B.B.—Bardot Talks" is a reference to the actress Brigitte Bardot and "Garbo Talks!" The silent film actress Greta Garbo was famous for her taciturnity and carefully cultivated mystique, and the film *Anna Christie* (1930), which contained Garbo's first onscreen words, was billed with the words "Garbo Talks!" It is also a reference to the fact that in *1984*, Big Brother never appeared in public and seldom gave speeches.
- *The Naked Truth* is a reference to the British film *The Naked Truth* (1957), about the blackmailing publisher of a gossip magazine, *The Naked Truth*. The cover of the magazine seen here is identical to the one in the film.
- The figure on the cover of *The Naked Truth* is the 1950s Invisible Man—see Page 148 below.
- *Joycamp Harlots* may be a reference to the "Joy Division," the Jewish women forced to become prostitutes in the German death camps during World War Two. "Joycamp Harlot" is the kind of death-obsessed pornography which would emerge in a country ruled by Big Brother.
- *The Daily Brute* is a reference to Evelyn Waugh's *Scoop* and is mentioned on Page 4 above.
- "Hank Janson" is a reference to Stephen D. Frances's pseudonym, "Hank Janson." As "Janson," Frances wrote over 100 hardboiled novels. (Frances chose "Hank Janson" on the grounds that it sounded suitably American, and everyone—i.e., the British reading public—knew that only Americans could write proper hardboiled novels.)
- *Daily Twopence* is a reference to Waugh's *Scoop*. In the novel,

the *Daily Twopence* is a competitor to the *Daily Brute*.

- *The Beast* is a reference to Waugh's Scoop. In the novel, *The Daily Beast* is *The Daily Brute*'s main rival.
- I'm not sure what "—tichrist"—obviously *Antichrist*—might be a reference to.
- The "Vitamalt Cho—" sign at the top is a reference to George Orwell's *Keep the Aspidistra Flying* (1936). In the novel, Vitamalt Chocolate is one of the treats which oppresses the impoverished protagonist—he wants it and cannot afford it, and he hates it as well.
- "Cyprolax Hair Ton—" is a reference to Orwell's *Keep the Aspidistra Flying*. In the novel, Cyprolax Tonic is one of the products the protagonist must sell, as part of his advertising agency day job.
- "—ntom —llion" may be a reference to the film *Phantom Stallion* (1954), a Western.
- *Weird Date* is very much in the style of the 1940s spicy pulps, but there wasn't one by that name. "Weird Date," however, is one of the comics in Michael Chabon's *The Amazing Adventures of Kavalier and Klay* (2000), a novel about the early years of the comic book industry.
- "Bat" is in all likelihood not a reference to Batman to but to one of the many pulp and British story paper characters by that name.
- "Nick Stacy" is a reference to Will Eisner's comic book character The Spirit. In the July 20, 1947 newspaper section of *The Spirit*, a comic strip artist, Hector Ghoul, creates a parody of Dick Tracy named "Nick Stacy." Stacy is an extremely violent, extremely hardboiled detective.
- *Phallos*, similar to "phallus," is a likely title for a 1950s spicy magazine.
- "Rubber Goods: —cket of 3: Spartan Heros X" is a reference to British comics artist Frank Bellamy's "Heros the Spartan" comic strip in *Eagle* from 1962–1965. Heros the Spartan is an adventure story set in Roman times. The ad on this page is for a condom, with "Spartan" replacing "Trojan" as the brand name of the condom.
- I'm not sure what *Secrets of Paris by Night* might be a reference to. Possibly this is one of the bowdlerized and/or rewritten versions of Eugène Sue's *Mysteries of Paris* (1843) which were common in the 1940s and 1950s.
- *Jelly Result* is a reference to Steve Aylett's *Lint* (2005), a very funny novel about a science fiction author, Jeff Lint, whose second novel is *Jelly Result*.
- *Blackshirt* is a reference to the cracksman and Gentleman Thief of that name, created by "Bruce Graeme" (a.k.a. Graham

Jeffries) and appearing in dozens of novels and short story collections from 1924 to 1969. "Blackshirt" was also the name of Italian fascist groups following World War One, with the name also being used to describe the members of the British fascist group the Legion of Fascists. Most likely the Blackshirt of the world of *League* is a combination of the two.

- "Castle Hill Labs VD Scare" is a reference to the TV series *The Invisible Man* (1958–1960), in which in which there is an explosion at Castle Hill Labs. Also see Page 148 below.
- I think *Clint* is a reference to the 1960s injunction, in American comics, against characters having "Clint" as a first name, on the grounds that, when drawn as "CLINT," it might appear as quite a different word to the casual viewer.
- *The Winged Avenger*, mentioned above on Page 8, is, in an episode of *The Avengers*, a killer vigilante superhero who appears to make the leap from comic books to real life.
- *Flick* is, like *Clint*, a magazine whose title, when drawn as "FLICK," appears to be quite a different word.
- *The Trump* can be seen in *Black Dossier*, Pages 29–48.
- *Selwyn Pike* is mentioned above, on Page 29, Panel 2.
- "Me Con?" is a reference to the Mekon, the opponent of British space hero Dan Dare, mentioned on Page 10, Panel 8. The figure here is drawn like the Mekon.
- The *Bradgate Argus* is probably a reference to the *Argus*, the daily newspaper for Sussex. The *Argus* puts out different editions for different areas of Sussex, and in the world of *Dossier* it probably puts out an edition for Bradgate.
- *J. Arthur* and *Hand Shandy* are British slang phrases for masturbation.
- *True Sweat* is a reference to the British term "true sweat" for the Men's Adventure magazines of the 1950s and 1960s.

Kevin O'Neill notes:

La Mode Magazine featured in a very funny Phil Silvers *Sgt. Bilko* episode about a new army uniform scam.

The Bat, I believe, first appeared in the Dean Martin-Jerry Lewis movie *Artists and Models* (1955), set partially in a Hollywood version of the comic book business. Dean was a comic artist and Shirley MacLaine was his model!

Antichrist, *Primrose Quarterly*, *Culture Quick Scrapbook*, and *Secrets of Paris* are all from George Orwell's *Keep the Aspidistra Flying*.

Scandalous is from the Terry-Thomas movie *The Naked Truth* (1957).

Panel 2. Mildly dirty postcards like this were common in the 1950s, though never sold in respectable establishments. They were known as "French postcards."

The artist's name is given as "Kano." This may be a reference to "Kalo," the *New Yorker* cartoonist invented by "Seth" (a.k.a. Gregory Gallant) and featured in the graphic novel *It's a Good Life If You Don't Weaken* (1996). In the novel, Kalo's cartoons are similar to Kano's here.

Kevin O'Neill notes:

> Postcard artist name I've used is Kayo (or K.O. for Kevin O'Neill). The style is pure Donald McGill (1875-1962). Much loved (and prosecuted), his saucy postcards are the essence of the classic British seaside experience.
>
> The vicar on the card behind is from a McGill whose caption read...
> "That was a splendid sermon you gave about 'the foolish virgins,' vicar. I'll never be one again!"

Panel 3. "Bove—" is a reference to Bovex, another of the products mentioned in Orwell's *Keep the Aspidistra Flying*. Chapter One of the novel describes this poster: "A spectacled rat-faced clerk, with patent-leather hair, sitting at a cafe table grinning over a white mug of Bovex. 'Corner Table enjoys his meal with Bovex', the legend ran."

Panel 4. "Seaview" may be a reference to the BBC comedy *Seaview* (1983–1985), about a seaside hotel.

Page 94. Panel 1. This is the Cornelius family again, from Page 20, Panels 2–8. I'm not sure why the figure in the middle is frozen solid, however.

The rolled-up comic book in Jerry or Franky's back pocket is *The Trump*.

Panel 2. M is contemplating the bust of Moriarty on Page 14, Panel 1.

In *1984*, rooms are equipped with "telescreens" (large televisions) through which the Party can broadcast and can spy on people. This office, being M's, would have had a very large telescreen. The bricked-over space is probably where the telescreen went.

Panel 3. Presumably, the two pictures on the left of the panel and the picture on the far right are of the Famous Five. The picture Bunter is holding is his sister, Bessie. The picture above and to Bunter's right, however, appears to be Anthony Buckeridge's J. C. T. Jennings, who appeared in twenty-five novels from 1950–1994. Jennings is an impulsive, spirited schoolboy.

Kevin O'Neill notes:
> Left to right behind Bunter are Harry Wharton, Lord Mauleverer, and Bob Cherry.

Page 95. Panel 1. A wrapper for one of the "Heros the Spartan" condoms advertised on Page 93, Panel 1 can be seen in the lower right-hand corner.

Page 96. The "Iron Mountains" around the North Pole are a reference to the Iron Mountains in the anonymously-written *Voyage au Centre de la Terre* (1821).

Regarding the humanoid animals in the boxes in the upper right, see Pages 178 and following.

The eye-in-the-pyramid, which also appears on the American dollar bill, represents the All-Seeing Eye of God and of the Freemasons.

The box-and-parachute below the eye-in-the-pyramid is the craft used by Dyrcona to go to the countries of the Sun in Hercule Savinien Cyrano de Bergerac's *L'histoire Des États et Empires du Soleil* (1662).

The blinking police box is the T.A.R.D.I.S. (Time And Relative Dimension In Space), Dr. Who's time- and spacecraft in *Doctor Who*.

"See now the symmetry of God's design…
Fit only for the dead, or disappeared."
This poem is clearly Prospero's account of visiting the Blazing World in 1695, as described in *League* v2, and strikes an ominous note.

"Here, by the testament of Captain Clegg…"
Captain Clegg, seen on Page 44, Panel 4, is a member of the 18th-century League of Extraordinary Gentlemen.

"…is found the Streaming Kingdoms, wherein transformed spirits of drowned mariners are ruled by an intelligence called only 'His Imperial Wetness.'"
The Streaming Kingdom is from Jules Supervielle's *L'Enfant de la Haute Mer* (1931). The Streaming Kingdom is an aquatic kingdom under the English Channel, near the mouth of the Seine. It is inhabited by water-breathing humans who must drown before they can enter the Kingdom. The Kingdom is ruled by a creature called His Royal Wetness.

Captain Clegg's encounter with the Streaming Kingdom is mentioned in *League* v2.

"…the much talked of 'water-babes.'"
The "water-babies" appeared in Charles Kingsley's *The Water-Babies* (1863). *The Water-Babies* is about Tom, a chimney sweep, who accidentally falls in a river. His body dies, but his soul is changed into a "water baby" by a group of faeries.

"—L.G."
"L.G." stands for Lemuel Gulliver, from Swift's *Gulliver's Travels*. Gulliver was a member of the 18th-century League.

I'm unsure whether the Emmanuel College, Cambridge stamp is a reference to anything in particular or simply a hint that this map can be found in the Emmanuel College Library, in the way that similar rarities can be found at the Bodleian Library at Oxford or in the British Library.

I don't know what the symbols in the lower left mean. Perhaps the third symbol, a fractured Masonic compass and right angle, is a hint that ordinary mathematics don't work in the Blazing World?

1666 is the date when Margaret Cavendish's *The Blazing World* was published. 1695 is the date when this map was published, as is mentioned on Page 25.

The man in the glass ball is the Time Traveller from H. G. Wells's *The Time Machine* (1895).

"The Radiance in these climes is of two partes,
One Red like Mars, the other Venus-green,
With variously glass'd pince-nez required
comprised of ruby and of em'rald both.
Thus furnished, we may fill our eyes and ears
With lights and musics come from higher spheres."
In other words, these extradimensional places are only visible through the use of 3-D glasses which have red and green filters. Note that the skeleton head above this passage has a red and a green eye.

The skeleton's hand, pointing to the Blazing World, is a riff on the cliché of pirate films in which the map of buried treasure has a drawing of a skeleton on it, similarly pointing the way.

Kevin O'Neill notes:
> Emmanuel College Cambridge is associated with Lemuel Gulliver (according to Swift), and he would have passed it into the library collection.
>
> The man in the glass ball is the space traveller from "Les Estats et empires du soleil" (1662).

Page 97/*Shadows in the Steam* 1. "Managed to save a copy of this from Litpol's furnaces."
There is no "Litpol" mentioned in *1984*, but it is probably a

Newspeak abbreviation for "Literature Police," hence the mention of its job of burning books.

"Meesons and Co. Limited" is a reference to H. Rider Haggard's *Mr. Meeson's Will* (1888), a crime novel about Mr. Meeson, an unscrupulous publisher.

Page 98/*Shadows in the Steam* 2. "…universally acclaimed professor of mathematics, the esteemed James Moriarty, since deceased."
Professor Moriarty is the archenemy of Sherlock Holmes.

"…the Hunnish 'Luft-Piraten,' Captain Mors…"
"Captain Mors" is the lead character of *Der Luftpirat und Sein Lenkbares Luftschiff*, a German dime novel published from 1908–1911. Captain Mors, the "Man with the Mask," is a Captain Nemo-like character, fleeing from mankind with a crew of Indians and involved in a prolonged fight against tyranny and evil, on Earth as well as on Venus, Mars, and the rest of the solar system. Captain Mors was mentioned in *League* v1 and v2.

"…his French rival, the repulsive Monsieur Robur."
"Robur" is the creation of Jules Verne and appeared in two books: *Robur le Conquerant* (1886) and *Maître du Monde* (1904). In *Robur the Conqueror*, Robur, a brilliant engineer and vehement proponent of heavier-than-air travel, invents a technologically advanced "flying machine," the Albatross, and uses it to kidnap several partisans of lighter-than-air travel and take them around the world. In *Master of the World*, Robur returns, now a dangerous megalomaniac intent on conquering the world. Robur was mentioned in *League* v1 and v2.

Verne never specified that Robur was French, but it would be in character for British intelligence to assume he was.

"…the purchase of heliotropes, imported from the remote nation of Bengodi…"
Bengodi appears in Giovanni Boccaccio's *Decameron* (1353), a very influential collection of Italian stories, some of which were later used by Chaucer in his *Canterbury Tales*. The notion of heliotropes

as a source for the Invisible Man's invisibility was raised by Moore in *League* v2.

"…the probably-invented 'horla' creature that the French claimed to have captured in the later 1880s."
The Horla, an invisible monster, was created by Guy de Maupassant and appeared in "The Horla" (1885).

"…unpleasant graveyard desecrations up in the vicinity of Highgate Cemetery, with decapitated corpses and the like in evidence."
This is clearly meant to refer to Bram Stoker's *Dracula*, but in the novel the cemetery scenes take place in Kingstead, not Highgate. There is a real Highgate Cemetery, in Highgate in London, and the fictional Kingstead Cemetery is supposed to be based on Highgate Cemetery. Moore is likely referencing the "Highgate Vampire" phenomenon of the late 1960s and early 1970s, in which, in proper urban legend style, a supernatural creature was seen in the cemetery, and in which a corpse was supposedly decapitated.

Page 99/*Shadows in the Steam* 3. "…I had arranged to meet with her beside the lake there in St. James's Park."
St. James's Park is the meeting place of many spies in cold war fiction.

"…the group of islands called the Riallaro Archipelago…"
The Riallaro Archipelago appears in John Macmillan Brown's *Riallaro, the Archipelago of Exiles* (1901) and *Limanora, the Island of Progress* (1903), both about island utopias near the Antarctic.

Page 100/*Shadows in the Steam* 4. "One, I think, was a Malay, another being a tall Negro with the elegant bone-structure and near-indigo complexion that I most associate with Africa's Ivory Coast."
These two are crew members from the *Pequod*, from Melville's *Moby-Dick*. The "tall Negro" is Daggoo, and the Malay is Queequeg.

"There was an older man that I assumed to be American whose voice had a New England twang about it…"
As seen in *League* v1 and v2, Ishmael, from Melville's *Moby-Dick*, is one of Captain Nemo's crewmen.

"…and a fellow similarly aged, dressed up in what appeared to be an ancient, threadbare uniform such as were common during the Sepoy Rebellion."
Perhaps this is Nemo himself?

"…a young and rather well-built Englishman whose name, I later learned, was Jack."
As seen in *League* v1 and v2, Broad Arrow Jack, from the E. Harcourt Burrage 1886 serial of the same name, is a member of Nemo's crew.

"…a lovely Indian woman… and the small child she held swaddled in her arms… who had the biggest, brownest and most knowing eyes that I have ever seen. I later learned that these two were the estranged wife and daughter of the man I had been sent to find…."
This is Nemo's wife and daughter. The daughter, per *League* v2, is named "Janni" and will appear in *League* v3, a.k.a. *Century*.

Page 101/*Shadows in the Steam* 5. **Panel 1**. The writing on the paper is Devanāgarī, the main script used in the Hindi, Marathi, and Sanskrit languages, and transliterates as "kaptān nīmo / prins dakār"—that is, "Captain Nemo, Prince Dakkar."

Panel 2. "Captain Kettle" is a reference to the short, cigar-smoking, red-bearded, pugnacious, brutal seaman Captain Kettle, created by C. J. Cutcliffe Hyne and appearing in stories, a novel, and several films from 1895 to the 1920s.

Page 103/*Shadows in the Steam* 7. "…a disastrous circumnavigation of Antarctica attempted three years previously…."
This was described at some length in *League* v2.

"It seems to me the British Empire has always encountered difficulty in distinguishing between its heroes and its monsters…."
This quote was used on the back cover of the first issue of *League*.

Page 104. The "Golden Rivet" is a bit of naval folklore. Supposedly, every ship has one rivet made of gold, and old sailors like to send young sailors on snipe hunts to find the golden rivet. Sometimes the search for the golden rivet is meant to get a young and attractive sailor alone so as to have sex with him (British naval tradition being, per Churchill, nothing but rum, sodomy, and the lash).

Pages 106–107. I'm combining panels and the text from the Key here.
Panel 1. "…the late eccentric visionary Selwyn Cavor, driving force behind 1901's lunar expedition and the subsequent annexation of the moon as part of the British Empire."
In H. G. Wells's *The First Men in the Moon*, Professor Selwyn Cavor is the inventor of "cavorite," a gravity-canceling alloy ("this possible substance opaque to gravitation") which Cavor and his friend Mr. Bedford, the narrator of the novel, use to travel to the moon. In the novel, the moon is inhabited by malign Selenties. The novel ends with Cavor trapped on the moon and the revelation that the Selenites' ruler, the Grand Lunar, is malign. The "subsequent annexation" answers the question about what Great Britain's response to this revelation would be.

Panel 2. "…Napoleonic naval hero Horatio Hornblower…."
Horatio Hornblower is the hero of eleven novels, from 1937–1967, by C. S. Forester. Hornblower is an officer in the Royal Navy and performs various heroics in the Napoleonic Wars.

In our world, the statue in Trafalgar Square is of Lord Nelson (1758–1805), to celebrate his victory in the Battle of Trafalgar (1805). Horatio's appearance here in place of Nelson is another of Moore's replacements of real people for fictional ones, implying that, as in the unfinished novel *Hornblower And The Crisis* (1967), it was Hornblower rather than Nelson who was most responsible for the British victory at Trafalgar.

Panel 3. "The Diogenes Club"
The Diogenes Club is a gentleman's club in the Sherlock Holmes stories. Quoting Sherlock Holmes, in "The Adventure of the Greek Interpreter" (1893):

> There are many men in London, you know, who, some from shyness, some from misanthropy, have no wish for the company of their fellows. Yet they are not averse to comfortable chairs and the latest periodicals. It is for the convenience of these that the Diogenes Club was started, and it now contains the most unsociable and unclubable men in town. No member is permitted to take the least notice of any other one. Save in the Stranger's Room, no talking is, under any circumstances, allowed, and three offences, if brought to the notice of the committee, render the talker liable to expulsion. My brother was one of the founders, and I have myself found it a very soothing atmosphere.

"…with a surprising number of Prime Ministers and cabinet members frequently popping in for a chat."
Despite the Club's purpose as a place of silence, Sherlock Holmes does visit his brother Mycroft at the Club, in "The Adventure of the Greek Interpreter," and (according to the text) has consulted with him on various cases in the past. Given Mycroft's brilliance—and as mentioned in "The Adventure of the Bruce Partington Plans" (1912), Mycroft's role as "the most indispensable man in the country… the conclusions of every department are passed to him, and he is the central exchange, the clearing-house, which makes out the balance"—it's natural that high-ranking government officials would visit him.

Panel 5. "…with a blackface actor impersonating the Captain…."
Given the English-reading public's traditional discomfort with Nemo's identity as an angry Indian, it should come as no surprise that far more white men have portrayed Nemo than non-whites. In fact, depending on how one defines "white," Omar Sharif (half-Egyptian, half-French) was the first non-white actor to portray

Nemo, in the 1973 French miniseries *L'Île Mystérieuse*. The first Indian to portray Nemo was Nasiruddin Shah, in the 2003 film of *League of Extraordinary Gentlemen*. Few of these actors appeared in darkface, however, which was a stage convention. The 1916 adaptation of *20,000 Leagues Under the Sea* had Allen Holubar, as Nemo, in blackface.

Panel 7. I don't believe that the writing in the panel is more than squiggles.

"...neighbourhood's good fortune to a local philanthropist, a doctor who protects the area."
This is a reference to Fu Manchu, from Sax Rohmer's novels. In the novels, Limehouse is under his rule.

"Here be South Londoners" is a reference to medieval maps on which "Here be Dragons" would be written on unknown areas of the map. Its use in reference to Londoners south of the Thames is a jibe at the way those north of the Thames have always regarded those south of the river.

Page 108. "...unsettling reports concerning the New England town of Arkham, Massachusetts."
In H. P. Lovecraft's stories, Arkham is a city, located on the North Shore of Massachusetts, which is the home to Miskatonic University. Arkham is a fictional city based on Salem, Massachusetts.

"Returning during the September of that same year after some unpleasant exploits..."
Those exploits were described in *League* v2.

"...the communitarian Phalanstery movement, then but recently established in the western English county Avondale."
A "phalanstery" is a self-sustaining commune. Avondale is from Grant Allen's "The Child of the Phalanstery" (1884) and is a well-managed phalanstery with the unfortunate habit of killing all crippled or deformed children.

"…in the lost land of Zuvendis…."
Zuvendis appears in H. Rider Haggard's *Allan Quatermain* (1887).

"…the incarcerated lunatic Dr Eric Bellman…."
Dr. Eric Bellman appears in Lewis Carroll's poem "The Hunting of the Snark" (1876). In the poem, Bellman and the Bellman Expedition go hunting for a snark, only to find that the gentle snark is in fact the dreaded boojum.

"…the recently-resurfaced brother of Mycroft Holmes at his home in Fulworth."
The brother of Mycroft Holmes is of course Sherlock Holmes, and the recent resurfacing is Holmes's return from apparent death, chronicled in "The Adventure of the Empty House" (1903).

"…the Anglo-Russian Convention…."
The Anglo-Russian Convention took place from October 1905 to August 1907, at which time an entente was reached essentially ending the Great Game of espionage, addressing Afghanistan and Tibet, and dividing Persia, the cause of much Russian–British antagonism, into three spheres of influence.

"…a dockside hotel worker and sometime prostitute named Diver…."
This is a reference to Jenny Diver, from John Gay's *Beggar's Opera* (1728), *Polly* (1728), and Bertolt Brecht's *Three Penny Opera* (1928). In *Three Penny Opera*, Jenny Diver sings "Pirate Jenny," about "the Black Freighter" which is coming to punish the guilty and take her away from her miserable life. "Pirate Jenny" was an influence on the "Tales Of The Black Frigate" section in Moore's *Watchmen*.

Page 109. "Zebed, Marsh & Sons of Innsmouth."
In H. P. Lovecraft's "The Shadow Over Innsmouth" (1936), Captain Marsh was the man who in the 1830s brought the worship of the Deep Ones back to the Massachusetts town of Innsmouth. His family remained a power in Innsmouth until the 1930s.

    The fishlike appearance on the faces of the fishmongers is

the "Innsmouth Look," a facial malformation indicative of their genetic descent from the Deep Ones.

"Curwen Street Market Square"
Curwen Street was introduced in August Derleth's "The House on Curwen Street" (1944), a Cthulhu Mythos story. Curwen Street was named after the wicked sorcerer in Lovecraft's *The Case of Charles Dexter Ward* (1941).

"Celebrate Wicker Rapist Day in Coradine"
In Julius Caesar's *Commentaries About the Gallic Wars*, he says that the Druids made a wicker statue, put human beings inside it, and set it on fire as human sacrifice. The modern world is more familiar with the burning of the Wicker Man from the 1973 British and 2006 American films of that name. Coradine is in W. H. Hudson's *A Crystal Age* (1887) and is a kind of utopia set in northern Scotland.

"Milosis Cemetery, Zuvendis"
This is the supposed grave of Allan Quatermain. The grave to the right, with the axe sticking out of it, is the grave of Umslopogaas, Quatermain's friend.

"The Fantippo Daily Mail. Hut Prices Plummet. Us Foreigners to Blame"
"Fantippo" appears in Hugh Lofting's *Doctor Dolittle's Post Office* (1924) and *Doctor Dolittle and the Secret Lake* (1949). Fantippo is a kingdom in West Africa which adopted the English postal system after Fantippo's ruler, King Koko, heard about the system and was impressed by it. The "Daily Mail" is a jibe at the reactionary British tabloid *Daily Mail*, which is racist in its treatment of immigration issues and has in recent months spent a great deal of time talking about soaring housing prices in the U.K.

Page 110. Lorimer E. Brackett was a publisher of picture postcards of Monhegan, Maine. The stylized font of "Post Card, Lorimer E. Brackett, Arkham, Mass." is in the style of Brackett.

"Met one R. Carter who took us to a ruin near Dunwich—beastly business. Mina almost abducted by something ghastly...."

"R. Carter" is Randolph Carter, who appeared in five of Lovecraft's stories. Carter, who Lovecraft partially based on himself, is a morose man who has adventures in various dreamlands. The near-abduction is described in *League* v1.

"Please excuse the jerky handwriting as I am currently racked with grief."

This is a reference to an old joke, possibly one appearing on the seaside postcards seen on Page 93, Panel 2, about a letter from a mother to son which reads something like, "Your poor father is suffering from a bout of erotomania and cannot be restrained from making love to me at inopportune moments whatever I am doing at any time of day or night. Please excuse shaky handwriting." The reader is free to draw his or her own conclusions about why Mina would have jerky handwriting in this case.

Page 111. "Octavia"
Octavia appears in Italo Calvino's *Invisible Cities* (1972), in which Marco Polo tells Kublai Khan about several fabulous cities in the Khan's empire.

"Greetings from Sussex"
See the notes to Page 112.

"L'Opera de Paris"
This is a reference to Gaston Leroux's *The Phantom of the Opera* (1911), with the unmasked, grotesque Phantom appearing in the upper right corner of the photo. If anyone else in this painting is a reference, I'm unaware of it.

"A Royal Occasion"
This image is a reference to a painting of some kind, I believe, but I've been unable to locate the original.

A number of the characters in this scene are from Enid Blyton's twenty-four Noddy novels and eight Noddy television shows, from 1949 to the present. Noddy is a little wooden doll who lives in Toyland and has various adventures. One of his friends is

Big-Ears the gnome, who can be seen in shadow in the lower left. The two yellow bears on the right are Tessie Bear and Master Tubby Bear, two more of Noddy's friends.

Page 112. "Sussex is dreadful, but I've met the gentleman I came here to visit. Yes, it's really him."
In Doyle's "The Adventure of the Second Stain" (1904), Sherlock Holmes has retired to the Sussex Downs to raise bees.

"Dear Tom, Well, it's over, though in truth they very nearly finished us. Fantomas was a horror, and the albino almost as bad."
See Page 113.

Page 113. The characters in the image are Dr. Mabuse, Dr. Caligari, unknown, Dr. Rotwang, and Maria.

Dr. Mabuse was created by Norbert Jacques and appeared in three novels and eight films from 1921 to 1964. Mabuse is a German criminal mastermind intent on world domination; worse still, he is a psychiatrist who uses his psychiatric knowledge and abilities at hypnotism for his own nefarious ends.

Dr. Caligari was created by Hans Janowitz and Carl Mayer and appeared in the film *Das Cabinet des Dr. Caligari* (1920). Dr. Caligari is the head of an insane asylum in a rural village in the mountains of Germany.

Dr. Rotwang was created by Fritz Lang and Thea von Harbou and appeared in the film *Metropolis* (1927). Dr. Rotwang is a mad scientist in the city of Metropolis.

Maria was created by Fritz Lang and Thea von Harbou and appeared in *Metropolis*. She is an android created by Rotwang to foment rebellion among the workers of Metropolis.

The sheet of paper to the right of Mabuse has the letter "M" on it. This is a reference to the Fritz Lang and Thea von Harbou film *M* (1931), about a child murderer in Berlin. The presence of the paper with the letter M on it here may be because the group is investigating the murders or because policeman Karl Beckert investigates both the child murderer in *M* and Mabuse in the first Mabuse film.

"...it is indeed possible that this Teutonic group played some part in the sinister activities that plagued the coronation of King George VI in 1910."
This will be covered in more detail in *League* v3, a.k.a. *Century*.

"...including a mesmerised assassin...."
In *Das Cabinet des Dr. Caligari*, the good doctor uses his hypnosis to manipulate one of his patients, Cesare, into carrying out murders while sleepwalking.

"...the ingenious criminal mastermind Arsene Lupin...."
Arsène Lupin was created by Maurice Leblanc and appeared in a number of stories and twenty novels and short story collections from 1905 to 1939. Lupin is the "Prince of Thieves," the archetypal Gentleman Thief of popular culture.

"The international arch-villain Monsieur Zenith, for example, was a pure albino who used drugs that overcame the weaknesses of his condition and indeed allowed him physical abilities beyond the ordinary."
In the Sexton Blake stories, Zenith uses opium to relieve himself of the boredom of life. In Michael Moorcock's Elric books, Elric (who, as mentioned above on Page 46, Panel 2, was inspired by Zenith) takes drugs to fortify himself. In recent stories, such as those in his *Metatemporal Detective* (2007) collection, Monsieur Zenith is shown to be a dream that Elric once had.

"...the unnerving Nyctalope. This creature, more some new, sophisticated breed of animal than man, had beating in his breast a manmade heart superior to the human model. He could breathe with equal ease in both our normal atmosphere and also underwater, and his eyes were such that the most stygian, impenetrable darkness seemed to him as brightly lit as if in the full glare of noon."
The Nyctalope was created by Jean de La Hire and appeared in sixteen novels from 1908 to 1954. He is the adventurer Léo Sainte-

Claire ("Jean de Sainclair" in some novels), who fights a wide variety of exotic evils with the help of a stalwart band of assistants. (In some ways the Nyctalope is Doc Savage *avant la lettre*.) The Nyctalope once fought a water-breathing creature but cannot himself breathe underwater.

"...the horror Fantomas."
Fantômas was created by Pierre Souvestre and Marcel Allain and appeared in forty-three novels from 1911 to 1963. Fantômas is "the Lord of Terror" and "the Genius of Evil," a French crime boss who murders with abandon and aplomb.

"It also seems he was precocious in the guarding of his true identity, in that those few early acquaintances of Fantomas who lived to tell the tale could not between them give an accurate description of the man."
Fantômas is a master of disguise and no one ever knows what he looks like.

Page 114. "...something in the voice and movements of this quite demonic being seemed to indicate that Fantomas might be a woman."
Fantômas is on occasion impersonated by his daughter Hélène.

"...the tomb of Launcelot up in Northumberland..."
Bamburgh Castle, in Northumberland, stands on the site of an earlier fort, built in the middle of the 5th century. The original fort's name was "Din Guayrdi." This name was taken by the Arthurian romancers, including Malory, and given to Launcelot as his home. Launcelot's tomb being there is referred to in *League* v2.

"...the kingdom of Evarchia."
Evarchia appears in Brigid Brophy's *Palace Without Chairs* (1978), a modern-day fairy tale set in an imaginary Eastern European socialist monarchy.

"Jean Robur, however, was no first-time aeronaut as the Professor had been, nor was his craft powered by Cavorite, which Robur had dismissed as 'unscientific.'"

One of the reasons that Jules Verne disliked H. G. Wells was that Verne attempted to base his creations on facts and hard science, while Wells took a looser approach. The classic quote from Verne about this is "I get my voyagers to the Moon with gun cotten—something you can buy in any store and Mr Wells uses a totally mythical substance! Pah! Where is this Cavorite? Let him produce it!" Clearly Robur is voicing Verne's views.

"...the monstrously disfigured madman Erik had resided while he carried out his terror campaign as the Opera's so-called 'Phantom.'"
Erik is the Phantom of the Opera.

Page 115. "...a subterranean Graveyard of Unwritten Books..." The Graveyard of Unwritten Books was created by Nedim Gürsel and appeared in *Son Tramway* (1900). The Graveyard, also known as the "Well of Locks," is the home of all books forbidden by authorities across the world.

"...or an underground land lit up by luminous balloons...."
This is a reference to André Maurois's *Patapoufs et Filifers* (1930), one of Maurois's juvenilia. In the novel, there is a giant underground cavern lit by balloons.

"...Jean Robur's airship shot down at the battle of the Somme...."
At the end of *Maître du Monde*, Robur's ship crashes into the sea, but his body is never found, although he is presumed dead.

The figures in the image are: the Nyctalope, Arsène Lupin, Robur, Zenith the Albino, and Fantômas.

Page 116. "What Ho, Gods of the Abyss" is written in the wonderful style of P. G. Wodehouse, and is a loving pastiche of Wodehouse's Jeeves and Wooster stories and novels, combined with the concepts of H. P. Lovecraft.

The idea of combining Wodehouse and Lovecraft has been done before, by Yr. Humble Annotator in "Cthulhu Fhtagn, Eh

Wot, Ha Ha!" (1996) and by Peter Cannon in *Scream for Jeeves* (1994).

"...that same Augustus, he of the Fink-Nottles...."
Augustus "Gussie" Fink-Nottle is a friend and schoolmate of Bertie Wooster. Gussie is described as a "teetotal bachelor with a face like a fish," which may be the Innsmouth Look (see Page 109) and would explain why he was chosen by the Old Ones in this story.

"...my Aunt Dahlia...."
Bertie's Aunt Dahlia Travers is rough but affectionate toward Bertie.

"...cross-country runs at dear old Malvern House, when I was younger."
Bertie and Gussie attended Malvern House Preparatory School.

"...my regrettable Aunt Agatha who uses battery-acid as a gargle and shaves with a lathe...."
Bertie's Aunt Agatha Gregson is quite fearsome: "When Aunt Agatha wants you to do a thing you do it, or else you find yourself wondering why those fellows in the olden days made such a fuss when they had trouble with the Spanish Inquisition."

"'...I may write a piece on for *Milady's Boudoir*.'"
Milady's Boudoir is a weekly woman's newspaper that Aunt Dahlia runs.

Page 117. "...a symptom of Peabody's illness, as I later learned, had made him sensitive to light...."
See below.

"...I was reminded by his rasping buzz...."
See below.

"'...its blossoms shall with certainty attract the Shambler in Darkness.'"
This very Lovecraftian-sounding creature is Moore's invention, although it may be a reference to Robert Bloch's "Shambler From the Stars" mentioned on Page 26 above.

"…my intelligence contained in an appropriate vessel."
See below.

"…an endearing rogue called something like 'Cool Lulu'…"
"Cool Lulu" is a Woosterian spin on Lovecraft's alien god Cthulhu.

"…sleeping and dreaming at a place called Riley…."
"Riley" is a Woosterian spin on Lovecraft's sunken city R'Lyeh.

"…some old goat who had misspent his youth so badly that he had a thousand young…"
Lovecraft's alien Shug-Niggurath is the "Black Goat of the Woods with a Thousand Young."

"…the three-lobed burning eye…."
The three-lobed burning eye is one of the avatars of Lovecraft's Nyarlathotep.

"Here he nodded to some dusty copper cylinders on a high shelf…."
The mentions on this page of Peabody's sensitivity to light, rasping voice, intelligence contained in a vessel, and copper cylinders are all references to Lovecraft's "The Whisperer in Darkness," in which a race of aliens, the Mi-Go, remove humans' brains and place them in cylinders so that the humans can travel across space. The Mi-Go then occupy the humans' bodies, during which time their voices are raspy and they are sensitive to light.

"…he might get in contact with a remote cousin of his, on the Silversmith side of his family…."
Jeeves's uncle is Charlie Silversmith, a butler at Deverill Hall.

"…the town of Goatswood, close to Brichester, for the occasion."
Goatswood and Brichester are in the Severn Valley, which in the stories of Ramsey Campbell is a location for many Cthulhu Mythos activities.

"...three or four feet long and roughly barrel shaped, its head resembling an elaborately ugly starfish and some ghastly tattered things that jutted from what we assumed to be its torso, these resembling fins or wings...."

This is an Elder Thing, which are mentioned in various H. P. Lovecraft stories and appeared in his *At the Mountains of Madness* (1936). The Elder Things are an alien species who were the first aliens to visit Earth.

Page 119. "The foursome from the Museum were in combat with the brute, the girlish-looking chap Orlando hacking gamely at it with a large and terribly impressive sword...."

The sword Orlando uses here, and which can be seen in the illustration in the lower right, may be the same sword seen on the cover of *Black Dossier*. If so, the discoloration and corroded edge would be the result of the blade coming into contact with the alien flesh.

Kevin O'Neill notes:
> Orlando is pictured as if drawn by someone who has not seen Excalibur so has illustrated a conventional sword.

Page 121. **Panel 3**. Courtfield is the town nearest to Greyfriars.

Kevin O'Neill notes:
> The telephone number shown is the correct one for Greyfriars. My friend, the writer/collector Norman Wright, provided invaluable Greyfriars information for us.

Panel 6. And so is finally explained the "Mother" Bunter got his postal orders from.

Page 122. Panel 1. "Roy Carson Horror!"
Roy Carson is a British hardboiled detective created by Denis McLoughlin and appearing in *Roy Carson Comic* #1–#44.

"'Splash' Kirby Exclusive"
Arthur "Splash" Kirby is a reporter for the *Daily Post* in various Sexton Blake stories.

"Friardale Gazette"
Greyfriars School is just to the north of the village of Friardale.

If the mother and children seen here are a reference to anyone, I'm unaware of it.

Kevin O'Neill notes:
> The concerned parents are sending young *Mike* from *The Knockout Comic* (1945-57) into disgrace. The *Mike* strip, drawn by Eric Roberts, was unusual in that he had a girlfriend, Dimps, a unique feature in post-war British comics. The consequences of such bomb site adventures are obvious to behold!
>
> The *Friardale Gazette*, lower right, was featured in the Greyfriars stories.

Panel 2. The girl or woman in the lower left would seem to be Vera, from the Giles Family (see Page 12, Panel 7 above).

Kevin O'Neill notes:
> Just behind Mina is Bert Cert from the *Daily Mirror* strip *The Flutters*. In front of Mina, giving the eye to Vera, is *Romeo Brown* (1954-62), another *Daily Mirror* strip character.

Panel 5. Kevin O'Neill notes:
> Passenger in background is reading *Sporting Snips*, also featured in the Greyfriars stories. Author Frank Richards, a.k.a. Charles Hamilton, was an inveterate gambler.

Panel 6. "How shall we reach Dunbayne from Birmingham, incidentally?"
See Page 170, Panel 1 below.

Page 123. Panel 2. The bus driver may be Stan Butler, from the British comedy *On the Buses* (1969–1973).

Panel 3. "Norma Desmond" is a reference to the aging actress in Billy Wilder's *Sunset Boulevard* (1950).

Kevin O'Neill notes:
> *Woman's Dream* is a fictional magazine briefly seen in the British film *Left Right and Centre* (1959).

Panel 4. Ambridge and Borchester are towns in the BBC radio soap *The Archers* (1951–present).

These two children were previously seen on Page 82, Panel 1.

Pages 124–125. The squat gray building in the upper left of the panel is the Space Gun from *Things to Come* (1936), the film version of H. G. Wells's *The Shape of Things to Come*, mentioned on Page 16 above. The Space Gun is used to fire a manned capsule into space.

The gray ship on the left-hand side of the panel, above the man with the pipe, may be from *Things to Come*.

The man with the pipe and his shorter companion are Dan Dare (smoking his ever-present pipe) and his sidekick Digby.

The ship next to it, with the "Kingfisher-8" insignia, is a reference to *Dan Dare*. The Kingfisher was the first manned rocket sent to Venus, but it was mysteriously destroyed, leading to Dan Dare's trip to Venus and encounter with the Mekon.

I'm unsure what the blue ship to the right of *Kingfisher-8* is a reference to.

The red ship in the lower right-hand corner of Page 124 is the titular vehicle from Gerry Anderson's TV show *Supercar*. The figure raising its hands in front of Supercar is Mitch, the pet monkey of Jimmy Gibson, a ten-year-old member of the Supercar team. To the rear of Supercar, in the lower left-hand corner of Page 125, can be seen Mike Mercury, Supercar's test pilot.

I'm not sure what the horizontal green craft (with the "BP" initials, presumably for British Petroleum) or the large horizontal blue craft are references to.

The small, light blue ship on the long track in the upper center of Page 124 is the *Fireball XL5*, from the British TV series *Fireball XL5*. *Fireball XL5* was a Gerry and Sylvia Anderson flying-marionettes-in-the-future show.

The white rocket commencing liftoff in the upper right-hand corner of Page 124 is the rocket from the movie *Flight to Mars*, seen on the cover of *Dossier*.

The green, vertical rocket in the upper half of Page 125 is from the "Space Ace" comic strip and various comics from 1953–1963. "Space Ace" is about a Texas sheriff, Ace Hart, who is given immunity to radioactivity by a fortuitous meteorite fall and becomes "Ace Hart—Space Squadron Commander." The green ship here is his *LS1*.

The apparent ship to its right is the Skylon tower from the Festival of Britain, mentioned above on Page 1.

The red, horizontal ship with the "Alpha 7" insignia appeared in an issue of *Adventure Annual* in the 1950s.

The small gray craft just above *Alpha 7* is Dan Dare's ship *Anastasia*.

The sign in the bottom right, reading "Danger, space ships taking off. Do not pass this point" appeared in the first episode of *Dan Dare*.

The bald man wearing the trench coat is Masterspy from *Supercar*, seen on Page 77, Panel 7.

Kevin O'Neill notes:
> Grey craft from left of Dan Dare and Digby is from *Eagle Annual* story "The Vanishing Scientists."

The blue ship to the right of Kingfisher-8 is in the style of the Captain Condor spaceships (*Lion, 1952-64)*, though perhaps a little more elaborate.

BP or British Petroleum fuel tankers were common enough in the 1950s, so a rocket fuel variant seemed to work well.

The pale blue/white rocket about to take off is from the 1956 *Journey Into Space* comic strip.

The red Alpha-7 is a continuation of the Alpha-3 that appeared in the text story *Destination Venus* by Jacques Pendower in the 1954 *New Spaceways* comic annual.

On the lower extreme left is an astronaut wearing a space suit in the style of those worn in the British film *Man in the Moon* (1960), starring Kenneth More.

Page 125. Panel 4. "Ordinary airplane pilot Gary Haliday at your service."

This is a reference to the BBC TV series *Garry Halliday* (1959), about two pilots, Garry Halliday and Bill Dodds, in pursuit of the criminal mastermind The Voice.

Haliday is holding one of the "I-Spy" books mentioned above on Page 88, Panel 4. There was no *I-Spy Rockets*, however.

Kevin O'Neill notes:
Girl in lower right is simply another St. Trinian's minx.

Page 126. Panel 1. "Well, I'm only a rocket-spotter, really, but I know a bit."

This is a reference to the British tradition of trainspotting and planespotting: ordinary citizens keeping notes on the various types of trains and planes they have spotted.

Panel 3. "We read about that when we were in the *States*. See-through robots made out of Perspex or something, all with names like Ronald, or Roderick..."

In *Fireball XL5*, the transparent robot Robert is the Fireball's pilot. Another robot with a see-through head made of Perspex was Robby the Robot, from the film *Forbidden Planet* (1956). "Roderick" is probably a reference to John Sladek's Roderick the Robot, from *Roderick* (1980) and *Roderick at Random* (1983). Roderick the Robot is the first intelligent robot to be built and has various misadventures.

The two boys in the lower left are Danny and Plug of the Bash Street Boys, mentioned above on Page 10, Panel 4.

The girl wielding the hockey stick is one of the feral schoolgirls from Ronald Searle's St. Trinian's School, from five books and six films from 1948 to 2007. The taller woman behind the feral schoolgirl is Alastair Sim in his role as either Amelia Fritton (in *Blue Murder at St. Trinian's* [1957]) or Millicent Fritton (in *The Belles of St. Trinian's* [1957]).

The boy running from the girl with the hockey stick is nigel molesworth from Ronald Searle's five books from 1953 to 1958. nigel molesworth is a schoolboy at St. Custard's who writes on various topics.

I believe that the girl in the lower right is the female member of the Bisto Kids, a ragamuffin boy and girl created by Wilfrid Owen in 1919 to sell the British Bisto foods.

Panels 3–4. "That's right. The X-Ls are American made."
"Well, I suppose they'd *have* to be. Who *else* thinks 'extra' stars with an *X*?"
"X" standing for "extra" is certainly an Americanism—hence Professor Xavier, of Marvel Comics' X-Men, calling his team the "X-Men" because they have an "extra" power—but this may also be a swipe at Hollywood, which abbreviated "League of Extraordinary Gentlemen" as "LXG."

Panel 5. "...somebody famous, like Morgan or Hawke or someone."
Morgan is Captain Morgan, mentioned on Page 10, Panel 8. Hawke

is Jeff Hawke, from the comic strip "Jeff Hawke, Space Rider" (1954–1975). Jeff Hawke, in the *XP5* rocket, goes 3,000 miles beyond the Moon and meets the Lords of the Universe, and then embarks on even wider-ranging adventures.

Panel 6. The older gentleman in the lower right-hand corner is Professor Popkiss, from *Supercar*. Popkiss was cocreator of the Supercar.

Page 127. Panel 2. The portly man wearing a monocle is Harris Tweed, created by John Ryan (who created Captain Pugwash, who was seen in *League* v2). "Harris Tweed, Special Agent," later "Harris Tweed, Extra Special Agent," later "Harris Tweed, Super Sleuth," appeared in the British comic *Eagle* from 1950–1956. Tweed is a bumbling, bluff, blundering detective and later spy who has an excellent reputation as a crime-fighter and spy-catcher, despite being incompetent at it.

I believe that the boy with the astronaut helmet is Boy, Tweed's youthful assistant, who is always responsible for getting Tweed out of the jams that Tweed gets himself into.

The mask on the child at the right is of a Worker Treen, the aliens ruled by the Mekon on Venus in the Dan Dare universe.

Panel 3. The seated alien is the Mekon. His head is so large that he cannot move himself, so he needs the hovering saucer he sits in to do it.

Kevin O'Neill notes:
> Green saucer-shaped craft above Mina's head is from Sydney Jordan's first *Jeff Hawke* strip—*Daily Express,* February 15th, 1955 (also visible in panel 6).

Panel 4. "Interplan— Police Patrol" is a reference to the Interplanetary Police Patrol, of which Captain Vic Valiant was the "Ace" in *Space Comics* (1953–1955).

"Kemlo" is a reference to the fifteen Kemlo books by "E. C. Eliot," a.k.a. Reginald Alec Martin. Kemlo and his friends live on Satellite Belt K, orbiting around the Earth.

The tentacled alien is the creature from the film *Fiend Without a Face*, seen above on Page 48, Panel 3.

Panel 5. "…the Westminster Abbey Fungus-Astronaut…."
This is a reference to Nigel Kneale's *The Quatermass Experiment*, in which a British spaceship thought to be lost crashes in Wimbledon. One of the astronauts turns out to be infected with a dangerous fungus alien and is eventually cornered in Westminster Abbey.

Page 128. Panel 1. This scene may be an homage to a highway scene in the film *Brazil*.

Kevin O'Neill notes:
> "Waggo with tail appeal" ad appears in the film *Man in the Moon* (1960).

Panel 7. The older, white-haired gentleman may be Dan Dare's sidekick Digby, last seen on Page 124.

Page 129. Panel 1. "He probably misses *Goldstein* and the Four-Minute *Hate*…."
In *1984*, the "Two Minute Hate" is a daily ritual in which Party members must watch a film showing Emmanuel Goldstein (see Page 16, Panel 8) and other enemies of the Party, and express their hatred for them.

Panel 2. The woman wearing pink may be Lady Penelope Creighton-Ward, most effective of the spies on the Gerry and Sylvia Anderson marionette adventure series on BBC, *Thunderbirds* (1965–1966).

Panels 3 and 7. Note the antennae sticking out of the heads of the male and female icons above the restrooms.

Page 130. Panel 1. The man in center right is wearing a button on which is the same character seen above on Page 16, Panel 9.

Kevin O'Neill notes:
> The man is wearing Freedonia button.

Panel 8. "Don't fancy a wager on Melchester hammering those Fulchester scoundrels, I suppose?"
The Melchester Rovers, mentioned on Page 9, Panel 1, is the team for which "Roy of the Rovers" plays. Fulchester is a fictional British town featured on the British TV series *Crown Court* (1972–1984) and in the British comic *Viz* (1979–present). One of the strips in *Viz*, "Billy the Fish" (1983–present), features the football team Fulchester United F.C., which is a parody of the Melchester Rovers.

If the two gentlemen in lower center of the panel are a reference to anyone, I'm unaware of it.

Kevin O'Neill notes:
> The two men in the lower center simply fear the anti-Semitic Hugo.

Page 131. Panel 1. These creatures are the Lazoones, mentioned above on Page 48, Panel 4. The Lazune who "talked with a lisp" is presumably Zoonie, the companion/pet of Venus and Steve Zodiac on *Fireball XL5*. The "others bit it to death" because, presumably, his lisp, slow drawl, and constant parroting of "Welcome Home" undoubtedly drove the other Lazoons to murder him.

Panel 3. The fat man is Harris Tweed—see the note to Page 127, Panel 2.

Page 133. Panel 1. "Indian wrestling" is an old English phrase for the martial arts, based on the English exposure to *pehlwani*, the Indian sport of wrestling.

Panel 4. "Anzia New Famine"
This may be a reference to the Azanian Empire, in Evelyn Waugh's *Black Mischief* (1932). Azania was mentioned in *League* v2.

Kevin O'Neill notes:
> Yes, Anzia is a *Black Mischief* reference.

Page 134. Panel 3. "Dixie Coll— Lesbian Expose."
This is a reference to the Wolf Mankowitz and Julian More play "Expresso Bongo" (1958, filmed in 1959). In the play, Dixie Collins is a young pop singer who helps protagonist Bert Rudge get out of a bad contract.

Page 136. Panel 1. Presumably these spaceships are further references, but I have not been able to identify them.

Kevin O'Neill notes:
> Blue space ship has heart symbol, seen on artist Ron Turner's Space Ace space craft, *Lone Star Annual* No. 5 (1955). I designed a less futuristic ship than Turner's to fit into the general look of the period. Ron Turner was an astonishing and inventive artist, a recluse we were told at IPC Magazines when I worked there as an office boy—in fact, one of my early jobs was doing the two colour separations on his *Wondercar* strip that appeared in *Whizzer and Chips* in the early 1970s.

Page 137. Panel 1. "...these oversized Dinky Toys."
Dinky Toys are a British brand of toy cars. Dinky was also the company responsible for producing toy models of the vehicles seen on the various Gerry and Sylvia Anderson series.

Panel 2. This car is one of the "space jeeps" which Dan Dare drove.

Panel 3. Kevin O'Neill notes:
> Allan is assembling a double-barreled Martian hither gun.

Page 138. Panels 1–2. I don't recognize the spaceships, if they are references.

Kevin O'Neill notes:
> Gray spacecraft marked UK-1 is the prototype British moon lander shown in the British film *Man in the Moon* (1960).

Page 139. Panel 4. "I read it in that dirty magazine you bought in America. *Stagman*, wasn't it?"

Stagman appears in John Sladek's *The Müller-Fokker Effect* (1973). In the novel, *Stagman* is a *Playboy* magazine analogue which is only successful because of its owner's frustrated libido.

Hugh Hefner's original choice for the title of *Playboy* was *Stag Party*.

Panel 5. "...stories by Kennaston..."

In James Branch Cabell's *The Cream of the Jest* (1917), writer Felix Kennaston's work begins to infect his reality.

"...Trout...."

In the novels of Kurt Vonnegut, Kilgore Trout is a hack writer of science fiction whose stories only appear in pornographic magazines.

"You just ogled that 'Montana Wildhack' floozy in the fold-out bit."

In Kurt Vonnegut's *Slaughterhouse-Five*, Montana Wildhack is a porn actress who is kidnapped by the Tralfamadorians and forced to mate with Billy Pilgrim.

Panel 6. "...you weren't much on the Stagman Club, all those girls with the deer antlers...."

The Playboy Club makes its waitresses wear bunny ears, so it's logical that in the Stagman Club, the waitresses would wear deer antlers.

Page 140. Panel 1. Roger the Robot's appearance is a reference to Robert the Robot on *Fireball XL5*.

Panels 3-5. Kevin O'Neill notes:
> Green jump-suited ground crew have "S" symbol on backs,

representing Captain Condor's Space Patrol (*Lion Annual* 1959).

Page 141. Panel 1. "I've seen brainier-looking Airfix kits." Airfix is a British manufacturer of scale model kits of planes.

Pages 142–143. Presumably these spaceships are more references.

The yellow helicopter is a helijet from the Dan Dare stories.

The building in the lower right is the Space City Control Tower from *Fireball XL5*.

The flat, flying platform in the lower right is a Hiller VZ-1 Pawnee, created in our world by the U.S. military in 1953 but abandoned due to its lack of military applications.

The figure in the lower right-hand corner is Dan Dare. The figure to the left of Dare is Christopher Philip "Flamer" Spry, a student who becomes Dare's sidekick on Dare's later adventures.

Kevin O'Neill notes:
> Yellow spaceship top left is a U.S. Space Patrol craft—cereal giveaway in 1953.
>
> Small red helicopter belongs to Harry and Colin Stars of *Diamond Raiders of Coral Isle* by Roy Leighton (*Lion Annual* 1959).
>
> To left of Dare is not Flamer Spry but Jason, a young crewmember of Captain Condor's Space Patrol.

Page 144. Panel 1. "Jona— Curs— on Brit— Na—" This is a reference to the lead character in the comic strip "Jonah" (*Beano*, 1958–1963; *Dandy*, 1993–1997). In British naval parlance, a "Jonah" is a cursed sailor who dooms whatever ship he is on. The comic strip Jonah goes one further and sinks not only every ship he sets foot on, but other ships in the area.

"Spider Man From Mars"
This is a reference to Michael Moorcock's *Blades of Mars* (1965), the middle novel of Moorcock's "Kane of Old Mars" trilogy, mentioned in *League* v2. In *Blades of Mars*, Michael Kane confronts a race of Martian spider-men.

The "Spider Man" has the face and haircut of Peter Parker, the alternate identity of Spider-Man in Marvel Comics.

Kevin O'Neill notes:
> *Spider Man From Mars* is a fictional movie poster seen fleetingly in British film *Left Right and Centre*. I should have added Troy McClure's name for *Boffo Laffs*.

Page 145. Panel 2. This was the uniform worn on *Fireball XL5*.

Page 146. "When They Sound The Last All Clear" is a reference to a popular 1941 song from British vocalist Vera Lynn (1917–present).

"...a self-styled 'surrealist sportsman' who suffered from chronic dwarfism and whose first or last name was apparently Engelbrecht."
This is a reference to Maurice Richardson's *The Exploits of Engelbrecht* (1950), in which the surrealist sportsman dwarf Engelbrecht boxes with a grandfather clock, goes on a witch hunt, and has various wonderful surrealist adventures.

"...a stocky, unkempt Negro with a very deep voice..."
See Page 166 below.

"...a Mr. Norton, an intelligence gatherer sometimes referred to as 'the prisoner of London.'"
This is a reference to Iain Sinclair's *Slow Chocolate Autopsy* (1997), about Norton, who can travel in time but is stuck within the physical confines of London.

"...the apparent dynasty of black-clad burrowing bandits..."
This is a reference to Terry Patrick's The Black Sapper, who

appeared in the British comics *Rover* and *Hotspur* for decades beginning in 1929. The Black Sapper is an inventor/thief, dressed all in black, who uses an enormous burrowing machine, the Earthworm, to commit crime. There being a dynasty of Sappers would explain the Sapper's longevity.

"...or an early manifestation of elusive international criminal mastermind The Voice."
This is probably a reference to the Voice, the archenemy of Garry Halliday, seen above on Page 125, Panel 4.

The cartoon in the lower left is a reference to the cautionary posters produced during World War Two. One of the British posters read, "Be Like Dad and Keep Mum." The woman and the man with the checkered cap are Flo and Andy Capp, from Reginald Smythe's comic strip "Andy Capp" (1957–present). Andy Capp is a working-class British drunk, and Flo is his long-suffering wife. The man taking money from Andy Capp is George Baker's Sad Sack, from comic strips and comic books, 1942–1976. Sad Sack is a gormless American Army private.

Page 147. The "Watch out—Adenoid's about!" cartoon is a reference to the "Careless Talk Costs Lives" propaganda campaign of the British government during World War Two. The posters of that campaign were drawn by "Fougasse," the pseudonym of Cyril Kenneth Bird (1887–1965), whose art O'Neill is imitating here.

"Adenoid" is a reference to Adenoid Hynkel, of the film *The Great Dictator*. As mentioned on Page 47, Panel 1, in the world of *Dossier*, World War Two was caused not by Adolf Hitler and Germany but by Adenoid Hynkel and the country of Tomania. Hynkel is the "Der Fooey" of Tomania, which may explain the "Fooey" signature in the upper left-hand corner of the poster.

The Hynkel balloon is a reference to the scene in *The Great Dictator* in which Hynkel dances a little ballet with a balloon which represents the world.

The phrase "Watch out—Adenoid's about" may also be a reference to Thomas Pynchon's *Gravity's Rainbow* (1973), in which a giant adenoid threatens London during World War Two. (Pynchon was likely referring back to *The Great Dictator* as well.)

"…the architect Nicholas Dyer's creepy church…."

This is a reference to Peter Ackroyd's *Hawksmoor* (1985), in which British architect Nicholas Hawksmoor (c. 1661–1736) is reimagined as Nicholas Dyer.

"He believed that in all probability the challenge would come from someone installed by Military Intelligence within the Labour Party, probably someone from a solid military background and intensely charismatic with a splendid chance of winning a post war election."

In our world, in 1945, Labour Party candidate Clement Atlee (1883–1967), known as "Major Atlee" because of his rank during World War One, replaced Winston Churchill (the Prime Minister in this passage).

"He broke off with a haunted look there in his bloodshot gundog eyes, as if he'd said too much, and lit one of those caber-sized cigars…."

This is a good description of Winston Churchill, who was, in our world, concerned about the possibility of a Labour Party-backed dictatorial bureaucracy.

Page 148. The four figures here are Worrals, William Samson Jr., the Iron Warrior, and the Invisible Man, with Professor Grey and the Iron Fish in the background.

Worrals is described above on Page 25.

William Samson Jr. is Wolf of Kabul, mentioned above on Page 14, Panel 1.

The Iron Warrior appeared in *Thrill Comics* (1940–1945) and *New Funnies* (1948). The Iron Warrior is a giant robot, controlled by Rodney Dearth and used to find treasure in Africa.

This Invisible Man is Peter Brady, from the American TV series *The Invisible Man* (1958–1960). In the show, Peter Brady, a British scientist, is turned invisible in an accident.

Professor Grey and the Iron Fish are mentioned on Page 14, Panel 1.

"...Miss Warralson's previously unsuspected tribadism...."
"Tribadism" is an older term for "lesbianism." Although W. E. Johns never said that Worrals was a lesbian, she was pursued by handsome, accomplished fellow pilot Bill Ashton, who was in love with her. She never reciprocated his feelings and liked him only as a friend. Suspicions of being gay have been raised with less evidence than that....
    The "F" tattoo on Worrals's arm is for Freck—see Page 149, Panel 1.

"...a pairing of pirate-slaver James Soames and Italian master-criminal Count Zero."
In various issues of *The Magnet* (1908–1940), James Soames, a pirate and slaver, and an Italian master criminal named Count Zero clashed with Harry Wharton and the Greyfriars crew.

Page 149. Panel 1. "...her companion 'Frecks,' apparently an old school chum."
In the Worrals stories, Worrals's sidekick is her best friend and fellow pilot Betty "Frecks" Lovell.

Panel 2. "...his deadly cricket-bat wielding colleague Chung...."
Chung and his deadly cricket bat are described on Page 14, Panel 1.

Page 150/*Crazy Wide Forever* Cover. "The Crazy Wide Forever, by Sal Paradyse."
In Jack Kerouac's *On the Road*, Sal Paradise (Kerouac's fictional stand-in) and friend Dean Moriarty (stand-in for Kerouac's friend Neal Cassady) travel around America, having Beat adventures. The style of *The Crazy Wide Forever* is Moore's own creation, however, and is based on Kerouac's poetry more than his prose.
    The man in the mirror, wearing the hat, is visually similar to William S. Burroughs. His companion is visually similar to Jack Kerouac.

Kevin O'Neill notes:
> Pendant Books came from *Seinfeld,* I believe. The neckline
> logo I made up. I painted the cover art as if it had been left
> in the sun for several weeks.

Page 151/*Crazy Wide Forever* 1. "…Vanness Avenue…"
a.k.a. Van Ness Avenue in San Francisco, an important city for the
Beats.

"…what a sigh what a kick in the eye that's Satori…"
This is a play on the lyrics of the song "That's Amore," most
famously performed by Dean Martin in 1953. The most famous
lyrics from the song are: "When the moon hits your eye like a big
pizza-pie, that's Amore."
> Satori, in Buddhism, means enlightenment.
> "Satori" and "Kick in the Eye" are the titles of songs
performed by the band Bauhaus. Alan Moore has worked with
Kevin and David J. Haskins of Bauhaus on projects.

"…from the light the true view and descend into Maya again…"
In Buddhism, "maya" is the illusion of the material world.

"…her second skin skirt feet apart in a capital A…"
This description of Mina matches her appearance on the back cover
of *Black Dossier*.

"…the fresh breath of Now Tathagata Now…"
Tathāgata, in Buddhism, describes the quality of a human being
who has transcended the being/nonbeing dialectic.

"…wide crazy and bottomless em'rald Pacific with conches an
corals in columns of weed… through the full fathom five of her
stare…"
This is reference to Ariel's lines, in Shakespeare's *The Tempest*:
> Full fathom five thy father lies;
> Of his bones are coral made;
> Those are pearls that were his eyes;
> Nothing of him that does fade,

But doth suffer a sea-change
Into something rich and strange.

"...tells you she's Minnie but never mooched..."
This is a reference to the Cab Calloway song "Minnie the Moocher" (1931).

"...Captain Easy..."
This is a reference to the excellent Roy Crane comic strip "Washington Tubbs II" (later "Wash Tubbs," 1924–1983). "Wash Tubbs" is about the adventures of a teenage boy, George Washington Tubbs II, and his friend and sidekick, Captain Easy, in his own words a "beach-comber, boxer, cook, aviator, seaman, explorer, and soldier of artillery, infantry and cavalry."

"...Lone Ranger..."
This is a reference to the Lone Ranger, cowboy star of radio, television, novels, and comic books from 1933–1955. John Reid, Texas Ranger, is ambushed and left for dead. He heals, puts on a mask, and uses the family silver mine and his native friend Tonto to fight evils in the Old West.

"O little did we know but Dr. Sachs was settin fer us..."
"Dr. Sachs" is a reference to the titular character of Jack Kerouac's *Dr. Sax*, mentioned above on Page 25. Dr. Sax is a scientist who travels to Lowell, Massachusetts, to destroy the Great World Snake, a Jörmungandr-like monster.

"...an comin through the night air soup of cotton candy..."
See Page 152 below.

"...Ed Dunkel..."
This is a reference to Kerouac's *On the Road*. Ed Dunkel is Kerouac's fictional version of his friend Al Hinkle.

"...drums his mand'rin hypodermic fingernails..."
See Page 152 below.

Page 152/*Crazy Wide Forever* 2. "…an Dr. Sachs stirs alla that into his schnapps…"
In *Dr. Sax*, Sax works on creating a potion which will destroy the Great World Snake. Perhaps everything that Sachs is mixing into his schnapps here is a part of the potion?

"…Mahatma in the Mission…"
"Mahatma" is a Sanskrit word translating roughly to "saint" or "liberated one."

"…an some say as his tailored suit's got pictures painted on all over like a carny hoardin men…"
This, along with the "…an comin through the night air soup of cotton candy…" comment on Page 151, may mean that Dr. Sachs is also Mr. Dark, from Ray Bradbury's *Something Wicked This Way Comes* (1962). In the novel, Mr. Dark runs a traveling carnival whose air always smells of candy and who is himself covered with tattoos, one for each person who is bound to service at the carnival.

"…Fiji mermaid in a pickle jar…"
The "Fiji mermaid" was a common attraction in carnival sideshows. The "mermaid" is purportedly an actual mermaid, but was usually either a dugong or two animal bodies stitched together.

"…a map of Egypt an the martyrdom o blessed Cath'rin there…"
This is a reference to Saint Catherine of Alexandria (c. 287–c. 305 C.E.), one of the Fourteen Holy Helpers in the Catholic tradition. She was martyred in an attempt to convert the Roman Emperor Maxentius to Christianity.

"…Jack Dempsey on the other…"
Jack Dempsey (1895–1983) was an American boxer and heavyweight champion.

"…Borgia popes all roun his hatband…"
The Borgia popes were Alfonso de Borgia (1378–1458), a.k.a. Pope Callistus III (1455–1458), Roderic de Borgia (1431–1503), a.k.a. Pope Alexander VI (1492–1503), and Giovanni Battista Pamfili (1574–1655), a.k.a. Pope Innocent X (1644–1655). The Borgias

were a Spanish family who became infamous for corruption and wickedness.

"…Lusitania sinkin on his fine silk tie…"
The *Lusitania* was a British passenger liner sunk by a German submarine in 1915.

"…with them spider-crabs them peril-yeller claws…"
This may be a reference to the Robert W. Chambers story "The Maker of Moons" (1896), in which a Yellow Peril villain, Yue-Laou, controls a crab-like monster, the Xin.

"…me n Dean…"
"Dean" is Dean Moriarty, one of the main characters in Kerouac's *On the Road*.

"…n they're in *The Thin Man* English Al an she they're Willum Powell n Myrna Loy…"
This is a reference to the 1934 film version of the 1933 Dashiell Hammett novel *The Thin Man*. In the film, William Powell and Myrna Loy play Nick and Nora Charles, a husband-and-wife pair of detectives.

"…how a mad perfesser an a wily oriental demon come ta blows with airboats spoffin flame down on sum grum Victoriolan slum…"
This is an adequate summary of the events of *League* v1.

"…where has the devilish chinee an offspring sprung son of a son o that inhuman Fu man Dr. Sachs by name…"
In the world of *Dossier*, Dr. Sachs has not only a homonymic link to Fu Manchu, who was created by "Sax Rohmer"; Dr. Sachs is the grandson of Fu Manchu, hence Sachs's "mand'rin… fingernails," mentioned on Page 151.

"…his ole grandad's foe no reglar Joe but the Napoleon o crime n craft this mad perfesser Moriarty his own grandson his own line all unbeknown aint no one else but Dean machine oil mean Dean Moriarty…"
In other words, Dean Moriarty is the grandson of Professor Moriarty,

the archenemy of Sherlock Holmes and, in *League* v1, Fu Manchu and the League of Extraordinary Gentlemen.

***Pornsec SexJane* Page 1**. This is Moore and O'Neill's version of what a Tijuana Bible would be like in the England of *1984*. Tijuana Bibles were crudely produced pornographic comic books about celebrities and comic strip characters produced from the 1920s through the 1960s.

The entire *Pornsec SexJane* sequence may be a reference to the beginning of the Charlie Chaplin film *Modern Times* (1931), in which Chaplin's character goes mad when faced with too much work, demanded too quickly, on an assembly line.

The character on the left, #6079, is a reference to Winston Smith of Orwell's *1984*. Smith's number in the novel is "6079 Smith W."

The "Jane" of the title is the Jane mentioned on Page 22, Panel 6.
        The "36J" emblem on her uniform is likely a reference to her bra size.

The characters are working for Night Industries, as seen on the left, and are producing what look like parts of sex toys.

***Pornsec SexJane* Page 2**. "Damn them, Jane! They can't stifle human passion!"
This (and his statements on Pages 3 and 4) is a brief description of Winston Smith's feelings about Julia before being caught.

***Pornsec SexJane* Page 3**. The two characters "—lvy" and "Bumstead" are references to Comrades Ogilvy and Bumstead, two characters in *1984*.

***Pornsec SexJane* Page 4**. "Withers" is a reference to the British actress Googie Withers (1917–present), whom this character resembles.

"Syme" is a reference to Winston Smith's friend Syme in *1984*.

"Jones" is a reference to one of the three major traitors in *1984*.

***Pornsec SexJane* Page 5**. "2050" is not a reference to a particular character in *1984*, but, perhaps, to the projected date by which Newspeak will become the only language anyone understands.

"Parsons" is a reference to Winston Smith's neighbor in *1984*.

***Pornsec SexJane* Page 6**. "We are the dead" is what Winston and Julia tell each other the morning after their tryst, right before they are caught by the Thought Police in *1984*.

"Pastry" is a reference to British actor Richard Hearne (1908–1979), whose recurring stage and TV character was Mr. Pastry.

***Pornsec SexJane* Page 8**. "Later, 14 o'clock:"
In the world of *1984*, the old-fashioned twelve-hour clocks have been replaced with twenty-four-hour clocks.

The cage is full of rats. The prospect of having a cage of rats placed on his face is what finally breaks Winston in *1984*.

"Imagine a patent leather boot grinding on a human tongue, forever."
This is a sadomasochistic riff on the famous line from *1984*, "If you want a picture of the future, imagine a boot stamping on a human face—for ever."

Page 153/*Crazy Wide Forever* 3. "...th' monkey wrench flip..."
This is a reference to Neal Cassady's tendency to compulsively flip a monkey wrench, described in Tom Wolfe's *The Electric Kool-Aid Acid Test* (1968).

"...at the Spaghetti Fact'ry..."
This is a reference to the Old Spaghetti Factory Caffe, a pasta

factory-turned-hangout for beatniks in the 1950s and 1960s in North Beach in San Francisco.

"...Torquemada..."
Tomas de Torquemada (1420–1498) was the first Inquisitor General of Spain and a fanatical enemy of those he perceived as enemies of the Church.

"...Krupp..."
Krupp is the name of a famous German steel- and munitions-manufacturing family, but the reference here is probably to Alfred Krupp (1907–1967), an early member of the Nazi family who used slave labor to help the family business during World War Two.

"...Nero..."
Nero Claudius Caesar Augustus Germanicus (37–68) was Emperor of Rome from 54–68. He is a byword for historical tyranny.

"...Mephrisco Bayzeebub..."
This is a pun combining "'phrisco Bay," or "San Francisco Bay," with "Mephistopheles" and "Beelzebub." "Mephistopheles" is the name of the devil in the Faust myth (see Page 28). Beelzebub is the name of a demon in the Bible.

"...Lucifornia Satandreas Asmode o Day..."
This is a pun combining "California" and "San Andreas" with "Lucifer," "Satan," and "Asmodeus." The latter three are Biblical bad guys.

"...top hat hoo hah Haiti cemeterrians..."
This is a reference to Baron Samedi, who in the religion of Voodoo is a spirit of the dead. He always appears wearing a top hat.

"...shoot craps wit' jackalheads in Memphis alleyway..."
In Egyptian mythology, Anubis is the jackal-headed god of the afterlife. His principal temple was in the Egyptian city of Memphis.

"...clinches hiz biz wit' titan ole boy Greek godpappy baby eaters..."
In Greek mythology, the Titan Cronus, afraid that his children would overthrow him, ate them as infants.

"...where Great Cthula..."
This is a reference to Lovecraft's Cthulhu (see Page 26).

"...ole Yoggy Soggy..."
This is a reference to H. P. Lovecraft's Yog-Sothoth, an alien god who is locked outside our universe.

"...sweet sweet sweat o Dizzy's brow..."
This is a reference to Dizzy Gillespie (1917–1963), a jazz trumpeter.

"...dried fried hide o Rin Tin Tin..."
This is a reference to the fictional canine hero of movies, radio series, stories, and TV series from 1922 to 1959.

"...with Bull Hubbard..."
Jack Kerouac used "Bull Hubbard" as a fictional stand-in for William S. Burroughs (1914–1997) in various novels.

"...Plastic Man..."
Plastic Man, created by Jack Cole in 1941, is a stretchable, mutable superhero.

"...Dr. Sachs explain accordin t' sum ole Republic serial script..."
Republic Pictures produced a range of film serials in the 1930s and 1940s. One cliché of these serials is that the villain, like Dr. Sachs here, would explain his evil plan too early, so that the hero would have a chance to stop it. Alan Moore memorably riffed off this in *Watchmen*, when the "hero," Ozymandias, is pressed by the "villains," Night Owl and Rorschach, to explain his plan. Ozymandias's response: "'Do it?' Dan, I'm not a Republic serial villain. Do you seriously think I'd explain my master-stroke if there remained the slightest chance of you affecting its outcome? I did

it thirty-five minutes ago."

"...some Aztec virus junk..."
This and following references to the Aztecs and Mayans are references to William S. Burroughs's *The Soft Machine* (1961), in which Aztec and Mayan calendars and codices create visual and spoken viruses which allow the priest class to control the workers.

"...what's stewed n stilled fum foot long cennipedes..."
In William S. Burroughs's *The Naked Lunch* (1959), large black centipedes are ground up and used for a variety of icky purposes.

"...Quetzacoatl..."
In Aztec mythology, Quetzalcoatl is a god of sky and creation.

"...dybbuk..."
In Jewish folklore, a dybbuk is an evil ghost that possesses people.

"...known more lately 'z th' Nova Mob..."
In William S. Burroughs's "Nova Trilogy" (*The Soft Machine* [1961], *The Ticket that Exploded* [1962], and *Nova Express* [1964]), the Nova Mob is a villainous alien crime group whose purpose is to destroy worlds and who "always create as many insoluble conflicts as possible and always aggravate existing conflicts" toward this end.

"...fun guys fum Yuggoth..."
As mentioned on Page 26, "Yuggoth" is a Lovecraftian stand-in for Pluto. "Fun guys fum Yuggoth" is a pun on "Fungi from Yuggoth," which is another term for the Mi-go (see Page 117).

"...Narlyhooly haunter o' th' dark..."
"Narlyhooly" is a reference to Nyarlathotep. He is also known as "the Haunter of the Dark."

"...what done fer poor young Bobby Blake..."
See Page 26.

"...now calls hisself as th' Sublim'nal Kid..."
The Subliminal Kid appears in Burroughs's *Nova Express*. Based on Burroughs's lover, Ian Sommerville, the Subliminal Kid is a rebel who undermines the "reality" of the world.

"...jumps in an out TV commercials so's ya barely see..."
This is one of the Subliminal Kid's abilities.

"...ol' Hastur what they call Unnameable now..."
In Lovecraft's "The Whisperer in Darkness," Hastur (originally named and created by Ambrose Bierce in "Haïta the Shepherd" [1891]) is a supernatural being mentioned in a list of beings and places. Later writers developed Hastur into a Great Old One (see Page 26).

Hastur's title is given as "the Unspeakable One" and "He Who Is Not To Be Named."

"...answers to Mr. Bradley/Mr. Martin two ole waspy fruits in one suit..."
Mr. Bradley and Mr. Martin appear in Burroughs's "Nova Trilogy." They are members of the Nova Mob.

Page 154/*Crazy Wide Forever* 4. "...n Hamburger Mary..."
Hamburger Mary appears in Burroughs's "Nova Trilogy." She is a member of the Nova Mob.

"...sprayin flakes in Hector's cafeteria..."
Hector's cafeteria appears in Kerouac's *On The Road*.

"...in Booneville reformatory..."
The Booneville reformatory appears in Kerouac's *On The Road*.

"...an puddle slop like Continental Op..."
The Continental Op was created by Dashiell Hammett and appeared in thirty-six short stories and seven novels and short story collections from 1923 to 1947. The Op is a heavy fortysomething agent of the Continental Detective Agency in San Francisco.

Page 155/*Crazy Wide Forever* 5. "...fum Summer afore last *Immortal Love...*"
This is a reference to the song "Immortal Love" which appears on the vinyl album released with the Absolute edition of *Black Dossier*.

"...Hyman Solomon fuck sea-heart sailors inna washroom ut th' Port Authority scream 'feed me I'm a Jew'..."
In Kerouac's *On the Road*, Moriarty and Paradyse meet a hitchhiker: "He said his name was Hyman Solomon and that he walked all over the USA, knocking and sometimes kicking at Jewish doors and demanding money: 'Give me money to eat, I am a Jew.'"

"...n sing holy holy holy Willyum Blake almighty..."
In Allan Ginsburg's "Howl" (1956), the word "holy" is repeated several times.
William Blake (1757–1827) was an English poet and painter who was a favorite of Ginsburg's and is mentioned by name in "Howl."
"Holy holy holy Willyum Blake almighty" is also a spin on the lines "Holy, holy, holy! Lord God Almighty!" from Reginald Heber's hymn "Holy Holy Holy."

"...in th' beat up negro dawn..."
This is a reference to the first two lines of Ginsburg's "Howl": "I saw the best minds of my generation destroyed by madness, starving hysterical naked, dragging themselves through the negro streets at dawn looking for an angry fix..."

"...Tom Mix..."
Tom Mix (1880–1940) was a world-famous star of silent Western films.

"...Bill Boyd..."
William Boyd (1895–1972) became known for playing Hopalong Cassidy in over 60 movies and TV series from 1935 to 1954.

"…Floyd Patterson…"
Floyd Patterson (1935–2006) was a heavyweight boxing champion in the 1950s and 1960s.

"…o th' uncaged Nova mugwumps…"
In Burroughs's *Naked Lunch*, a mugwump is a nasty quasi-human thing, in Burroughs's words "obscene beyond any possible vile act or practice." A mugwump appeared in *League* v2.

"…Dr. Sachs that hero bold gon bad…"
In Kerouac's *Dr. Sax*, Dr. Sachs is the good guy, not the villain.

Page 156. "…your attempt to raise the party's flagging fortunes by re labelling it 'New Ingsoc'…."
This is a reference to British Prime Minister Tony Blair's recasting the Labour Party as "New Labour" in the mid-1990s.

"…government irregularities and illegalities…."
This is a reference to the series of British government scandals in the 1990s and 2000s.

"…even going so far as to claim that MI5 had been responsible for the release of the aforementioned incriminating documents to the Conservatives."
MI5 has in at least one case done exactly this in our world. In 1924, MI5 agents released a forged letter, the "Zinoviev Letter," to the *Daily Mail*. The Letter was purportedly written by a Communist International official and called for greater Communist activity in Great Britain. The Letter caused a sensation and led to the downfall of the Labour government of Ramsay MacDonald. As well, according to a BBC program, *The Plot Against Harold Wilson*, in 1974 MI5 officers, convinced that Prime Minister Harold Wilson was a Communist agent, attempted to use MI5's files on Wilson to release incriminating material about him to the British press.

"…small towns dotted about the country such as Maybury…"
Mayberry, North Carolina, is the site of the TV shows *The Andy Griffith Show* (1960–1968) and *Mayberry R.F.D.* (1968–1971),

and also appeared in an episode of *The Danny Thomas Show* (1953–1964).

"...or Riverdale..."
There are various real Riverdales, but in all likelihood the Riverdale mentioned here is the Riverdale which is the setting for the numerous stories in Archie Comics.

"...metropolitan environments like Central City..."
In DC Comics, Central City is the home city of the Flash. In Marvel Comics, Central City was the original home of the Fantastic Four. In the Spirit stories of Will Eisner, Central City is the home of the Spirit.

"...Gotham...."
In DC Comics, Gotham City is the home city of Batman, among others.

"...the supposed goddess of love called Venus..."
The Greek goddess Venus appeared as a superhero in the Atlas Comics *Venus* #1–#19 (1948–1952) and *Marvel Mystery Comics* #91 (1949). She was active in New York City, where Mina and Allan encounter her.

"...Gotham's by then elderly Crimson Avenger..."
The Crimson Avenger was possibly created by Jim Chambers and appeared in a number of DC comics beginning with *Detective Comics* #20 (Oct. 1938). Newspaper reporter Lee Travis puts on the costume of "The Crimson" to fight crime, aided by his Asian valet Wing. The Crimson Avenger predated the Batman and was arguably the first costumed crimefighter in DC Comics.

Page 157. "...film star Linda Turner's close associate the Black Cat..."
Linda Turner, a.k.a. the Black Cat, was created by Alfred Harvey and appeared in a number of comics beginning with *Pocket Comics* #1 (Aug. 1941). Linda Turner, the daughter of a movie star and a stuntman, became one of Hollywood's biggest stars but got bored

with the make-believe life of Hollywood and decided to fight crime instead as the Black Cat.

"...mental marvel Brain Boy..."
Brain Boy was created by Herb Castle and appeared in six comics in 1962 and 1963, beginning with *Four Color* #1330 (Apr./June 1962). When Matt Price was still only a fetus in his mother's womb, she was struck by electricity in a car accident. This gave Price various psychic powers, and when he turns eighteen he is recruited by the government to go to work for them, fighting evil.

"...and a thirteen-year-old orphan said to draw fantastic powers and abilities from an adjoining extra spatial region or dimension ruled by technologically advanced fly people."
This is a reference to the Fly, created by Joe Simon and Jack Kirby and appearing in a number of comics from 1959 to 1966 (and again in later iterations), beginning with *The Double Life of Private Strong* #1 (June 1959). Orphan Tommy Troy is hired to do odd jobs by Ben and Abigail March. Troy finds a ring in their attic, for the Marches are wizards, and the ring summons Turan, one of the Fly People, former rulers of the Earth. The Fly People were eventually reduced to common houseflies in a magical war, although a few, including Turan, escaped to another dimension. The ring can be used by Tommy to switch bodies with one of the Fly People, who has magical powers. Tommy uses the ring to fight crime.

"Seemingly, a Negro man from out of town had been held in the Maybury jail on morals charges, including an accusation of procuring, with his two white skinned female accomplices who were apparently twin sisters from the Netherlands."
See the notes to Page 166. This may also be a reference to the Drew and Josh Friedman comic strip, "The Andy Griffith Show" (1980), which portrayed an African-American appearing in Mayberry and being lynched by the natives.

"...one sheriff's deputy's account was 'exactly like one of them there hot air balloons, 'ceptin it weren't.'"
The speaker is Gomer Pyle, from *The Andy Griffith Show*. Pyle is occasionally deputized by Barney Fife.

As for the 'ceptin-it-weren't-a-balloon, see Page 168.

"...there was a frankly stupid rumour that for a brief period the self styled legendary adventurer evaded notice by the novel means of having been against his or her will transformed into an animal by sorcery."
This is a reference to Kathleen Hale's nineteen "Orlando the Marmalade Cat" novels (1938–1972). Hale's Orlando is an exceptionally intelligent and active cat, and he and his wife Grace have kittens, buy and run a farm, ride on flying carpets, travel to the moon, and have various other adventures.

"...our projects at Port Merion...."
The Prisoner, mentioned above on Page 14, Panel 1, was filmed at the Welsh village of Portmeirion.

"One of their Central Intelligence lot, F. Gordon Leiter...."
Felix Leiter appears in various James Bond novels as a C.I.A. agent who works with Bond on various cases. Leiter's real name is "Felix." The "Gordon" may come from a conflation of Leiter with Watergate rogue G. Gordon Liddy. In the American animated TV series *James Bond Jr.* (1991–1992) Bond's nephew, Bond Junior, attends a private school with Felix Leiter's son Gordon.

"My best to you and Julia...."
The love interest of Orwell's *1984* is Julia, a mechanic. At the end of the novel, Julia, like Winston, has betrayed her lover and been brainwashed to love Big Brother. Presumably she took up with her torturer O'Brien.

"I remain, of course, yours most sincerely...."
This is a reference to Orson Welles's trademark sign-off phrase in his radio shows: "I remain, as always, obediently yours." As mentioned on Page 78, Panel 9, Welles was the narrator of *The Lives of Harry Lime* radio show—and it is Robert Cherry, a.k.a. Harry Lime, who is writing here.

The image on the left is Mina and Allan with the Crimson Avenger's costume.

The center image is Mina and Allan with Billy Batson, the youthful alternate identity of the Fawcett superhero Captain Marvel. The reason that the people in the background are opening umbrellas is that Batson has just transformed from Captain Marvel to Batson, an act always accompanied by a roll of thunder.

The image on the right may be of Mina and Allan with Linda Turner.

Page 161. Panel 9. "Oh, for crying out loud. It just never bloody *stops*, does it?"
With Moore's departure from mainstream comics now a reality, there is a great temptation to see even minor things as a commentary by him on superhero comics. This line may be indicative of his feelings about the serial nature of comics and the endless demand for more stories, more adventure, and more danger for the unfortunates caught within superhero stories.

Page 162. Panel 1. "Gordon Bennett" is a euphemistic British expression, indicative of shock or surprise.

Panel 4. The "SF" on the side of the helicopter probably stands for Dan Dare's "Space Fleet."

Page 164. Panel 2. "Wij zullen het dadelijk voor u doen, onze dappere held. Wij zijn verzot op u."
"Waar gaat u heen, trotse kampioen der liefde?"
Translation from the Dutch: "We will do it for you at once, our brave hero. We adore you."
"Where are you going, proud champion of love?"

Regarding the dolls, see Page 166, Panel 1 below.

Panel 3. "Hij heeft een slecht humeur. Laten wij ons maar aankleden."
"He is in a bad mood. We ought to get dressed."

Linseed oil is used to keep wood supple.

Page 166. Panel 1. This is the Golliwog. He was created by Florence Kate Upton in *The Adventures of Two Dutch Dolls and a Golliwogg* (1895), about the adventures of several dolls on Christmas, the one day of the year in which dolls come to life and can have fun. Golliwog appeared in twelve sequels by Upton and in numerous sequels by Enid Blyton and other authors. The Golliwog (as it later became spelled) was a beloved children's character in Britain for several generations, although it is substantially less popular today.

The Golliwog was originally a rag doll drawn like a blackface minstrel doll, visually similar to O'Neill's portrayal here. Golliwog's features and the overtly racist portrayal of Golliwog in many of the non-Upton novels have led Golliwog to be seen as a racist character and "Golliwog" and "Wog" to be used as racial epithets. Upton detested the offensive way in which Blyton and other authors portrayed the Golliwog: "How can I convey any idea of the delight of that book and clearly separate it from later imitations of the Golliwogg… a mockery of his original noble-minded self, on those little labels some people stick on their Christmas parcels." And Upton's intention in the Golliwog novels was to portray a positive character. But Upton was no more free of racism than any other person of her era, and many people have seen racist elements in Upton's work. (For example, there is a minstrel caricature named "Sambo" in *Adventures of Two Dutch Dolls*.)

Golliwog's two companions, the "Dutch Dolls" of his first appearance, are Peggy and Sarah Jane Deutchland [sic]. As can be seen on Page 164, Panels 2–3, their appearance is overtly sexualized. This may be a reference to the work of artist Hans Bellmer (1902–1975), who created a series of pictures called "Die Puppe" ("The Doll") about sexually perverse dolls, or simply a reference to "Dutch Wives," the slang phrase for sex dolls.

Kevin O'Neill notes:
> Florence Upton's *Golliwogg* is a fascinating character, and his relationship with the Dutch dolls in the original books does have an odd subliminal sexual atmosphere, also

present in Arthur Rackham's work in a similar period.

Panel 4. The fact that Drummond is still on his feet while Bond and Peel are knocked off theirs may be indicative of how Moore feels about the old-style action heroes versus the newer generation (i.e., they made them tough back then).

Page 168. **Panel 1**. The Golliwog as a balloonist is a reference to Florence Upton's *The Golliwog's Air-Ship* (1902), in which the Golliwog and the wooden dolls Sarah Jane, Peg, Meg, and Midget go on a balloon trip together. If the design of the balloon is a reference to anything in particular, I'm unaware of it, although the shark face on the front is a very Kevin O'Neill-like touch.

Golliwog is the "bold, fearless black balloonist" mentioned in *League* v2.

Kevin O'Neill notes:
> Florence Upton's airship was cute but not adequate to our needs. I took my design cue from Alan's name for it—the *Rose of Nowhere*. The later view of the complete black balloon above it had a symbolist engraving eye motif.

Panel 3. The dresses that Peg and Sarah Jane are wearing are those that they wore in *The Adventures of Two Dutch Dolls and a Golliwogg*.

Page 169. **Panel 2**. It is typical of Bulldog Drummond that, though hateful and bigoted in many ways, his reaction to meeting two traditional English heroes is to believe them rather than what the government has told him.

Page 170. **Panel 1**. This is clearly the ruins of a castle, and it's been identified as in Dunbayne, which means this must be Dunbayne Castle, from Ann Radcliffe's *The Castles of Athlin and Dunbayne* (1789), one of Radcliffe's first Gothic novels.

Page 171. **Panel 6**. "Sodium morphate in his fucking *pie*?" Sodium morphate is a drug that slows the heart and smells like apples, and so putting it into an apple pie is an efficient method of assassination. Whom it has been used on depends on which conspiracy theory you read.

Panel 7. "Trick *cars*, trick *pens*, trick *cigarette lighters*... why can't you just *fight*?"
Bulldog Drummond never was one for gadgets, preferring more straightforward brutality. It is typical of his mindset to look down on newer heroes like Bond who rely on gadgets rather than fists.

The gun Bond is reaching for is a Walther PPK. Bond is known for using the Walther PPK, but he used a Beretta in his first five novels and switched to the PPK only at the beginning of *Dr. No*.

Kevin O'Neill notes:
> This sequence of Hugo thrashing Jimmy is a favourite of mine up alongside Griffin killing a policeman in volume one and Hyde killing Griffin in volume two. Of the three this had the most emotional reason for the shocking outburst of violence.

Page 173. Panel 2. "I'm going to need sturdier clothing if I stay in this business."
Many men of a certain age fondly remember Emma Peel's sturdy leather catsuit in *The Avengers*.

Page 174. Panel 1. The Golliwog's balloon is a visual reference to Odilon Redon's painting "L'oeil, Comme Un Ballon Bizarre Se Dirige Vers L'infini" (1882).

Kevin O'Neill notes:
> I modified the Redon image a little but a symbolist flourish seemed to fit the Golliwogg's nature.

Panel 5. "Heer Orlando is momenteel een dame."
"Mr. Orlando is a lady at the moment."

Page 175. Panel 1. "So Queen *Olympia* presented you with the dolls?"
As mentioned in *League* v2, Olympia, the doll from E. T. A. Hoffman's "The Sand-Man" (1817), became queen of Toyland.

Panel 2. "Wij hebben ons vrijwillig aangeboden. Zijn geslacht is kolossaal.
"We volunteered. His penis is enormous."

Panel 3. "…are these things *common* in your black-material cosmos?"
See the Interview for more on Golliwog's "black-material cosmos."

Panel 4. "Belted 'The Rose o' Nowhere' all on me jingle, did I."
The "Rose of Nowhere" is a phrase found in the mystical writings of Golden Dawn followers.
On Page 168, Panel 1, can be seen the roses which apparently power Golliwog's balloon, the "Rose of Nowhere."

Panel 5. "Ik denk dat die grote wolk daar de weg naar huis is."
"I think that big cloud ahead is the way home."

Pages 176–177. A number of the images in this sequence are standard optical illusions.

Standing on a small asteroid, next to Allan, Mina, and Golliwog, is the Little Prince, created by Antoine Saint-Exupéry and appearing in *Le Petit Prince* (1943). The image here is very similar to the original cover of *Le Petit Prince*.

The clown on Page 177 is Koko the Clown, a cartoon character created by Max Fleischer and appearing in numerous cartoons from 1919–1961.

The ship to the right of Koko may be the legendary Flying Dutchman, cursed to sail the oceans forever because its captain made a rash oath.

Page 178. Panel 1. The animal-headed creatures at the bottom of this panel and in the rest of the sequence are described in Margaret Cavendish's *The Blazing World*:

> The rest of the Inhabitants of that World, were men of several different sorts, shapes, figures, dispositions, and humors, as I have already made mention heretofore; some were Bear-men, some Worm-men, some Fish- or Mear-men, otherwise called Syrenes; some Bird-men, some Fly-men, some Ant-men, some Geese-men, some Spider-men, some Lice-men, some Fox-men, some Ape-men, some Jack-daw-men, some Magpie-men, some Parrot-men, some Satyrs, some Gyants, and many more, which I cannot all remember; and of these several sorts of men, each followed such a profession as was most proper for the nature of their species, which the Empress encouraged them in, especially those that had applied themselves to the study of several Arts and Sciences; for they were as ingenious and witty in the invention of profitable and useful Arts, as we are in our world, nay, more; and to that end she erected Schools, and founded several Societies.

Panel 2. Parts of the Blazing World, especially this and Page 179, Panel 1, may be visual homages to the Salvador Dali-designed dream sequence in the Hitchcock film *Spellbound* (1945).

"Er is nog zo'n plek, in de buurt van de zuidpool van der aarde."
"There is another place like this, near the South Pole of the Earth."

The two characters in the lower right-hand corner are Disney's Goofy and Donald Duck. To their left is A. A. Milne's Winnie the Pooh, defecating.

Kevin O'Neill notes:
> No Jess, it is just a regular dog man laying pavement logs. Or playing pooh-sticks as we probably didn't say in my south London youth.

Page 179. Panel 1. "…this South Pole location, Megapatagonia, is actually the same *place* as the Blazing World?"
Megapatagonia was created by Nicolas Edme Restif de la Bretonne and appeared in *La Découverte australe Par un Homme-volant* (1781). It is an archipelago which is exactly opposite France and so its culture is an inverse of the French, down to its capital "Sirap." Megapatagonia being the same as the Blazing World explains certain reversals, as mentioned below on Page 183.

Page 180. Panel 1. "Meteen, admiraal van genoegen."
"At once, admiral of pleasure."

On the right side of the panel is one of M. C. Escher's flying fish.

Panel 2. "Zusters! Het is zo prachtig om jullie te zien!"
"Sisters! It is so lovely to see you."

Panel 3. "Welkom, vurige piraat van het hart! We zullen sterven van geluk!"
"Welcome, fiery pirate of the heart! We will die from happiness!"

Page 181. Panels 1–4. Perhaps the giant walking by is Gulliver, as large in the Blazing World as he was on Lilliput?

Panel 2. "I was a bloody orange cat for simply *ages*."
See Page 157.

Page 182. Panel 1. The wrestling dwarf is Maurie Richardson's Engelbrecht, mentioned on Page 146. As mentioned on Page 183, Engelbrecht's opponent is Poetry. The words on Poetry's left arm are from Wordsworth's "I wandered lonely as a cloud" (1804), and the words on his right arm are from Felicia Dorothea Browne Hemans's "Casabianca" (1826).

Panel 2. The character at the top of the page is P. L. Travers's Mary Poppins.

Visible in the portal in this panel and the next three are the Faraway Tree and the House on the Borderland. The Faraway Tree was created by Enid Blyton and appeared in four novels from 1939–1951. The Faraway Tree is a magic tree at the top of which is a ladder which leads to magic lands. The House on the Borderland was created by W. H. Hodgson and appeared in *The House on the Borderland* (1908). The House on the Borderland is a gateway to another world.

In this panel, in the Faraway Tree section, can be seen what looks like the White Rabbit from Lewis Carroll's *Alice's Adventures in Wonderland* (1865).

"…the swine-things' *Borderland*…"
This is a reference to Hodgson's *The House on the Borderland*. The other world that the House on the Borderland is linked to is inhabited by evil swine monsters. (The swine monster can be seen on Panel 3 on this page and in Panels 1 and 2 on Page 183.)

"…the various realms of that peculiar tree in Buckinghamshire."
The tree is mentioned in *League* v2.

The words on Poetry's right and left arm are from Felicia Dorothea Browne Hemans's "Casabianca."

Panel 3. Perhaps coincidentally, the inhabitant of the Faraway Tree in the portal looks like one of the elves from the Keebler TV commercials. The Keebler elves live in a magic tree.

That may be Piglet, Winnie the Pooh's young companion, in the portal.

The words on Poetry are from Felicia Dorothea Browne Hemans's "Casabianca."

Page 183. **Panel 1**. The words on Poetry are from John Keats's "On First Looking Into Chapman's Homer" (1816).

The two children on the flying chair, who can be glimpsed in the portal on Page 182, Panel 3, are Mollie and Peter, who were created by Enid Blyton and appeared in the three "Wishing-Chair" stories from 1937–2000. Mollie and Peter find a magic chair in an antique shop and use it to visit places and have adventures.

In the portal can be seen Dame Washalot, from Blyton's "Faraway Tree" series. Dame Washalot is an eccentric inhabitant of the Faraway Tree.

Panel 2. The two characters in the portal are The Saucepan Man and Moonface, from Blyton's "Faraway Tree" series. The Saucepan Man is covered with saucepans and kettles tied to his body, and Moonface is another inhabitant of the Tree.

Panel 3. The winged thing in the upper part of the panel is a Flying Buttress.

Kevin O'Neill notes:
> The winged object is the leg of the flying chair in close-up.

Page 184. Panel 1. The flying character is Ace Hart, who appeared in the British comic *Super Thriller* #6 (1948). "Ace Hart, a young scientist, has been able to harness atomic energy to his own body, which gives him the strength of twenty men, and enables him to fly faster than a jet."

The character on the flying carpet on this page may be Baggy Pants, from the British comic *Dandy* (1956–1959). Baggy Pants is a genie-like magician.

Panel 2. The flying character is Commando Cody, who appeared in two movie serials in 1952 and 1953. Commando Cody is an inventor who creates an "atomic-powered rocket suit" and uses it to fight threats against humanity.

In the pool can be seen mermaids and water-babies from Charles Kingsley's *The Water Babies*, mentioned on Page 96.

Page 185. Panel 1. The figure sitting on the stairs is A. A. Milne's Winnie the Pooh, who is sitting halfway down the stairs, a reference to Milne's poem "Halfway Down" (1924).

The figure at the bottom of the page is the creature from Page 184, Panel 1. It has dived into the pool and caught a Water Baby in its mouth.

Kevin O'Neill notes:
> The Yellow Claw is standing under the stairs at the top of the page.

Panel 2. The creature seen in the window on this page, whose tentacles can be seen on Page 184, Panel 1, may be only an octopus, or it may be a reference to Pierre Dénys de Montfort's paintings of giant octopi and the Kraken.

Page 186. Panel 1. The figure with the fly head may be the protagonist of any of "The Fly" movies (there were five of them, from 1958–1989), whose head is swapped with that of a housefly in a teleportation accident.

Kevin O'Neill notes:
> The yellow-eyed fly admiring a ring is from *One Hundred Nonsense Pictures and Rhymes* by Edward Lear (1872).

The toad in the tuxedo may be Mr. Toad, from Kenneth Grahame's *The Wind in the Willows* (1908). Mr. Toad is an excitable and wealthy motorist (among other things).

The green-costumed figure below and to the right of might-be-Mr. Toad may be Turan, one of the Fly People who gave Tommy Troy his abilities, as mentioned on Page 157.

Panel 3. "Do give the Duke Toyland's regards. Truly, he is a philosopher of the heart's sorrows."
The "Duke" in this case is Prospero, and the "heart's sorrows" phrase is from *The Tempest*. The speaker is Adam, Frankenstein's

creation, who according to the second *League* mini-series married the Queen of Toyland.

The topless cat-headed woman is the Egyptian cat goddess Bast.

The dog next to Bast may be Dogtanian, from the cartoon *Dogtanian and the Three Muskehounds* (1981).

Kevin O'Neill notes:
> Just behind Orlando is Heros the Spartan.

Page 187. Panel 1. "I pray thee, do not rise."
This child, who is incapable of saying anything else, appears in from Marco Denevi's "La niña rosa" (1966).

At the top left of the panel, looking out over the skyline, is Marsman, from the British superhero comic *Marsman Comics* #1 (1948). Marsman is a Martian who comes to Earth to "make a report on Earth's social life and civilisation."

The child with the large hat may be Mysterious Pete, from Lyonel Feininger's comic strip "The Kin-der-Kids" (1906–1907). Mysterious Pete is a mysterious figure who gives messages and directions to the other characters in the comic strip.

The blond male in the lower right-hand section of the panel is Masterman, from the British superhero comic *Masterman* #1–#10 (1952–1953). Masterman is Bobby Fletcher, a boy who uses the Ring of Fate to turn into the superpowered, crime-fighting Masterman.

Kevin O'Neill notes:
> Yes, it is Mysterious Pete. Lyonel Feininger was bloody brilliant—the setting sun behind pages 186-187 I hope is in his spirit.
>
> Just below Masterman is author Michael Moorcock enjoying some alien refreshment—probably Martian hooch.

Panel 2. The character on the left side of the panel may be Johnston McCulley's Zorro, from stories, novels, comics, movies, and TV series, 1919–present. Don Diego de la Vega, foppish aristocrat in Spanish California, is actually the daring masked vigilante Zorro.

Above and to the right of Zorro may be the Lone Ranger, mentioned above on Page 151.

To the right of the woman speaking to the Lone Ranger is Captain Marvel, mentioned above on Page 157.

Captain Marvel is looking at Shazam, the wizard who grants him powers.

To the right of Captain Marvel is Thunderbolt Jaxon, who appeared in various British comics, 1949–1958. Jack Jaxon finds the magic belt of Thor, the Norse God of Thunder, and uses the belt to become Thunderbolt Jaxon, superpowered crimefighter.

To the right of Zorro, with her back to the viewer, may be the Disney film version of Snow White.

Snow White may be speaking to Charles Schulz's Charlie Brown and Linus.

Panel 3. The smirking boy in center left of the panel may be *Mad* magazine mascot Alfred E. Neuman.

The Elizabethan character may be Edmund Blackadder, from the second *Blackadder* series (see Page 46, Panel 3).

The woman standing behind Allan is the Marvel Comics character the Blonde Phantom, by day secretary Louise Grant, by night crime-fighting masked vigilante the Blonde Phantom.

Kevin O'Neill notes:
> About midway up is the Amalgamated Press version of Robin Hood, a staple of 1950s British annuals.

Page 188. Panel 4. "A-all the Just-So animals are still stampeding around loose, then?"
This is a reference to Rudyard Kipling's *Just So Stories For Little Children* (1902), thirteen stories about how various animals' features developed.

These animals are drawn in the style of Winsor McCay, and the narrow or thin panels of the entire Blazing World sequence are likely homages to McCay's classic comic strip "Little Nemo in Slumberland" (1905–1913), in which a little boy has adventures in Slumberland while he dreams.

Panel 5. "Come along, Fanny, dear. I'm going to dye my hair back to its former *brunette* so I don't clash with *Wilhelmina*."
This may be a reference to the movie *Bram Stoker's Dracula* (1992), in which Sadie Frost and Winona Ryder, the actresses who were playing Lucy Westenra and Mina Murray, respectively, were both brunettes, and Frost was forced by director Francis Ford Coppola to dye her hair red so that it would be easier to distinguish the two.

Page 189. Panel 1. Nyarlathotep says, "The three-lobed burning eye cares not." See the notes to Pages 26 and 117.

Panel 2. Nyarlathotep says, "The Lloigor are offended." In the Cthulhu Mythos, the Lloigor are a race of malign energy beings.

Panel 4. "Goodnight, sweet Duke."
This may be a reference to Horatio's comment to Hamlet in *Hamlet* (c. 1600), "Good night, sweet prince."

Page 190. Panel 1. "...our bead-game won...."
This may be a reference to Hermann Hesse's *Magister Ludi* (1943), in which the "Glass Bead Game" is a game in which players simulate reality.

Kevin O'Neill notes:
> Just below and beside Ariel are three characters from Booth

Tarkington's *Beasley's Christmas* (1909). Their inclusion was a special request from Melinda Gebbie, for whom the book was a childhood favourite.

Panel 3. The character breaking frame in the lower right-hand corner is Mighty Moth, who appeared in an eponymous comic strip in the British comic *TV Comic* from 1959–1984. Mighty Moth is a moth who fights evil.

Page 191. Panel 1. "Two sketching hands, each one the other draws: The fantasies thou've fashioned fashion thee."
This is a reference to the M. C. Escher lithograph "Drawing Hands" (1948).

Page 192. It's fitting that Ariel breaks the frame here.

ALAN MOORE INTERVIEW

Jess Nevins: Was there a specific point during the writing of the earlier *League* books that inspired you to do the *Black Dossier* in the formats it's in, or was it more of an organic evolution of the idea?

Alan Moore: I think, probably, it was more of an organic evolution than a specific point. What actually happened was that it was at the end of the second *League* book and I think that Kevin was just finishing up the endpapers and the tiny little bits of design work that were needed for the Absolute edition or for the hardback edition of the second volume. And we'd been talking over the phone, and he had said in a jocular manner that he supposed he was out of work at the moment, and after I put the phone down I was so touched by the vision of Kevin having to go down to the Job Centre the following morning and learn new skills at his time of life that I just couldn't bear the thought of that happening, so I phoned him up and told him that I'd had an idea for a kind of fill-in book that Kevin could work on while I was finishing up the various other projects that I had to finish up before thinking about Book Three. Initially, the idea was that we could maybe put together a sourcebook, but we could perhaps make it interesting, and it perhaps wouldn't be too demanding a job, and that this would give Kevin something agreeable to do until I was finished with the other commitments. What happened was, once I sat down and started thinking about the idea of a sourcebook, I realized that none of them are actually any good, and that's mainly because they don't actually have a narrative element tying them together. So the idea came to me that it might be possible to do a kind of self-referential sourcebook, where you could have a narrative that involved the retrieval of the sourcebook itself, and then a chase, in order to get it out of the country and safely home. So this was what I started to put together, and it sort of grew in the telling. Once I realized that we weren't, strictly speaking, doing a sourcebook any more, but neither, strictly speaking, were we doing a comic book, I became aware that it had turned into something fairly new, that it was certainly unlike anything that I'd worked on before, and that there were possibilities for us to include all sorts of things. We talked about the idea of the record, which should be coming out in the larger edition, which should be due out in a month or so—

JN: That's good news. There's been a lot of interest from fans in the record and a lot of them were disappointed that it didn't get included in the—

AM: That's nice. It was from the beginning meant to be part of the package, along with all the other things. And right at the beginning of the project, when Kevin had agreed that he'd like to do it, when we talked to Wildstorm about it, they were delighted, and promised Kevin that he would have as long as he wanted to do the artwork, and that the book wouldn't be solicited until he was finished, which sounded like a perfectly sane and reasonable way of dealing with Kevin, where, quite frankly, if he wants to take as long as he wants on a piece of artwork, that is as long as it will take. And that is perfectly fine by me, the end result is always spectacular. These things can't be rushed. So we embarked upon the *Black Dossier* and it carried on getting more and more entertaining for us as we went along, really. It was a much longer job than we'd originally imagined, but we're both very pleased with the amount of unusual material we've managed to get into there.

JN: That sort of leads into the question of, what exactly went wrong? Why did DC end up treating what had been a very successful set of books for them and a very successful writer–artist team—why did they end up treating you all so badly? I know you've been asked this before, but—

AM: Surprisingly few times, actually. And I probably still don't have a better answer for it. Yes, they have treated me and Kevin, particularly over this past year Kevin, very badly indeed. They have treated us in I suppose what is not an unsurprising manner, given that most of our previous dealings with them have seemed to be on their part kind of neurotic and incompetent. I think that what happened upon this occasion was that after I had somehow got through five years of working for Wildstorm/DC, in which we had had issues pulped at the whim of the publisher, in which I'd had stories refused, again at the whim of the publisher, and yes this has been irritating and it's been annoying, but then, like I say, this is the kind of behavior I have come to expect from these people. At the end of that, I had been very clear with the way Wildstorm, at least, had produced the first two volumes. I'd said to them, I was happy for Wildstorm to continue publishing the *League* until such a point as I was reminded that the people who owned Wildstorm were DC Comics, who have treated me very badly in the past and who I don't want really to work for and haven't done since the mid-1980s.

Now, what basically seemed to happen was that when that ridiculous business with the *V for Vendetta* film suddenly erupted, which I considered to be a very strong reminder that the *League of Extraordinary Gentlemen* was being published by DC Comics, who were owned by Warner Brothers, who were making all of these statements about me which were actually untrue, and so I said, fair enough, I gave them the opportunity to make a modest retraction, correction, and clarification upon the statements that they'd been making about me. Which was no more than the simple honest truth. But that was, perhaps, a little more than I should have expected. When they tell the truth, it makes their tongues turn black and fall out or something like that. So I said, fair enough, we will finish the *Black Dossier*, this will be the last book that we shall be doing for you, we will be published in the future by Top Shelf. Now, this was the point at which I had just finished the writing of the book. This was the beginning of Kevin's troubles. He immediately started to get a barrage of phone calls that were frankly hostile. And far from saying that he would have until he had got the last page finished before the book was solicited, they were now saying that they'd suddenly, out of the blue, made up a completely spurious date by which this book must be published. They were demanding of Kevin—which is ridiculous, for these frankly talentless nonentities to demand something of an artist of Kevin's stature, when they have already promised him a completely different form of treatment—but they seemed to have suddenly decided that they were going to teach us a lesson. They were asking Kevin to turn out a page a day to meet their completely spurious deadline, even if the work was bad and suffered as a result.

At one point, when Kevin had finished all of the work, including the 3-D section, which he'd finished early, because he wanted them to have plenty of time to get it to Ray Zone, who was already very eager to start work on it, and we knew that it was going to be a complex job, so we wanted to give the production people plenty of time to get to work upon the 3-D section—so having finished that, Kevin was about to start upon the final piece for the *Dossier*, which was the Orlando section, which he'd left to the last. At this point somebody at DC said, "Listen, if you left out that entire section, you'd be back on schedule!" Which Kevin told them, in no uncertain terms, that that was inane, ridiculous, and wasn't going to happen. I don't think that anybody there had ever read it. I don't know whether there was anybody there who was literate enough to read it. I suspect that most of the scripts that I've sent them have gone unread until they had pictures accompanying them, at which point, maybe, somebody would get around to actually reading through something and understanding it. They clearly didn't have any idea as to how all of the various bits of information in the *Dossier* fitted together. They didn't have any idea that you couldn't just leave out twenty-five crucial pages of it and have it still be the same book. Or maybe they did. Either, that is a sign of incredible stupidity, illiteracy, and incompetence, or—to be generous about it—it might have been intentional. It might have been that DC were thinking something along the lines—this would be incredibly petty, spiteful, and childish, but they may have been thinking along the lines of, that they were incredibly offended that we should have taken this very lucrative title away from them because, actually, we own it, unlike any of the other things that I've ever done for that wretched company. We've taken this away from them after their bad behavior. Which was not one incident but which was several incidents throughout the entire of my regrettable period with them, particularly this last ABC period.

Now, they seemed to have been so irked by that, that I think they perhaps decided that it would be in their best interests to sabotage the *Black Dossier* so that the book's readers, who would probably buy it, expecting it to be good, then would be terribly disappointed, when it turned out to be substandard. I think they had perhaps hoped that the readership, if that had been the case, would have thought, well, obviously, Kevin and I had completely run out of ideas on the book, that our hearts weren't in it, and that there probably wouldn't be a great deal of point in picking up the book when Volume Three came out from Top Shelf. I think that they did that for a number of reasons—like I say, I think they were hoping to somehow disadvantage Chris Staros and any future volumes of the book. I think that they also—it has to be said that a lot of this seems to have intensified since there was that wretched poll in *Time* magazine, which is a magazine we don't get over here and isn't of very much importance to us, but as I understand it from the excited people who phoned me up—excited people from DC and Wildstorm—to tell me that *Watchmen* had been voted, I think it was, number one for a couple of weeks and ended up somewhere at number five or something. Which is ludicrous, because I myself can think of a great number of American novels and great literary works that really should have been up there.

JN: It's flattering, certainly, but—

AM: It's inane. Where's Steinbeck? Where's Faulkner?

JN: Where's Pynchon?

AM: It's inane. And also, *Watchmen* isn't even American. It was published by an American company, but despite that list of names in the back of the book, there were only three people who really worked on it, and they were all British. I tend to think that—from what I heard, that was the only "graphic novel" that appeared in the entire list. Now, like I say, we don't tend to pay much attention to lists like that over here, but I got the impression that over there, at least at DC Comics, it was important to them. And I should think also probably a little bit galling. Because if you did pay attention to lists like that, then that would kind of imply that in sixty or seventy years, the American comic industry hadn't been able to create a single work that had been taken to by the general public to the degree that *Watchmen* had. Which would be quite damning,

I would have thought, if you do pay attention to these things. So I wondered whether the fact that the *Black Dossier* was the work it was had had some bearing upon the way that it was treated. It struck me that maybe it made a lot of DC's other products look kind of lazy and a little bit illiterate. I don't know whether that's the case, but that's the only thing that I could think of. Because otherwise their behavior is kind of senseless and extraordinary. Like I say, I'm not at all surprised that their behavior is senseless and extraordinary, but on this particular occasion they seem to be acting even more unfathomably than usual. Unless it is all just another one of DC's cunning plans which always end up terribly. They're a bit like Donald Rumsfeld's cunning plans. They never work and they just leave an embarrassing mess, which I'm pretty sure that they'll probably manage to do again over this new *Watchmen* film. But that's completely off the subject. So, yeah, they gave us the runaround something rotten, particularly Kevin, who certainly didn't deserve any of the treatment he got from these clowns. That has completely decided me—

Well, that's only half the story, really. This was the story up until last summer. At that point when DC had finally made all of the irritating, carping changes and omissions that they were going to make—they were going to leave out the record, they were going to not be bringing it out in the initial large format that I'd been assured they would be bringing it out in, and apparently they'd been completely unable to understand simple instructions like leaving the edges of the Fanny Hill pages sealed. This was after they'd gone to the trouble—when I'd suggested that we have a section in the style of John Cleland, and I'd said, what might be fun is if we actually had the edges of the pages sealed like they did in old books. It was just an idle suggestion. I'd have been perfectly happy if they'd said, no, we can't do that. What they had said was, yeah, we can do that, definitely, but we'll need a heavier grade of paper. So I said, well, if the economics work out, let's go for it. We got the heavier grade of paper, but by that time there was apparently nobody at DC or Wildstorm who understood what we meant by leaving the edges of the pages uncut in the way that they did with old Victorian books. It got published with all of the edges of the pages open despite all of the references in the text to them being closed.

So there was the way that we had been promised that the book was coming out. We'd already suffered lots of disappointments and been told that, no, it wouldn't be a big book, no, there wouldn't be a single enclosed. But, around about last summer, it was ready to come out. It had been through an exhaustive process with DC's lawyers, who had cleared the book for publication—this was publication in the U.K., in Canada, in all those other places where it never eventually came out. So this was the situation until a few weeks before it was due to go to print. This was last summer. At this point another petty talentless American entertainment industry figure enters the picture. It transpires—allegedly, we've heard this from somebody who was working at DC on the *Black Dossier*—now, I've got no real reason to believe anybody over there involved in that business at the moment, but if what we heard was true, and I've got no reason to believe that it isn't—then around about last summer a movie producer that me and Kevin had both had some unpleasant dealings with—this was the person who had, according to Twentieth Century Fox's lawyers, been responsible for sending the alleged joke e-mails to the plaintiff in that ridiculous *League of Extraordinary Gentlemen* lawsuit that came up a couple of years ago, if you remember, when Twentieth Century Fox was being sued—

JN: I don't think I heard the story of the joke e-mails.

AM: Well, during this case, a couple of the plaintiffs, a screenwriter and somebody else, had made the case that they had provided a screenplay which included a number of Victorian characters, none of whom were the Victorian characters in my comic book, but a couple of which were the Victorian characters that had been unnecessarily shoehorned into that wretched film. Now, on the strength of this, the plaintiffs had to bring a case, because they knew that the film had been based on my comic, they had to come up with an unlikely scenario in which the head of Twentieth Century Fox had stolen their screenplay, had got in touch with me, because apparently we're such good friends, and had asked me to write a graphic novel, purely to camouflage his theft of this screenwriter's screenplay. And apparently I'd agreed to this. This I found incredibly insulting, because as you know I've not got the greatest of regard for Hollywood screenwriters, so the thought that one of them was accusing me of getting my ideas from him or from Hollywood in general was profoundly insulting.

So I went down to London and in a basement room I made—I was on a video-link, and I put in a deposition, speaking for ten hours and being cross-examined, regarding the *League of Extraordinary Gentlemen*, my authorship of it, and when I'd come up with the idea, and all of this stuff. As it turned out, I needn't have gone down there for those ten hours, because it was already a lost cause anyway. Twentieth Century Fox had to settle out of court. I was told by Twentieth Century Fox's lawyers, on that occasion, that the reason they'd had to settle out of court was because the film's producer had sent joke e-mails—alleged joke e-mails—to the plaintiffs, stating that, yes, I had stolen all of my ideas from their screenplay. Now, that is actually libel. I was very very angry about it, and so the next time that this producer's office contacted me, I said that I never wanted to have any contact with this third-rate, sweaty buffoon, ever again. Kevin had already had similar dealings when he'd actually gone over there, more fool him, to have a look at the film in production, and he'd attended the premiere of it. After the premiere, when it had become pretty obvious that it was a colossal failure, Kevin—because he'd got on well with the director and some of the actors—Kevin had felt that he didn't really want to make any cutting or negative comments. So he'd been a nice guy about it and said, yeah, well, it was alright for an adventure film—something noncommittal like that. This had been taken by the film's producer and worked up into a veritable essay about how much Kevin enjoyed the film, how faithful a reproduction of our work it was. Which was then posted upon the Ain't It Cool website.

So both me and Kevin were by this point very very sick of this individual. And we both told him not to contact us again. Not to phone, not to contact us in any way. So apparently he had felt stung by this, that we should have spurned him, a Hollywood producer, for so trivial a matter as the fact that he'd lied about us, that he'd lied to us, that he'd libeled us. We should have been prepared to accept him back into our hearts, apparently. So when he found out that we didn't, and that actually, yes, we despised him, he decided to go to DC and to demand that they show him the *Black Dossier*. He apparently was asking all the way through the final stages of Kevin working on the book, but it wasn't until the book was finished, because me and Kevin, whenever there was a request, had just said no, tell him he hasn't got any right to look at it, he just made a terrible film out of the first book, he's got no right to look at this third one. But apparently the people at DC, who are in my experience generally craven in most circumstances, are particularly cowardly when it comes to a loud, voluble, pushy, third-rate sweaty American Hollywood movie producer. This was my experience of how they behaved in the Joel Silver affair, and it seems to have been how they behaved in this current set of circumstances. They allowed him and his lawyer, or one of his lawyers, to read through the book, at the end of which, he said that—I think he implied—this is what we were told—we were told that he had more or less implied that, because there were figures in the book that he recognized as characters from, say, popular movies, he was convinced, or he convinced DC, that if Hollywood were to find out about this book, and I should imagine with the heavy implication that he would make sure that Hollywood found out, then DC would be sued—despite the fact that DC's own legal department had gone through the book exhaustively and cleared it. This was the point at which Kevin was suddenly sent a huge list, a week before the print deadline, of changes that they wanted made. These were ridiculous. I think that Jim Lee got most of them thrown out, because they were obviously just complete nuisance time wasting, which we shouldn't have had to deal with at any point. But there were a number of them that they decided to stick with. And when they were suggesting that I change the names "Jeeves" and "Wooster" to some silly made-up names like, I dunno, "Jooves" and "Weester," perhaps, I by this point was reminded of the incident that I'd had with Cobweb, when we'd done that story about L. Ron Hubbard and John Whitesides Parsons, in which I'd gone through for a couple of hours that entire story with someone from DC's legal department, and at the end of it they'd said, yes, this is fine to publish, and at that instance Paul Levitz had stepped in and said that even though the legal department has assured me that this is fine to publish, I think that I'm still going to refuse to publish it, for his own, presumably petty reasons.

So, expecting something like that, I told them that, no, we weren't prepared to change the name "Jeeves" and "Wooster" just because they had suddenly and maliciously decided that they wanted to do so. This was before we had found out about the alleged interference from the Hollywood movie producer. So the end result was that, yes, the book came out in America. It didn't officially come out in Canada or England, although from what I understand a lot of shops have simply been aware that this was actually a bullshit legal decision and that they've been treating it as such. But I would remark that this movie producer is also a comic shop proprietor. His comic shop being in the United States, I don't know, whether perhaps, if he isn't refusing to sell it at all, and if he isn't refusing to make money out of this book that he obviously found so many offensive things in. Or perhaps he is, and it's only the retailers in Canada that have been disadvantaged. Not sure about that. But that is pretty much the long and sorry story about what happened to the *Black Dossier*. It has completely convinced me that outside of Top Shelf I don't really trust any comics companies, and effectively we're talking about American comics companies now. I don't trust them to be honest with us. It seems to me to be a sort of grubby, third-rate industry that may have had an opportunity to drag itself up out of the mud but couldn't really shuck off the sixty-year-old gangster practices and gangster attitudes that it had grown out of.

JN: And in the 1940s, ties with the gangsters who were involved in the publishing—

AM: Meyer Lansky and Legs Diamond and all the rest of them, yeah. Frank Costello. The whole bunch. That is what the comics industry grew out of. And they have never really bothered to throw off those associations or really those business practices. They've modified them slightly. They carry out their acts of violence in a more subtle and completely legal way, these days. But they're probably even more morally reprehensible. So, they have, basically, after all these years, finally managed to make me regret my involvement with American comics. All of the books that they own, I really have no interest in any more. Yes, they were great books, and I'm very glad that me and the artists were able to work on them so well and to do such a good job, but I've really got to consign them to the past, because I really want nothing to do with the comic industry any more. At the moment I'm cleaning out most of my comic collection. It's down to a couple of old 1960s comics, mostly Herbies. I've got rid of everything else. With the exception of the *League*, I'm pretty much out of comics. But, mercifully, and luckily, the *League* does exist, so I am enjoying—all of the enthusiasm I have for the comics medium is being poured into the *League*, into Volume Three and into the future books that we're already talking about. We were incredibly pleased with the way that the *Black Dossier* came out, in that, even though, yes, there were stupid, minor, pointless alterations made all the way through it, it was not the book that we had been promised, I think that it was such a good book, that even with the pissy little alterations that its publisher had insisted on, and the little bits of sabotage or attempted sabotage, I don't think that any of the people involved managed to do anything to really harm the book. They've only left their grubby fingerprints over it, to show how they treated the book. From my perspective, that's a fairly decent outcome.

JN: So what you're saying is that there's no chance of you writing for *Captain America*?

AM: I think that you probably could conclude that, yeah. No, I really don't want anything to do with the American comics scene any more. With the exception of Top Shelf, who have been a wonderful, reputable, fair, decent company to work for, and who have done a fantastic job on *Lost Girls*, which me and Kevin are both looking forward to having done on Volume Three. So, no, no *Captain America* in the foreseeable future.

JN: Changing gears somewhat, there seems to be more of your sense of humor displayed in the *Dossier* than in the earlier *League*. Was that just how the *Dossier* ended up being written, or was there somewhat of a sense of lightness on your part because of your impending departure from American comics?

AM: A bit of both. I think that once I became aware of the possibilities of the *Black Dossier*, this peculiar thing that wasn't quite a sourcebook and that wasn't quite a comic book, I think that

I started to take a kind of almost childish delight in the possibilities, the things that we could play with. Yeah, I should imagine that perhaps my sense of humor, such as it is, is perhaps more evident in the *Black Dossier* than in the early books. In the early books it tended to be confined to the letters page and the packaging, the various adverts and things like that, the messages from the editor. But with the *Black Dossier* it makes up a good chunk of the book—the P. G. Wodehouse, H. P. Lovecraft mashup, as you referred to it, was a lot of fun. The Shakespeare piece was a lot of fun. The piece that I most enjoyed was probably the *Crazy Wide Forever*, the Beat novel, that I gather was impenetrable to a lot of people. And it wasn't only the bits in the *Dossier* where we managed to get in a certain amount of humor. In the actual comic strip section, although there's some dark and depressing stuff that's going on there, there are some quite funny things going on as well, particularly in Kevin's backgrounds, and some of the illustrated details that he's added. It was a lot of fun to write, it was very liberating, we were throwing away most of the things that people found familiar about the *League of Extraordinary Gentlemen*. We were throwing away the Victorian milieu, which we thought would probably lose a lot of readers, because we assumed that people liked that High Victorian adventure and the more visual characters such as Hyde and Nemo and the Invisible Man, if you can call the Invisible Man a visual character. But with them out of the picture, and with the action moved to 1958, we figured that, yeah, we might lose a lot of readers who had been mainly along for the Victorian ride. But from what I hear it's actually selling better than the first two collected volumes did. Which kind of suggests that there is a group of readers out there who perhaps haven't looked at the *League* before who perhaps aren't that interested in the Victorian characters but who, in the *Black Dossier*, have come across characters that they're familiar with from their own century, from their own lifetimes. So maybe that is why the book does seem to be selling quite well. Yeah, it was a thing that kind of evolved. We wanted it to have a different feeling—partly, that was inevitable because of the 1958 section. But we wanted the whole book to have a different mood that was more appropriate to those times than the atmosphere of the first two Victorian books. So we're very pleased with how it turned out. We did manage to get quite a lot of laughs in there, some fairly obvious, some bits of broad humor, like the *1984*

Orwellian porno comic, which, yeah, that was broad humor. But there were some clever little bits and references that we found kind of funny and entertaining, but, don't know, they might have sailed completely over other people's heads. But there is a lot of deliberate humor in there, because we're reflecting a world of culture, of films and television and literature, which did have an increasing comic element, perhaps, by the 1950s.

JN: I thought it was interesting that the world in the *Dossier* is recovering from the government of Big Brother, and it's the late Fifties, and there are still shell marks on buildings, and ostensibly you'd think that this would be a sort of grim, gray environment, and yet there's—a lot of the *Dossier* is lighthearted, and I thought it was interesting that you could look at it as a grim book with lighthearted moments or a lighthearted book with grim themes.

AM: The way that we saw the whole crucial historical progression of our fictional Second World War, it struck us that Orwell had originally written *1984* in, what, 1947?

JN: 1947 and 1948.

AM: And I believe the original title for the book had been *1948*. This may be apocryphal, but I did hear that his original title had been *1948* and that he'd been told by the publishers that it was too soon, too contemporary, and that nobody would understand what he was trying to say, and so he changed the last two digits around and made it into *1984*. But, that aside, I think Orwell's book, it kind of reeks of the British 1940s. It is very much a kind of postwar, a book of postwar austerity, and greyness, and drabness, which still prevailed in the 1950s, when I was growing up. I was born in 1953, and I can remember the 1950s as a very dark time. Everything seemed to happen indoors, and you weren't—it seemed as if colors were rationed, so that you were only allowed, I dunno, black, grey, sepia. We didn't really have colors until the early 1960s. And, yeah, it was a very drab time. At the same time, there was all of this bright, postwar stuff starting to emerge. There was new technology. There were Dansette record players. There were different sorts of cars in the street—bubble cars and futuristic-looking things like that. There was new music emerging and we were playing it upon smaller radios that were portable. So there was the promise of a very new and futuristic world erupting out of the dark post-war shadows of a very battered England. And we tried to capture that in the *Dossier*, but in fictional terms. So, yes, we have got these very distressed-looking streets and buildings, and we've got the Birmingham Spaceport, which of course never existed in the real world, but it was obviously on our minds, the idea of space travel, in the Fifties, starting with Dan Dare in 1950 and including *Journey Into Space* and various other radio series and comic strips and text stories. So it seemed that, at least in our imaginations, in the 1950s, Britain was getting into space. And the idea of something as modern as the Birmingham Spaceport, it seemed to strike the right sort of contrast that things like the London Airport struck for me the first time that I saw London Airport in the early Sixties. It was like something from a different world, in contrast to the kind of streets and houses that I was familiar with. It was like a huge chunk of the future, and I think that I tried to capture some of that in the sequence in the *Dossier* with the Spaceport. It was that contrast that both me and Kevin were aware of, just what a contrast that was, when we were on the brink of the Sixties, when the war was about ten years behind us, when the Summer of Love was about ten years ahead of us—that we were between two times that were noticeably different, and I think we tried to capture that sense of being on the cusp in the *Dossier*.

JN: Do you feel like the *League* books are getting more British in their outlook? Or is it more or less constant? One of the things that struck me was that in Room 101 there's a cane resting against a wicker chair, and for American readers the cane probably wouldn't mean as much, but for British readers, the idea of a cane being in Room 101, the worst place in the world—probably a fair number of British readers are going to be aware of what caning means.

AM: Certainly British readers of my generation would be aware. The school that I went to, I remember—this was a grammar school—where the headmaster had previously been a deputy headmaster at a public school, which means something quite different over here to what it does in America. Over here "public school" means places like Eton and Rugby that are schools that you have to be fairly aristocratic and have high-fee-paying parents to ever dream of getting into. These are the sorts of schools who turn out a lot of Tory cabinet ministers, and increasingly a lot of Labour cabinet ministers. This deputy headmaster, from a public school, found it a terrible demotion to be working at an ordinary grammar school, which although it catered to the top stream of children of its age, was a step down from public school. And I remember in his office he had a glass case in which he had an assortment of canes for different occasions. This would be difficult to believe, I'm sure, for a lot of people these days, but, yes, you have the light canes that would sting, and if wielded with enough force might even draw blood, and you have the thicker, heavier canes that would bruise. I think it was probably Kevin's idea to stick the—I'd just said, generally, torture implements. I think I'd mentioned the rat cage that connects to the helmet because that was mentioned in *1984*, but I think most of the other things in there were Kevin's own inclusion. So maybe at one of those schools that he attended as a boy it was a kind of unpleasant memory for Kevin as well, perhaps that is why he put it in there. But the general point, it's probably fair to say that it is getting more English even though both of the first books were set predominantly in England, and that will probably—throughout the third volume that will probably continue to be the case, in that they will be predominantly set in England. But the third volume opens with scenes in the South Atlantic, and so it's not exclusively about England, and in the future there's always a possibility that we will spend one volume or part of it talking about at least one incarnation of the League's foreign travels. We've got a lot of material there to choose from when it comes to selecting what we want to talk about in future books. It's predominantly based in England, but at the same time it can be global, or who knows, even in the future perhaps interplanetary in its scope. We'll just have to see what Kevin and I feel like doing.

Obviously when it comes to something like the *Black Dossier* it's because me and Kevin have got an awful lot of connections with the 1950s. And yet we were both very young during that decade. A lot of it passed us by. So when we came to study it for the purposes of the *League*, we were surprised at actually how exotic it was. It seemed to us that the fictional world of the 1950s was every bit as exotic as the fictional world of the late Victorian period—that enough time has elapsed between now and then, between now and fifty years ago, that there's been as much change in society as there had been in the previous hundred and fifty years or so before that. Yeah, those days do seem a long way away, and they do seem exotic. The kind of way we thought then, the kind of fictions we entertained ourselves with then. All of these things do seem quite strange to us now. And that was what we found when were doing the *Black Dossier*, anyway, and I suppose that any time that we deal with is going to be as interesting to us, as exotic. When we do the third volume, the third part of Volume Three, that will be set in the present day, and I think that the fictional world of the present day, there's a way we can make it every bit as fascinating as that world a hundred years ago.

JN: One of the things that struck me about reading the *Dossier* is that it feels like a real love letter to 1950s and 1960s British science fiction and television, and of course for most American readers and even younger British readers that's going to be as alien as the Victorian literature. Was it just a fortuitous happpenstance that you started looking at popular fiction, British popular culture in the 1950s, or did you think, this is a neglected and overlooked piece of British popular culture, I'd like to celebrate it a bit?

AM: Yeah. That was partly it. We sort of settled… why did we settle on 1958? I think because we decided that seemed like an interesting date, it was near as damn it fifty years after the first two books, and I think that when we started looking at that year and thinking about it, we started to realize that there was all of the spy fiction, and, yes, a lot of it would emerge later, in the early or mid-Sixties, but for the purposes of our fictional world it would clearly have been around in the late Fifties, at least in its seed form. And so we tried to come up with a scenario that tied in as many of the different spy fictions as possible, and tried to make sense of all those disparate fictions in terms of our world, which led us to, via the Frank Richards/George Orwell feud, led us to Billy Bunter, so we were able to revisit all of that stuff. There was, when we thought about it, just a wealth of material. Some of the characters we reference are not ones we were particularly devoted to, but ones that we thought might be amusing—for example, when we showed the destruction of Pompeii, to include the British camp comedian Frankie Howerd, who starred in a bogus faux-Pompeii, in a very innuendo-laden British sitcom in the early Seventies called *Up Pompeii!* I think that in some of the Roman scenes in Orlando we've got "Carry On" film extras taking some of the roles. In the first World War, I think Rowan Atkinson's Captain Blackadder turns up in a cameo. There's something that's just interesting about taking these fairly minor characters from comedies and television and dropping them into these epic situations. We realized that, yes, some of the references would probably be completely foreign or alien to Americans, but there again, it's not really a world these days where the country that you're living in makes a huge amount of difference. If you want to find out about these things, thanks to your own web sites as much as anything, it is possible to find out what these things are referring to. And I think that a lot of our readers are probably literate enough concerning these matters to know where they can find the answers if they're particularly bothered in looking for them. We delighted in—I know that Kevin was finding old British newspaper strip characters that he was dropping into the background, some of which completely bewildered me. If people don't get those references, I don't think that it will spoil the story, because the story is fairly simple.

All we've done with the *Black Dossier*—I was thinking about this the other day—what we've basically done is to unpack the MacGuffin. Hitchcock's idea of a MacGuffin: something that everybody wants and which doesn't really matter that much in itself, but which fuels the entire story, gets everybody chasing each other and doing all the things they need to do for dramatic narrative. All that we've done with the *Black Dossier* is to take the MacGuffin, the Dossier that everybody's after and that people are chasing after, and we've unpacked it. We've let the reader, we've let the audience know, what is in the MacGuffin, in the locked suitcase. It seemed like an interesting way of working. And I don't think that readers who don't get all the references are necessarily going to be all that alienated from the story—I might be wrong there. But I think the story is fairly exciting, fairly easy to understand even if you don't know what all of the rocketships in the Spaceport are references to. Even if you don't know what the ship that Allan and Mina climb aboard is a reference to, or what its robot pilot is a reference to. I think there's an essential kind of adventure and comedy in the situation that is going to be conveyed anyway even if you don't know these things. You have to remember that me and Kevin and most people over here, we were reading *Mad Comics* and *Mad Magazine* back in the early Sixties, and, yeah, there were lots of references to American things that we'd got no idea about. But you kind of picked them up in context. I think most readers are probably at least as intelligent as me and Kevin were fifty years ago, so I should imagine that even if there are details that escape some people, that they'll still be able to enjoy the story on some level or other. We tried to make it so that it is enjoyable upon a number of levels, both by the literary professors and by the people who are just looking for an exciting, stomping good read. That was more or less our thinking regarding the inclusion of all these obscure characters from cinema and television.

JN: You mentioned the Frank Richards/George Orwell feud. I've described your treatment of Billy Bunter as "Orwellian," but people don't seem to get that. Do you think Orwell would generally have approved of what you did?

AM: I wouldn't go that far. I'd like to think that he might have smirked. He might have lifted his moustache at one corner, perhaps. We were just intrigued by the fact—well, two facts, really: that Orwell had always said that the secret state, totalitarian apparatchiks in *1984*, the O'Briens and people like that, he'd based them, the Thought Police, all of these terrifying agents of repression, he'd based them upon the prefects at Eton, the public school that Orwell attended. That seemed to me to be resonant. It seemed to suggest that there was a connection there, between *1984* and the public school system. When I found out about the feud between Frank Richards and Orwell—it was pretty one-sided. Frank Richards a writer of schoolboy fiction who turned out hundreds of Billy Bunter books to pay off his gambling debts. He was a chronic gambling addict who was losing all of his advances at the roulette and blackjack tables and who would have to turn out another three

Greyfriars novels to pay the bills. Orwell had written this stinging little essay in which he—correctly—pointed out that the Greyfriars books were full of nationalism, a kind of misplaced celebration of the days of Empire, racism, and all sorts of things. Terribly hurt that the illustrious George Orwell should have picked upon his harmless little schoolboy stories, Frank Richards ill-advisedly wrote a reply in which he tried to defend his books against Orwell's criticisms, including his statement that "Mr. Orwell apparently takes objection with my treatment of foreigners as being figures of fun or amusement. But—they are!" Which is obviously perhaps not the best argument to leave to posterity.

So we were interested in putting those things together, and also because it led on to other things. There was a chain of interesting little connections. The fictional school Greyfriars was set in the fictional town of Bradgate, which is down on the south coast, according to Richards's books. Now, Bradgate was actually a surrogate for Broadstairs—Broadstairs in Kent, where Richards lived. And Kevin went down, he took a couple of days down in Broadstairs, so he could get the references right. It is a little wind-swept British seaside town, and there are a number of steps running up from the beach to the clifftop. And, at least by reputation—I think that Kevin said there were forty-something—but at least by reputation and tradition, there are supposed to be thirty-nine steps leading from the beach to the clifftop. And these are the same thirty-nine steps that John Buchan had written his novel *The Thirty-Nine Steps* to commemorate. So we were able to bring that in, and generally weave an interesting web, using characters from Greyfriars. I found an invaluable book, that Kevin found. It must have been published by some incredibly devoted Billy Bunter fans, and it was a hardback prospectus of Greyfriars School. It was fantastic. It had got maps of the school and where it was situated. I think we moved it a little bit closer to the clifftop, but we didn't really violate anything that Richards had set up. It had got ground plans of the school, details of its history, including the date when Queen Elizabeth was supposed to have visited it, which we referred to with the fictional Queen Gloriana, and there was a list of all the boys who had supposedly attended the school during the time that Billy Bunter and his friends were there. And we found a Francis Wavery, which was so close to the name

Waverley, which I was interested in bringing into the mix, because of *The Man From U.N.C.L.E.* connection, with Mr. Waverley, the head of the department. So I figured that maybe Wavery was a misprint, and perhaps he had a middle name. Perhaps it was Francis Alexander Waverley. It's little things like that, things that nobody who was sane would even notice, but in the kind of mindset that we've had to get into for the *Black Dossier* it's kind of neat the way that you can tie all these tiny little threads to make a bigger tapestry. So I don't know whether Orwell would have approved. I think he probably would have done on some level. If he'd have bothered reading a comic at all, I don't know. He certainly might have approved of our castigation of the British public school system and our suggestion that it was a breeding ground for spies and traitors.

JN: There has been some controversy among some fans about your portrayal of James Bond. They refuse to believe that he's as hateful and misogynistic as he was portrayed in the *Dossier*, despite the way that Fleming wrote him.

AM: They need to go back to the books, really. I would have thought there would have been plenty of unpleasant episodes in those early books, particularly in the *Spy Who Loved Me*, which was so misogynistic and strange that they had to make up a completely new story when they brought it to the screen. I'm sorry if James Bond fans are offended by that, but I think that the James Bond figure has always been a fairly hateful misogynist, and in his earliest incarnation was much more so than the revised and bowdlerized figures that have appeared on the screen since then. James Bond is not a very pleasant figure, certainly not in the very early books, and I am not entirely sure that the bloke who wrote him was a very pleasant figure, either. I think that there was a lot of funny stuff that Ian Fleming was getting out of his system with James Bond, and I think that given the way that James Bond has become such a male fantasy figure, that he's probably got quite a lot to answer for. We tried to make our James Bond as authentic as possible. In Ian Fleming's original chronology of the character, he was born, I think, in 1918, which would have made him forty years old, with the scars and the appearance that Kevin has depicted in our character, all being from Fleming's books. And even the new version of the clichéd "shaken, not stirred" line, because in the books he asks for his martinis "stirred, not shaken," because, apparently, it was believed that shaking a cocktail would "bruise" the alcohol. So we just changed it back to Fleming's original from what it had been in the films, and I think we did a very authentic job, but obviously if people are attached for some reason to the screen version of James Bond then they would find our version offensive. But no more offensive than we found the original Ian Fleming James Bond, I can assure you.

JN: There's always a temptation to read symbolism into everything and to read various characters' comments as metaphor. Was there any intentional symbolism in Bond killing Drummond or in Allan Quatermain's comments about Bond, was it a metaphor for anything, or am I just—

AM: In a certain way, there was a sort of line of descent that was being explored there. Allan Quatermain probably begat Bulldog Drummond, in that Sapper's hero was very much in the same sort of vein as Haggard's. He was probably a successor, a more brutal successor to the Haggard tradition. But in terms of the British adventure hero, it probably goes something like Allan Quatermain begets Bulldog Drummond who begets James Bond. And I think that these are three figures in a tradition—yeah, James Bond is definitely the heir to Drummond, so in that final brutal execution scene you've got perhaps the new pretender claiming the throne. And in Allan's comments about, "Is this what it's come to? The British adventure hero?" there is a certain amount of disdain for the degeneration of what in Allan's eyes had been a noble institution, down to these violent treacherous womanizing thugs and quasi-rapists, as represented by the Jimmy figure. There was a certain degree of poignance, shall we say, in both of those things. I was aware that we were talking about representatives of three different generations of one tradition, in a way, so putting them into a story together, yeah, that had got a certain resonance for me.

JN: A couple of fans were intrigued by your description of Ajax and the other Homeric figures and thought that they were almost a prototypical League. Have you thought about doing a *League*-like retelling of the classic myths?

AM: No, but that isn't to say that there might not be a "Tales of Orlando" at some point in the future in which we could go into more detail into some of the classical situations which are alluded to in a panel or two in the "Life of Orlando," so I guess that could happen. Although I had such a lot of fun doing the "Life of Orlando" because I could at least glancingly handle things like the Trojan War and things like that. My characterization of the various Greek demigods who fought at Troy was all backed up by Steve Moore, who is amongst many other things a really, really gifted classical scholar. And he said that, yes, pretty much, this is the way that Homer tends to portray these figures. So it seemed appropriate. It's a great deal of fun dealing with titanic figures like that. So if the opportunity arises, who knows? There might be some historic epics at some point in the future that would deal with some figures from classical mythology. It's possible.

JN: I know that fans are always wondering about things that might have inspired you to do something in the *Dossier*, and I found one thing that, I didn't think you'd read, but you might have, and I was wondering if there was any chance you'd read it, and it had any—it provided you with any inspiration. There was an 1891 French novel, *Memoires d'une Procureuse Anglaise*, set in an English brothel. It was reissued in 1972 in Finland, with an added section, of Lord Peter Wimsey and Bertie Wooster having a competition in the brothel of who can seduce a virgin faster. Have you seen it?

AM: No, but it sounds brilliant. So this was Lord Peter Wimsey and who else?

JN: Bertie Wooster.

AM: Bertie Wooster! Jesus, this is—no, I haven't seen that, but I'm not at all surprised it exists. Largely thanks to some of your excavations I've become aware of almost how redundant the *League* is, how most of these authors or other authors seem to have been cross-fertilizing these characters for centuries. I think that all that the *League* seems to be doing is just bringing what has been a prevalent urge in literature and culture for an awful long time to its logical conclusion. But, no, that is fantastic, Jess, I'd never heard of that. So this is a kind of light pornography or a racy narrative that concludes with Lord Peter Wimsey and Bertie Wooster competing to seduce a virgin.

JN: Yeah, it's hard to think about writing something original when there are already things out there like that. I wonder, how could I ever top that?

AM: Yeah, that is very bizarre. Like I say, you've turned up some really odd linkages between these disparate characters that have surprised me. I sometimes do feel with the *League* that in some ways we're responding to the original urges of those authors, that those original stories seem to have wanted to join hands, that the characters in them seem to be itching to break into other people's stories, and that in the hands of other writers, and pastiche writers, sometimes in the hands of the authors themselves, that they would do. I think it's great. I think it's a healthy sign for a field of literature when its characters are running around unsupervised like that. I think that's glorious. No, I shall have to look out for that one.

JN: Do you find something particularly attractive about Orlando as a character, or is the attraction primarily that you can use Orlando to write a story set in any time in human history?

AM: Well, of course, that is a very very big advantage to the character of Orlando. I must admit that as we've started to—primarily in the *Dossier*—as we've started to include bits about Orlando I've become a little fond of him or her as a character, because there is something so ridiculous and vain about the character, at least as we portray him. I thought it would be interesting initially to simply link up the Virginia Woolf Orlando with, say, Ariosto's original and a couple of the other Orlandos that have been around, including Orlando the Marmalade Cat in that brief reference at the end. I just thought, yeah, what if it's been one Orlando all along. I think we've both become fond of Orlando as a character. This is particularly true in the third volume of the *League*, where Orlando features quite a lot. And I wouldn't say that he's a very likeable character, but he's a very interesting character. In fact, we kind of implied throughout an awful lot of this third volume that if you're around Orlando for any length of his time you'll have heard most of his anecdotes at least twenty times, and that he's very vain and that he rather tends to get on people's nerves, especially when he's in his male form. So it's an interesting character to work with, and also it's very much the universal soldier, which is also, I suppose, not dissimilar from Mike Moorcock's Eternal Champion, but this one working fairly—pretty much within human history as it is normally defined. And that facet has been very useful, particularly in this third book.

Book Three opens in 2008, 2009, probably 2008, with Orlando enlisted in the British Army, still involved in trying to pull out of Qumar, which I believe is the Iraq substitute that is mentioned in the *West Wing*, which is something that I don't watch, but I have my spies who are always on the lookout for fictional countries, rock bands, anything. So we're going to be opening with Book Three of Volume Three with a very terse scene in Qumar in which we will get to see close-up what kind of creature Orlando is after these thousands of years. With this third book—it's very dark. It's a lot more grown up than even the *Dossier*. We seem to have foregone the boys' adventure comics tradition of having to keep the physical action moving all the time, and that's made a big difference. The rhythms of this third volume are much more like those of, say, Bertolt Brecht's *Threepenny Opera*, which is not mainly about people racing around and having fist fights. So it's got a different pace, a different feel, and that's something that we're hoping to explore. And Orlando is one of the *Dossier*'s new characters we introduce more in the third book. But, yes, I have got a certain affection for him or her. And it's very useful to have two or three immortal characters if you're going to project this book as far into the future as me and Kevin might do. At least in terms of science fiction, the future is mapped pretty conclusively, as well. There are all sorts of future worlds that we might decide to set some future version of the League amongst. I think it would be good to have Orlando around then, although, who knows? The fact that these characters are immortal doesn't necessarily mean that they can't die. I didn't get the impression that Orlando would be invulnerable to decapitation or being run through or being blown up. I got the impression that he'd been very very lucky, unlike characters such as, say, Gerald Kersh's Corporal Cuckoo, another immortal who we may have Orlando running into in this third volume. 'Cause in the services, it could happen. We have quite a bit of fun with Orlando. I wouldn't say that he's an incredibly likeable character, or that me and Kevin particularly like him, but he's great fun, and he adds an interestingly louche spark to the narrative.

JN: As you might imagine, the appearance and the use of the Golliwog has been somewhat controversial with American fans. Can you touch on your inspiration for using him, and—also, actually, a pure fanboy question: Where did his shout and speaking style come from?

AM: The first part of that question is probably easier to answer than the second part. The first part was that Kevin had turned up some material concerning Florence M. Upton's original Golliwog. Now, it seemed to us on looking over this material that the Golliwog as a figure had been grossly misrepresented. It seemed to us that Florence M. Upton's use of the word "Golliwog" preceded the later British use of the term "wog," to mean somebody of foreign extraction. I think that she used the word "Golliwog" simply because it was a funny-sounding word, like, for example, "polliwog." That may have been the inspiration. However she derived the term, the character of the Golliwog in those early books was, at least as far as we could see, one of the first black role models that you could name as such to ever appear in Western fiction. At the time, there were—you'd have your Uncle Toms and your Nigger Jims and you might even have the odd Umslopogaas, but these were fairly menial and in retrospect, even if well-intentioned, were fairly demeaning roles for black characters. Whereas the Golliwog was traveling fearlessly all around the world in a balloon, he was his own master, he'd got this string of continually naked, for the most part, Dutch dolls accompanying him everywhere. He seemed to be a self-determining and valiant character who succeeded in everything he did, which was far from the norm for black characters of any kind in fiction.

So what we thought we'd like to do is take this perhaps needlessly controversial figure, strip him of the minstrel clothes that he was later, and not in any of Florence M. Upton's narratives, but he was later dressed in, to take all of those elements away, to restore him to the original figure, to give him a bit more of an interesting hot air balloon. We invented the *Rose of Nowhere*. But we wanted to make this a memorable character, and when it came to writing his dialogue—I'm not sure what I was trying to do, actually. I just thought myself into the role. I decided that he was probably incredibly heavy, that he was maybe made out of baryonic material, out of the hypothesized "black matter" that we suspect ninety percent of the missing mass of the universe is composed of. So I've got a kind of backstory in my head about how he started off in this baryonic universe, how he traveled to our world, how he landed in Toyland, how he acquired the Dutch dolls—there may very well be an "Adventures of the Golliwog" special at some point in the future. It's something me and Kevin have talked about. But having this pretty impressive character, I wanted to jazz him up a little bit. So, regarding the shout, that was probably inspired by, at least in part, by the movie *The Shout*, surprisingly enough, which is a very good Australian movie in which I believe Alan Bates plays a mysterious, messianic escaped mental patient, who claims to have powers learned from aboriginal shamans, including the power to shout somebody dead. And there is a mesmerizing scene where he takes a disbelieving recording engineer out into the remote countryside, positions himself on top of a hill, with the recording engineer on top of a nearby hill, and after giving the recording engineer instructions to cover his ears, he shouts, and it's a marvelous scene, you can see—they actually used the sounds of about five jets taking off, a nuclear explosion, and several other things, all mixed into this shout, and there's sheep just falling downhill, dead. It's a spectacular scene which tends to stick in the mind. So when I wanted the Golliwog to have some kind of offensive power, it struck me that, I don't know, baryonic vocal chords might be capable of registering notes so low that they could almost be used as a sonic weapon.

So that was where the shout came from. The actual language that he talks in, I kind of made that up as I went along, and when I'd sent a couple of pages to Kevin, he got back to me and said that he thought that it was appropriate, because there wasn't an awful lot of dialogue in the Florence M. Upton books, it was mostly just reported speech in text underneath the pictures, but one of the things that she established was that the Golliwog actually was the King of Pankywank, which I know it's only one nonsense word, but which seemed to have the same kind of feel as some of the Golliwog dialogue that I'd already written. So we took that as a sign that I was on the right track, and we gave the Golliwog—I wanted to give him a very distinctive voice, I wanted to make him piratical in his nature, and not piratical in the human sense. I wanted this to suggest something of a boundless energy and spirit that had come from a different world entirely and is navigating our own with fearlessness and vigor. We mainly wanted to dispel any racist notions. It was the same reason that we got rid of the minstrel clothing that people associate with the Golliwog, although as I say it was nowhere present in Florence M. Upton's original. And by giving him this distinctive form of speech, which is very entertaining both to write and I hope to read, we wanted to further distance our character from any Golliwog that the readers may have previously come across. So that was why we gave him such an unusual speech pattern, although where it came from, I can't exactly say. It just seemed to fit with the character, it seemed almost a form of poetry that he was talking, some sort of colloquial poetry, with bursts of song and resonant, unfathomable phrases. The Golliwog is a character that doesn't make an appearance in Volume Three but which we're thinking about for Volume Four.

JN: Some fans have read the final sequence of the *Dossier* where Prospero gives his speech as autobiography, the bearded magus withdrawing from the world and being unshackled from mundane authorities. How much did you intend it to be autobiographical, if at all?

AM: I didn't intend it to be autobiographical at all, no. I do happen to be a magus, I do happen to be English, I do happen to have largely withdrawn from—certainly from the comics world, although I'm still fairly present in this material world, where I'm sitting now. I think most people around Northampton are always surprised when I'm described as a recluse. I guess that there are similarities: Yeah, we've both got beards. But, no, I wasn't thinking about me at all. I was mostly thinking purely about the fascinating figure of Prospero, who as we construe him in the *Black Dossier* is connected with both Christopher Marlowe's Faust and Ben Jonson's John Suttle, the Alchemist, or I think he was just called Suttle, I think we added the John, because we wanted to try and underline all of these three figures were based on Elizabeth the First's astrologer and magician John Dee, and so that final sequence with Prospero, it wasn't even Prospero saying "I am retiring from the world," and indeed Prospero makes an appearance in Volume Three of the *League*, in the third book. But it was purely meant as a triumphal statement on behalf of the world of fiction. I was using Prospero as a spokesperson for my ideas concerning fiction and how important that world is, how dependent we are upon it, how it can hardly be regarded as fictional at all when it has such far-reaching effects on the nonfictional, physical world. So that was mainly why we put Prospero in such a strong role. And also, right at the end, we'd previously established that Prospero speaks in iambic pentameter, and I wanted the final scene of the book to be able to go out with a really rousing final speech delivered in full Shakespearean flow, that would be able to sum up what kind of statement the *Dossier* is trying to make, taken as a whole, all of its individual parts. And if you had to sum it up succinctly into one statement it would probably be pretty much what Prospero says. He's saying that the world of fiction is vital to the human world and fortunately the world of fiction is eternal and is beyond the reach of all mortal authorities, and where it can continue to carry on its work uninterrupted by mundane problems. So I suppose at least in that regard me and Prospero at least have that much in common. But I don't feel that I am withdrawing from my sense of engagement with the world. I'm working harder now than I've ever done before. I am turning out more stuff. I know that people aren't seeing it, because I'm two-thirds of the way of a three quarter of a million word novel, which will be finished in another couple of years, and so then people will be able to see what I've been doing.

ABOUT THE AUTHOR

Jess Nevins, a reference librarian at the University of California at Riverside, is the author of *Heroes & Monsters* and *A Blazing World*, the previous companion editions to the popular graphic novel series *The League of Extraordinary Gentlemen*, as well as the critically-acclaimed *Encyclopedia of Fantastic Victoriana* and the *Pulp Magazines Holdings Directory*. His forthcoming books include *The Encyclopedia of Pulp Heroes* and *The Encyclopedia of Golden Age Detectives*.

Photo by Alicia Germer Nevins